WEALDSTONE

C000128893

WEALDSTONE

CROSSROADS

by

David W. Adams

WEALDSTONE CROSSROADS

WEALDSTONE

This story is a work of fiction. Names, characters, places and incidents are either the product of the authors imagination or are used fictitiously or in reference. Any resemblance to persons living or dead, or locales are purely coincidental.

Copyright © 2023 David W. Adams

Front & Rear Cover images compiled from public domain images from Google Images, Unsplash and Flikr by David W. Adams.

All rights reserved. No parts of this story, including the cover, may be reproduced or used in any manner without written permission of the copyright owners except for the use of quotations in book reviews.

All uses of the title 'Wealdstone : Crossroads' as depicted in this instance are included within the copyright.

Wealdstone : Crossroads first published 2023 via KDP.

Also available from this author

The Dark Corner

Return to the Dark Corner

Wealdstone

Resurrection

(all titles available through Amazon)

WEALDSTONE CROSSROADS

For Molly,

My beautiful little girl.

I'd take on all the worlds for you.

Love Daddy.

WEALDSTONE CROSSROADS

FOREWORD

Welcome back.

I must be honest; I didn't think I would be returning to this little town so soon. But then again, life is like a roadmap. Eventually all roads lead back to where it started.

When I recently re-read the first four books in this universe, I realised the love that I had for them, and it felt like coming home again. Initially, I had no idea that I had inadvertently written Resurrection into the same universe. Then again, if you can believe it, I had never actually read the full finished product. I asked my wife Charlotte to read it and if it was given the seal of approval, I'd publish it. So that's what I did!

And it was from that discovery that I decided I wanted to expand these connected tales outside of Wealdstone. Resurrection was just the first and if you have read it, you will know that the Epilogue of that book is also preparing for the second branch away from Wealdstone. But more about that at the end of this book!

When I decided that I was going to begin some serious universe building, I decided to make a plan. I know. Me and plans don't normally go together. I have lost count of the number of times I have had to edit the back of an already released book to change the date I gave for the next one or change the title or some random shit that a *real* author shouldn't need to do!

But this time, I did it in a pictorial style in the form of my version of the Marvel MCU Release slate you get at Comic-Cons.

7

It looks great if I do say so myself. I would show you, but as we know I tend to get ahead of myself a little!

Needless to say, I know the name of every book I intend to write from now until 2027. I know, right? I actually have it planned! I will however share one detail with you, and that is that this whole collection of books I am going to build, will come together in a huge climax.

And I will reveal the title of that book to you very soon. Because I've already got it written and a logo made and everything. Again, can we appreciate how cool plans are!?

But now for where we have gotten to at this point.

Wealdstone Crossroads is my vehicle to extend the arc of some of our well established characters but also to introduce new ones and take some of them in a completely different direction. Where that will lead going forward, only time will tell.

This book is exciting for me because I get to blend my love of writing in this universe, horror and sci-fi all together, and even leading into fantasy by the end of it. I was inspired for this book by so many different aspects, and I hope that I have done them justice.

This is the fifth book in a planned total of at least fifteen. Well, that's how far I've gotten so far. Who knows there may be more. But I have planned for fifteen, with the final one being designed to bring everything full circle.

But for now, please enjoy the ride and as ever please do get in touch on social media with me and let me know your thoughts, or any suggestions you may like to see in the series going forward.

While I do have initial ideas, and all the titles decided, I'm always willing to accept input from my readers. And if I choose an idea you suggest, you may get mentioned in the next book!

Before I waffle on too long, I just want to say that I have created a character in this book dedicated to someone who had a huge influence on me as a child, and I will go into detail in the afterword at the end of the book but see if you can figure it out.

Welcome back to Wealdstone.

WEALDSTONE CROSSROADS

PROLOGUE

The dirt shifted beneath the heavy footsteps sending clouds of dust up into the night sky, shimmering in the light of the full moon. A shot rang out and echoed across the valley, bats bursting from the trees circling wildly unsure of which direction to go. Several other sets of footfalls now joined that of the first man, increasing in speed.

Another shot pierced the air, and the man quickly diverted down to his left towards the edge of the river. A third shot hit the surface of the water nearby spraying him, before a fourth shot hit right next to his feet. He couldn't stop. They couldn't make him go back. He had to get as far away as possible. Away from *him*.

"Get your ass back here Tommy!" came a shout from somewhere in the dark.

Tommy could hear slithering in a nearby bush, but this was no time to worry about snakes. He twisted his foot on a rock, and stumbled, just catching the edge of the water, and making a loud splash with his left foot.

"Over there, by the river!" came another voice.

"Shit!" exclaimed Tommy, affording himself a quick look over his shoulder.

He saw four or five flashlights scanning the wilderness, two of them flashed across his face causing him to squint and raise his hand to shield his eyes.

11

"There!" the first man shouted.

A fifth shot rang out and Tommy felt the searing pain as it burst through his right shoulder, sending him crashing to the ground in pain. He scrambled against the loose surface attempting to get back up, but it was too late. The men had caught up with him, and as he lifted himself to his feet, he was met with a forceful fist directly to his lower jaw, sending him straight back down again.

One of the gang placed his dust covered boot directly onto Tommy's shoulder wound and he cried out in pain, trying to lift the boot away, but he couldn't fight back. A new set of footsteps could now be heard approaching slowly, which seemed to catch the attention of the gang of men that had been pursuing Tommy.

As the steps became louder, and the person approached, the gang parted and through the middle stepped a very tall man, easily over six feet in height, slender but with broad shoulders, and a greying goatee beard. The moonlight was reflected in a pair of darkened glasses lenses, and as the man stood in front of Tommy, looking down at him, he could see his own pained expression looking back at him.

"Why all the trouble, Tommy?" asked the man as he scratched his fingernails against his stubbled cheek.

Tommy gave no reply. This man signalled to the one standing on Tommy's shoulder and the force of the boot intensified.

"I said, why all this trouble?" the man repeated.

"I won't go back, Monarch. You can't make me go back!"

Tommy's raspy voice seemed to carry on the breeze, but only garnered a slight grimace from the man known as Monarch.

"Why would you forsake our community? Have we not provided for you? Have we not fed and sheltered you? Have you not embraced the wonders of the Crossroads? You are our brother, Tommy. Are we not yours?"

Again, Tommy fought against the boot, and again was forced back down in pain. Monarch knelt and leaned in, removing his glasses as he did so. His eyes searched left and right over Tommy's face almost looking for some sort of explanation.

"Well?" Monarch asked.

"What you're doing here, Monarch, is unforgiveable! These... these things... these doorways... you're brainwashing these people!"

Monarch sighed, and rested an elbow on his left knee, holding his hand over his forehead.

"I'm disappointed in you, Tommy. I thought we all strived for the same goals. I thought we all sought the power that this opportunity provides. And when they come... they will find us ready to serve them. And when they do, there will be nobody left here to stop us."

Monarch raised himself back to full height and returned his glasses to his eyes. He looked towards the man holding Tommy down.

"Take him to the third door... and guide him through."

Tommy's face was now filled with terror and his eyes glowed white in the darkness as they grew wide.

"Not the third door, Monarch please! Not that one!"

Tommy had seen two others of the settlement sent through that doorway and he remembered the screams.

"I'll come back, I'll do as you say, I promise!"

The man nodded, and as Monarch turned and began walking away, Tommy was pulled to his feet, and grabbed by a second man. With his fate seemingly sealed, his defiance returned.

"NO! Monarch, you have no idea what's through those doorways! You don't know what's coming! You are NOT a God!"

Monarch didn't look back and didn't say another word. Tommy was dragged back towards the settlement, writhing, and twisting to no avail. The valley was soon silent again and the only evidence that anyone had been there was a few footprints in the dirt.

After a few minutes, there was a distant scream, and a flash of green light popped above the settlement.

And then, once more, all was silent.

1

This wasn't the best bar that Kristin had been to in her life, but it was probably her favourite. The walls had that dark mahogany wood that they stopped using for construction in the 1980's. Interesting style choice considering this town was only twenty years old.

"Another?" asked the bartender.

"Yeah sure, why not."

He was a friendly face in an otherwise depressing place. A man of around seventy years of age, white beard and swept back hair to match. There was a glint in his wise blue eyes that made Kristin feel like he was a safe place. A person you could trust.

Trinity Bay hadn't exactly had an easy time of it. Originally built to house military personnel and their families, the place had been neglected since they left and had fallen into the hands of drug runners. Which would have been bad enough, had those drug runners been human.

"Can I ask you something ma'am?" asked the barman.

Kristin looked up from her already emptied glass and nodded.

"Is your friend always like that?"

Kristin sighed and turned to look in the direction of her rather tipsy wife, currently having a full on conversation with a dart board.

"Only when she's celebrating," came Kristin's reply. "It's been a tough few years, so I let her have the little wins, you know? Keeps us from arguing."

The barman, Will, according to his name tag, tilted his head to the side, and nodded to himself.

"Don't I know it. There's been talk of a new set of lawmen coming to clean up this forsaken place for the last five years. Even began attracting new business interests with the news. Some huge great megastore on the edge of town opened last Christmas. Nothing came of it though."

"Oh?" asked Kristin.

Will started polishing a glass before replying.

"Some kids were found strung up inside on Christmas Eve morning. All dead. After that, the company went bust and the store shut down. Shortest store opening I ever knew. Wasn't even in business by New Years."

Kristin raised her eyebrows. Sounded like her kind of business, but the way things had been going, she was glad she missed that one.

"Can I ask you something, Will?" asked Kristin.

Will nodded.

"Why didn't you leave this place? I mean you've got so many other places you could set up a bar. Why stay here?"

He was overcome with a kind of nostalgic look, and Kristin thought she saw his eyes well up a little.

"This is my home. Me and my wife Marina moved here when I was deployed down by the docks as a mechanic."

"A mechanic? Like what, fixing planes and stuff?"

16

Will laughed.

"Fixing everything. I was nearly fifty and my heart just wasn't in the fighting side of it anymore, literally."

He tapped his chest to indicate either his age or a heart condition. Kristin smiled as he continued.

"So, I retrained. Marina said it was a bit late in life to go back to school, but by the time I was finished I could pull apart the engine of a Super Galaxy plane and rebuilt it from scratch if I had to. Plus, the laws around this place were, let's say, relaxed. It let me earn a few extra bucks on the side."

Kristin nodded, trying not to be too distracted when she heard Kathryn fall over and then apologise to the dartboard from the floor. She was reminded of the amount of tension that had plagued their relationship in the last few years and chose to pay attention to Will for a while instead.

"Yeah there are some screwy laws here. No official jurisdiction, so no police force claims any. Pretty good way to avoid responsibility."

Will nodded.

"Yeah, well when she died, I opened the bar and when I hung her picture up in my office, I just felt like she was here with me."

"Yeah, she's here. They all keep us company. We just don't see them."

Will was expressing a look of acceptance but mild confusion at the same time, as if Kristin's statement wasn't necessarily wistful, but more matter of fact. His thought process was interrupted by the arrival of Kathryn to the bar, who was rubbing her lower back.

"Well, I think I should probably get this young lady a cup of coffee," offered Will.

17

"Yeah that's probably a good idea, thanks."

Kathryn leaned on the bar as she sat on the stool next to Kristin. She ran her hands over her face several times to wake up. She only remembered having three drinks, but alas had forgotten that they had been triple measures.

"So, how you feeling?" asked Kristin.

"Like I've been run over with a snow plow," came the muffled reply from between Kathryn's hands.

"You know you're a lightweight, Kat. You're like this after every mission."

The mission in question had been one of emergency. They had received a rather panicky call from someone they knew from home. Elliot had been the previous manager of Sisko's back in Wealdstone before the events involving the pain wraiths. He had gotten in touch with them saying his restaurant had been turned over by what he described as 'vampire thugs' but before he could elaborate, the line had gone dead.

Short on resources, and team members, they drove out to find the town virtually locked down. It had taken them three weeks to flush out the vampires and take them down. But the job was done, and the town was safe. Except Elliot. They found him torn apart outside his restaurant. But with no police force, at least they didn't have to come up with a cover story.

"There we go madam, freshly ground from the beans of a Javan volcanic island."

"Thank you very much," Kathryn replied, taking a very large and very quick gulp from the cup.

"How the hell do you do that without burning your mouth?" her wife asked.

"Hey I can't hold my drink, but I have a Teflon inside. I could drink from a kettle if I wanted to."

Will was beginning to wonder if he'd encountered some kind of super-hero types the longer he was around these two. He had heard them murmur about vampires, but he thought they were talking about Comic-Con. Now he wasn't so sure.

Kathryn began to feel a little more stable as she finished the coffee and ordered another, but Will became distracted as the door opened and a tall lady with long brown hair, a red checked shirt over a white vest top and a sidearm on her hip entered the bar.

"Well, I'll be damned," he said. "Beth Ford."

Kristin and Kathryn were both somewhat taken aback by this very beautiful woman who was now standing alongside them. They ignored the fact that Kathryn's phone was ringing and watched as Will moved from behind the bar to give the woman a hug.

"Hey Will, I was hoping you were still here," she replied.

"It must have been about fifteen years since I saw you. You've grown!"

Will immediately knew that had been a stupid thing to say, but Beth laughed it off anyway.

"My Dad convinced me to come back. And I'm not the only one. Which is why I'm here. I need a drink."

"You mean?"

Beth nodded.

"I'll fix you something… strong."

19

Will walked away leaving the three women alone. Beth sat on a stool three down from Kathryn, and although she started by staring at the bar, she could feel eyes on her, and turned to see she was the object of attention.

"Can I help you ladies?" she asked.

What Kristin wanted to say was something along the lines of 'I wouldn't mind helping myself to you,' but she was conscious of her wife's presence and so opted to be more subtle.

"No, just having a drink, having a nice conversation with Will about the weird loopholes this town has."

Beth smiled and shook her head.

"Loopholes doesn't cover it, darlin'."

The southern drawl made Kristin lose her next sentence somewhere between her brain and her lips. Kathryn, however, was still not yet fully sober.

"May I just say on behalf of me and my lovely wife here, that you are a simply fantastic piece of ass."

Will had just turned the corner with Beth's drink and stopped in his tracks, Kristin also in a state of shock. The level of embarrassment running through her right now was off the charts. She opted for the typical face palm attempting to shield her from the void of despair.

Beth on the other hand, was very much amused.

"Why thank you beautiful. You're not so bad yourself."

With literally no idea how she had managed to dodge that bullet, Kristin excused herself and made her way to the bathroom, and Will resumed his journey to the bar and handed Beth her drink.

20

"Beth here, was one of the military kids. I knew her mom, Faith. Unlike the rest of us, she had the good sense to leave town and make a life for herself."

"If I had good sense, Will, I wouldn't be back. And I wouldn't be reliving the nightmare that is Jason Harper."

This time, Kathryn felt her phone vibrating and the faint sound of the *Yellowstone* theme echoing in her pocket.

"Excuse me for a moment."

Kathryn strolled over to the far end of the bar and sat in a booth under a missing light bulb. The screen showed a familiar but unexpected caller ID.

"Annie? Hey long time no…"

"Kat, I'm sorry but there's no time for pleasantries. Although it is good to hear your voice. We have a serious issue."

Kristin returned from the bathroom, and although briefly distracted by Beth once more, noticed Kathryn had moved and walked over to sit beside her.

"Why? What's wrong?"

Kristin mouthed the same words to Kathryn, who in turn mouthed back Annie's name.

"Well, if you can believe it, there's something a little off the scale brewing in Wealdstone."

Kathryn rolled her eyes in a 'so what else is new' way, but before she could respond, Annie continued.

"And there's something else."

21

A pause followed.

"What else?" Kathryn asked, rather impatiently.

The response she got was not what she wanted to hear and made her go white and a shiver run down her spine.

"Grace is missing."

2

The journey back from Trinity Bay had been a long one. Kristin and Kathryn had barely spoken despite the near five hour travel time. While her wife had more or less sobered up by that point, there was still some unspoken thing between them. And it wasn't going away.

As they reached the welcome sign for Wealdstone, Kristin pulled over in the dirt layby at the side of the road and switched off the engine, staring out the windscreen as she spoke.

"So when are we going to talk about this?"

Kathryn kept her eyes down and spoke with her chin pressed to her chest. She had no desire to go over past conflicts for the hundredth time.

"Talk about what? Look I thought we were moving on from all that."

Kristin began to get angrier at her wife's apparent ease at moving past something that was boring through the very core of their marriage.

"How can we move past something that you won't even acknowledge?"

"What do you want me to say?"

"How about I'm sorry? I'm sorry that I almost fucked my ex-boyfriend! I'm sorry that I kept it a secret for three years! I'm sorry that I spend as much time away from my wife as I can to avoid the uncomfortable situation. Oh, and let's not forget I'm sorry for getting drunk all the time!"

When Jack had died during the battle with Jasmine three years previously, Kathryn had tried to forget the incident in question. She carried on working with the team, fighting the demons both literal and figurative and continued to try and make it work between her and Kristin.

But the truth had been revealed when she had one too many celebratory drinks at Sisko's, and Kimberley had asked her how well she had known Jack before he died. The response she gave was 'very well indeed'. Kimberley had asked if she had ever thought about looking him up and she had replied with a drunken smile that she had very nearly done more than that 'recently'.

Since then, the relationship had been strained, and with all the trouble and loss Grace had suffered in the past year she had chosen to distance herself from both of them. At some point in the journey home, they had both prayed that they weren't part of the reason she was now missing.

"I'm sorry, Kristin. I can't explain what happened. I only know that some kind of feeling surrounded me and there was something comforting about the familiarity of him. I just figured that as we never actually went through with it, I could forget it and move on."

Kristin batted away a tear before Kathryn could see it.

"Yeah well it would have if you weren't such a drunk these days."

Kathryn had no defence for that. She had been drinking a lot more than she had ever done over the past year or so. Deep down she knew that there were problems. Perhaps there were now too many to fix.

"I am sorry Kris. I…"

Kathryn couldn't quite say the words she had said at the end of every conversation when they were first together. Kristin swiped away another tear. This one had not gone unnoticed. Kathryn reached over and placed a hand on Kristin's thigh, but she batted it away and sniffled.

"Let's just go find our niece shall we."

24

She turned the key in the ignition and pulled back onto the road. No more words were spoken in the drive down the hill into town, and while there was only a maximum three feet gap between the two of them, it felt like a chasm.

And it was getting wider.

3

Annie felt a little awkward being in the same room as everybody again. It had been over a year since they were last all together. They had grown to be a powerful team of women and they were battling whatever came their way without issue. But internal issues had splintered them all apart. Annie had been tasked with working for the British Museum after the battle with Jasmine, but she had been asked to stay by both Kathryn and Kristin and so had passed on the job. But after the rift grew between them, it began to push the rest of them away too, and she had spent the last fourteen months working in Montana with a small group of like-minded students trying to learn to develop her witchcraft.

Kimberley was stood propped up against the door frame in the dining room of Kathryn and Kristin's house staring out the window. She had chosen to assume the form of her previous host in tribute to Jack. She had kept her long blonde hair, but lately had started putting it up into a bun. The married couple were sat on opposite chairs, and of course Grace was noticeably absent. As awkward as it was, the scene did resemble some familiarity. Annie was stood in front of a digital whiteboard with a map of town and a layout of what they knew so far. Rather than make conversation, she decided to just press ahead.

"Okay, so here's what we've got. We've been having reports of people disappearing on and off for the last eight months as you know, but we've found no leads. Well while you were chasing vampire drug dealers in Trinity Bay, we got a lead."

She tapped the screen and brought up a CCTV image of a tall, slender man wearing dark sunglasses.

"This man we believe goes by the name Monarch. He has been seen in town on numerous occasions near to the time where a family member or acquaintance has been reported as missing. Grace followed him to a settlement on the edge of town called 'Crossroads.'"

Kristin volunteered some information.

"Yeah I heard of that place, they found it during the rebuild of the town. Like an Old West setup. A main street, stores, houses. Used to be a tourist attraction about fifty years ago, then it got abandoned."

Annie nodded before swiping to the next image.

"Well, it isn't abandoned anymore."

The image was an aerial video taken with a drone that showed at least one-hundred people moving between buildings, all seemingly wearing older clothes and no signs of technology of any kind. No cars, no electricity even.

"How the hell did nobody notice that was there? I mean that's a whole community."

Kimberley offered her first contribution to the discussion. Kathryn replied.

"What happened to Grace?"

Annie swiped again but the screen was frozen. No matter how many buttons she clicked, she couldn't get the thing to work. She took a deep breath, closed her eyes, and moved her hands in front of her. The group were captivated by the blue lights and swathes of energy coming from the tips of her fingers. As they watched, the glowing ribbons moved into the computer, before exiting it again and creating a three dimensional recreation of the information Annie had been attempting to show them.

As the group smiled and continued to look on in shock, Annie was quite nonchalant.

"What? You don't think I've been sitting on my ass while you three have been having all the fun do you?"

She managed a wry little smile having known full well the reaction she would get. In fact, that was one of the reasons she had done it rather than simply turn the computer off and on again. Now the surprise was over, she continued, and as she waved her hands, the images altered as she told the story.

"After Grace followed Monarch back to Crossroads, she came back to prepare for an undercover mission. Unlike the three of you, she had managed to keep a fairly low profile after Jasmine's antics so the chances of her being recognised were smaller."

"Hey," said Kimberley in protest. "That was only one building. And I apologised to the owner."

Kathryn and Kristin shared a laugh for what felt like the first time in a long time. They glanced at each other, but the smiles quickly dissipated, and they got back on task.

"Yes, well. She managed to speak to someone near the entrance and gather some intel that this Monarch character was the leader of the community, and that he believed there were doors. Gateways. Ways for things to come through to our world from other realms."

The others suddenly displayed a look of concern. They had been there before, and it didn't end well. Almost in response, Annie held up her hand.

"Don't worry, nobody mentioned pain wraiths."

A collective sigh of relief made its way around the room. Kathryn stood up and began to stretch her legs.

"So, how is this possible? I thought the gateway to other realms was closed?"

Kimberley's turn to speak came, but she was reluctant to admit the information she now volunteered.

"That may be my fault."

The others looked around at each other before settling on her.

"When the gateway was being sealed, Ariella used the last of her diminishing power to hold the rift open long enough for me to escape. I think that by coming back through, I may have caused… damage."

Annie seemed quick to dismiss the idea.

"No, that's not it, don't worry."

Kimberley, whilst relieved, was unsure how she could be so certain.

"How can you know that?"

Annie just smiled.

"Just call me Giles."

The only one in the room to get the reference was Kristin.

"So which one of us is *Buffy*?" she asked smiling.

Annie smiled back and waved her hands once more to display an image of where she had been staying in Montana.

"That's… a lot of books Annie."

Kathryn was now looking at what seemed like a very large library with more books than she could even begin to count. It resembled the scene from the original *Beauty and the Beast* when Belle is first introduced to her favourite room in the castle.

"Yeah well, I figured we had a super-human, two *Sarah Connors* and a pain wraith. I would give it a shot at being a nerdy *Scarlet Witch*."

Another giggle from everybody, before Annie turned serious again.

"There are records of sightings of these doorways all over the world. The first one was said to be discovered over two millennia ago. They are believed to be doorways into other realms or plains of existence and guarded by a spiritual being who keeps them secure."

Kimberley had heard of these doorways whilst in the Realm of Screams.

"I never believed them to be real. I had heard stories of them whilst I was a child, but I dismissed them as fairy tales."

Annie continued.

"Well, there was a sighting as recently as the 1970s in Southern California at a place called Catalina Island. A resident of the island wandered down to the beach during a storm and took shelter in one of the caverns. Once inside, he saw what he described as a 'green doorway' almost superimposed on the rock. When he saw eyes glowing either side of the door, he ran. Nearly drowned getting back to land."

"Why didn't he go back?" asked Kristin.

"When nobody on the island believed him, he went back but the doorway was gone."

"And what you're saying is that this Crossroads place, seems to have one?" asked Kimberley.

Annie shook her head.

"Not one. Several. Conflicting reports have placed it at six."

Kimberley nodded.

"So, while I didn't cause them, I probably helped amplify the effect."

Annie nodded.

"That's my theory. Your powerful levels of energy are present all the time. It's how you keep your physical form without occupying another body, in the same way Jasmine and Ariella did. But that energy is almost free-floating, and it impacts other environments."

Kathryn nodded.

"I have always noticed I'm never low on phone battery when I'm near you."

Kimberley gave her a look, and Kathryn held up her hands apologetically.

"The only other problem we have is that the doors appear to have lost their guardians. When I learned of Grace's disappearance yesterday, I did some digging and I found the only other two mentions of these doorways I could find was that once somebody had gone through them, they closed."

The concern returned.

"So, without these mystical guardians, there's nobody to keep the door open."

31

Annie nodded.

"Or guarded."

The group as a whole were beginning to realise what this meant.

Kristin started the confirmation of suspicion.

"So, somebody, or something has killed the spiritual guardians of these doorways, which means…"

"Which means," Kathryn interrupted, "if Grace was pushed through one of these doorways, it's gone. And so is she."

"I'm afraid so," replied Annie.

There was a moment of quiet, and Kathryn paced around her dining room attempting to formulate a plan. Despite the group being less connected than they once were, she was still the de facto team leader. But much to her dismay, it was Kristin who appeared to take charge.

"Okay, so we know where she was going, we know who is responsible for taking the people out of the town. Whoever this Monarch guy is, do we think he is some kind of non-human entity?"

Kathryn's shoulders slumped a little as the group seemed to rally around that idea. Obviously, it was a good surmising, but she now felt her place on the team had been devalued.

"Well, he can't be a wraith," said Kimberley. "I'd know. There's a sort of… Spidey sense. The only way to mask that is to inhabit another body, and as far as we know he hasn't done that right?"

Annie nodded.

"No. He definitely isn't a face from the normal Wealdstone population. He's new. But so far there is no evidence to suggest he isn't human."

Kathryn slammed her hand down on the dining table, drawing everyone's attention.

"Well, there's only one thing for it."

She stood tall, reached into her jacket, and pulled out her revolver.

"We'll just have to go ask him."

4

The church was full, without a single seat empty. Each row had a mix of women, men and children all wearing the same dull, off-white clothing on top, braces, and dark grey trousers on the bottom. The women wore dusty grey cloth sandals and the men and the children wore black shiny loafers. Many of the men had chosen to wear hats, but as they sat at the pew, they removed them as a sign of respect.

The church itself was untouched by modern influence. The walls were damp and stained, the roof had several holes where the sunlight could peak through, and the previously stained glass windows were now dark or broken. The only light was coming from avenues of white candles along the centre aisle and across the altar.

The crowd were talking quietly amongst themselves when the doors to the church opened, and Monarch entered. Behind him were two of the men who had chased down the escaped man from two days prior, and two others were stationed either side of the entrance. Monarch walked slowly down the aisle, looking around as he did so, still sporting his dark glasses, and as he did so, the crowd reduced to a low murmur before going silent altogether.

The majority of the crowd appeared as though they feared him. They shrunk down and they attempted to avoid his gaze. There were a few who stood tall and placed their hands on their hearts as he passed, and in return they received a gentle nod from the man himself.

When he reached the altar, the doors were closed and locked, and Monarch turned to face the crowd, standing between two large flaming torches. He brushed a wrinkle out of his pristine white shirt and stood with his hands clasped together in front of him in prayer.

34

"May we be grateful."

As he began to speak, after each line, the crowd repeated his words.

"May we be grateful."

"For the bountiful lives we have been given."

"For the bountiful lives we have been given."

"We guard this powerful gateway with our lives, so that we may be of service to the Gods on the other side."

The repetition from the crowd continued as the words being spoken by Monarch diverted from the normal kind of prayer to the more cult-like. They were putty in his hands, their spirits crushed beyond measure. Every word was designed to subjugate them and every word was a lie.

"Three years ago this very night, we were shown a glimpse into another realm when the Violet Spirits descended on us to purify this world! They were driven back by those too afraid to seek redemption! And we say no more!"

"No more!"

"The other Gods will come. And they will punish the deserters. They will reward the righteous! And they will share their power!"

Enormous cheers from the crowd, despite the faces of many not matching the sound echoing around the hall of the church.

"We guard the gateways abandoned by their guardians and we wait. The realms of good, and the realms of evil. Some of you may be aware that another brother was lost two weeks ago."

A critical silence from the crowd.

35

"This man was a deserter. A coward. A non-believer! He came into our home. He took the food that we gave him. He took the clothes we provided, and he slept in the bed we honoured him with! And then? He attempted to abandon us!"

The two men who had accompanied Monarch into the church stamped a single foot hard on the wood of the floor, the sound reverberating throughout the room. Again, a second stamp. Then a third. The stamping continued until the whole crowd began joining the rhythm. As the thumping got louder, Monarch continued to speak, raising his voice in line with the increase in noise.

"Speak the laws of the Crossroads!"

The stomping became more rapid.

"We shall not steal!"

The crowd repeated. They continued throughout the list of Monarch's commandments as if he was the Lord Almighty himself.

"We shall not abandon! We shall not forsake the Gods of the realms! We will obey! We are one! We are united!"

As the final commandment was read, the stomping stopped and Monarch stood at the altar head raised to the roof, arms wide apart and his eyes closed as if chanting these rules had taken every sap of his energy.

"Well that there is some mighty fine bullshit."

The crowd gasped audibly, and Monarch snapped his head back down, looking over the top of his glasses to see that the doors to the church were now wide open, and the two unconscious bodies of his guards were laying either side. And standing in the middle were four women.

36

"But then again, I've heard worse. I mean have you actually *read* the Bible?"

Kristin's sarcasm cut through the atmosphere like a knife. Monarch's throat was turning a dark shade of red as the rage began to build within. The crowd began to filter out of a side door as the team moved further into the church, Kristin holding a shotgun over her left shoulder, Kathryn with a modified pistol in each hand, and Kimberley with small sparks of purple lightning shooting between her fingers.

"Who dares to enter my sanctuary? Assault my brothers? And challenge our beliefs?"

The two men beside Monarch drew their weapons and aimed them square at the group, who stopped mid-way down the aisle.

"Well, I'm going to give you two options," began Kristin. "Either you tell me where my niece is, or I shoot your legs off, and drag you through the nearest one of these gateways of yours."

Even Annie, who was seemingly the only person unarmed, was impressed at how ballsy Kristin had become. She suspected the conflicts in the group had given her more of a gilded edge. And she liked it.

Monarch, however, simply smiled.

"So, you're the Aunt she spoke of."

Kathryn felt a tinge of rage shoot through her and moved forward, but Kristin, keeping as cool as possible, motioned for her to stay back. Yet another indication that she was no longer considered a leader.

"I'm one of them. And I'm guessing that she warned you what would happen if you didn't let her go."

Monarch reached up and removed his sunglasses and the image slightly surprised Kristin, who attempted to remain unmoved.

Monarch's eyes were golden.

He carefully folded them and placed them down very gently on a side table, before unbuttoning the top button of his collar, where a thin piece of chord could be seen leading down to a mass of some kind visible under his shirt.

"It was kind of hard to hear through the gargling of her blood."

5

12 DAYS EARLIER

The scene reminded her of *Casino Royale*. And not in a good way. The chair Grace was tied to was nothing more than a wicker frame with no seat in the middle. Her backside was wedged in the hole, and her ropes were so tight, her skin was wearing on her wrists and her ankles. Still unsure of how mere rope could be strong enough to contain her, she awaited the arrival of the man they called Monarch.

She took another look around the room. Fairly basic, kind of a port-a-cabin style, one single light bulb glowing above her head with a long pull cord to activate it. A window on two of the four walls, a door on the third, and a schematic of the area on the biggest wall. It was clearly somewhere outside of the settlement given the modern design and of course the electricity supply. Unable to remember too much before she had been captured, she did recall speaking to Annie on the phone about a new contact she had spoken with. Although given the fact that they were talking when she was attacked, the chances of Tommy surviving were slim.

While she was unconscious, it seemed as though her captors had removed her shoes, her jacket, and any of her personal belongings. Including her weapon. However, for some unexplained reason, they were all laid out on a long table in the corner of the room. As she stared at them trying to figure out why they would be left so near to her, mumbled voices could be heard outside. She had already heard a loud scream and figured it must have been Tommy's voice.

The rickety door opened and two broad shouldered, heavily built men in dark cloth jackets entered the room and flanked the door on either side. A moment passed, and then Monarch entered the cabin. In an attempt to get the immediate upper hand, Grace decided to speak first.

"So, when do I get my phone call?"

Monarch chuckled at the question as he meandered his way over to Grace's chair. She tensed against the ropes, but still, she could not break them.

"No phone call? Okay, how about my prison meal?"

This time the sarcasm was met with a violent reply. Monarch raised his right leg and brought his foot down so hard onto Grace's bare toes that she felt all five of them crack, the sound filling the cabin, followed by her screams. Monarch was very calm as he placed his foot gently down on the floor once more. He removed his dark glasses and began to polish one of the lenses on his shirt.

As she tried to regain composure and catch her breath, she could have sworn she saw a glow in his eyes, but before she could confirm it, he replaced the glasses onto his face before speaking.

"Who are you, young lady?" he asked in a manner so polite that it threw Grace off, considering his brutality just a moment before.

"Who wants to know," she said through gritted teeth.

"Oh... the boogeyman."

Monarch chuckled again as he gave his reply, thinking he was being witty. Grace wasn't buying it.

"I've seen worse than you, asshole. You're just a deranged nut job who thinks he's Jesus or some shit."

Monarch raised his eyebrows and turned back towards Grace.

40

"Oh? Is that right? Well, I certainly wouldn't want to disappoint you."

He once again reached for his glasses, this time removing them and handing them to one of his associates, revealing his golden eyes.

"Really? That's it? I fought vampires, werewolves, pain wraiths, and you think fancy contact lenses are going to impress me?"

Although Grace was speaking defiantly, inside she was terrified. But Monarch wasn't done yet. He slowly raised his arms to the side, and Grace saw his body tense up, the veins on his neck protruding, and as he did so, his mouth began to widen, and his teeth began to sharpen. Wisps of golden mist emanated from his body and swirled around the chair, and it was lifted from the ground.

"Well, let's try and impress you."

Monarch now spoke with a hiss as his face mutated into a demonic *Joker* face and with a deafening roar, Grace's chair was launched through one of the two windows in the cabin, taking out a large section of wall with it, and she hit the ground hard, rolling several times before coming to a stop.

She gasped wildly for air and looked down to notice a small bone protruding from her left knee. There was a very loud whooshing sound followed by the tearing of metal as Monarch seemingly floated through the side of the cabin landing six feet away before striding purposefully forwards. Grace struggled against the chair, which was now weakened by the impact, but just as she loosened one wrist, Monarch delivered a swift kick directly into her ribs and both her and the chair once again travelled through the air, this time landing on her back.

Grace coughed and spluttered, and she could taste blood. As Monarch approached her once more, she attempted to shout a warning to him.

"My Aunt's are going to come for you. They are going to tear you apart!" she shouted, before spitting out blood from her mouth.

Monarch leant down and pondered for a moment.

"Torn apart huh? That doesn't sound like a bad idea."

He gave Grace a sickening grin, before standing back to his full height, and once more raising his arms. The chair was lifted again into the air until Grace was several feet above Monarch directly opposite him. He gave a flick of each wrist, and the chair was ripped apart, leaving just Grace floating, restrained above the ground.

"Now, you're going to tell me what you're doing in my little community, or I'm going to take your advice."

Grace said nothing, still struggling for breath. Monarch sighed and gave a shrug of his shoulders. Another flick of the wrist and Grace's already broken knee snapped in the other direction. The scream was almost beyond audible range. Blood now poured from her wound and as she just managed to catch a breath, he asked her again.

"You caused me to send one of my brothers in arms away tonight. Unless you speak, I shall have to send you away too. Only you won't get quite as pleasant an end as he did."

Grace sucked in as much air as she could, before getting her words out.

"We were tracking the people disappearing from town," she said between coughs.

"Well, there's nobody missing. People have joined our community, but nobody is missing. We are a family here. United to serve those on the other side."

Despite her immense pain, Grace gave a laboured laugh.

42

"If you think there's some kind of God on the other side of those doorways, you're the architect of yet another delusional religion!"

Monarch appeared to anger at this, visibly. His eyes burned like fire, and as he took a large breath, he thrust his left arm out to the side, closed his fist, and yanked it back down.

As Grace's left arm was ripped clean of her body, she began to convulse. But she could not scream. Monarch was holding his finger to his lips, and no matter how hard her lungs wanted to let her bellow, she couldn't. Her mind went woozy, and her vision blurred. Her entire side was darkened with her blood and continued to drip onto the floor until a pool of it surrounded her. As she began to pass out, Monarch waved a hand swiftly in front of him, and an invisible slap ricocheted across Grace's face. A single drop of blood dripped from her nose as she righted her head centrally again.

"You are delusional my dear, if you thought you were ever going to make it out of here alive."

Grace, dangled in the sky like a ragdoll, and Monarch decided that enough was enough. He turned to speak to his associates who had joined him at his side.

"She is no threat. Dispose of her. But if anyone comes looking for her, I want them brought to me. Do you..."

Monarch was interrupted by what sounded like the breaking of bones behind him. There were more crunching noises followed by a very large intake of breath and a heavy thud. As he turned around, Grace was standing directly in front of him, completely reassembled and healed. In the momentary instance of time that he contemplated what had happened, Grace smiled at him, and thrust her hands forwards into his chest, sending him launching through the air with such an overwhelming force he crashed back through the hole in the cabin, and out the other side.

43

The two henchmen, bewildered by what they had just seen, hesitated a moment too long. Grace leapt towards them, tackling them both to the ground, one arm swinging into the face of each, before, in turn, placing a foot on each neck, and snapping it. Twisting metal could be heard coming from the cabin, and she knew she had lost her advantage. Whatever Monarch was, she was no match for him without the element of surprise. She felt under her shirt. Good. The amulet was still there. Her eyes searched the horizon for somewhere to hide, and she could hear the sound of running water, not far away.

Monarch tore his way through what was left of the cabin, to see Grace over a hundred yards away already, and getting further from his grasp. He let out another thunderous roar, spittle flying from his mouth across his jagged teeth, eyes burning once more, and he began leaping in bounds to cover more ground. He knew she was getting out of range of his powers and put everything he had into chasing her.

Grace reached the river and started to run along the flat bank. Her advanced abilities, even without the amulet, meant she covered a lot of ground fast, but she knew he was not far behind. She could hear him roaring, and the ground being pounded with each landing. As she tried to increase her speed, she saw something shimmering on the other side of the river. Ahead of her was a narrow part of the water and on the other side, appeared to be a glowing green line. It began to move and traced the shape of a door in the air.

Grace took a sharp left turn and waded into the shallow narrow river crossing, stumbling on a wet rock as she reached the other side. Monarch was now just yards behind her, and he thrust his hands out from his body in turn, and a golden string of light left the palm of his right hand and wrapped around Grace's left thigh like a rope. With one tug, he yanked her body to the ground, and her shoulder crunched on impact.

He leapt across the river and landed with a thud, sending dust cascading up into the air. Approaching Grace, his face slowly contorted back to

44

normal, and his eyes reduced their glow. He stood in front of her as she turned around and placed her palms behind her to try and prop herself up. Monarch slammed his boot onto her broken shoulder. Another scream of pain, but her cries of agony were ineffective on him by this point. They were almost like music.

However, curious, he removed his boot and waited a moment. Beneath Grace's shirt, a yellow glow began to brighten, and he heard the audible crunch of bone once more.

"What… what is that?" he asked.

Grace attempted to get up quickly now her shoulder was healed, but he landed a heavy punch to her jaw with his fist, sending her back down. He leaned forward, his eyes beginning to burn again, almost matching the glow of the amulet. He reached his hands forward and tore open Grace's shirt to reveal the pendant. Momentarily distracted by the large scar on her chest showing this creature had been in battle before, Grace shifted her weight, and slid beneath him.

He turned quickly, and launched his hand forward, but this time not towards one of Grace's limbs, but towards the pendant. As his energy hit her, Grace leapt through the illuminated green doorway and vanished. As she did so, the doorway itself changed from green to red, before vanishing altogether.

Grace had escaped. To where? He did not know. Despite the performance he displayed to those at Crossroads, he was no more knowledgeable than they were. But for now, he had a much more interesting question to answer. What was this magical object?

As he turned the amulet over in his hand, his menacing pointed grin returned, and he began to walk back towards Crossroads.

6

The left side of the church exploded with purple light, wood shards flying all around as Monarch landed in the dirt with a thud and a mild cracking sound as his back impacted the ground. Kimberley strolled through the new opening in the wall towards him as he stumbled to his feet.

Inside the church two loud gunshots rang out as Kristin took down the two guards, before Kathryn unloaded two modified silver bullets into each, just in case. Annie meanwhile, stayed back, her eyes closed and mumbling words under her breath. Kristin considered going to ask her what was going on, but as thin streams of blue light began to emerge from her shoulders and weave through the air, she decided she would leave her to it.

Monarch was yet to retaliate to the initial assault. He simply stood where he had fallen, his eyes glowing a softer yellow than previously, and his head tilting from side to side as he tried to assess what he was witnessing.

"You… are one of them."

His words caught Kimberley off guard.

"One of who?"

"The violet spirits. The ones who came to cleanse this world. Why do you fight me? We want the same thing."

Kristin and Kathryn joined Kimberley.

"We do *not* want the same things. I don't know what you are, but my people did not intend to cleanse this world. They don't want anything more to do with this realm. That's why they closed the gateway."

Slightly perturbed by her statement, Monarch narrowed his eyes.

"Believe what you want, traitor. The one called Jasmine was a visionary. And when the others come through, you'll see. My patience will be rewarded!"

Kimberley sighed, as the blue glow behind her in the church intensified.

"Nobody else is coming! The gateway was sealed! What don't you get?"

Monarch's mouth now began to spread into the twisted smile, and the teeth grew into their multiple points as he spat his reply.

"But the Realm of Screams isn't the *only* realm… is it?"

Letting out a deafening roar, Monarch leapt into the air, launching himself towards Kimberley. She reciprocated launching in front of a burst of purple energy, and the two of them collided mid air, exchanging punches and blasts of yellow and purple explosions, before Monarch reached out and grabbed Kimberley by the throat. As he intensified his grip, the purple flickering began to dissipate. As Kristin and Kathryn watched from below, they couldn't believe what they were seeing. What was this creature that could subdue a pain wraith?

Monarch's golden wisps of light began to wrap around Kimberley's body as the life began to drain from her. He leaned in close to her until his teeth were inches away from her face.

"I thought you people were Gods. Perhaps I was wrong. Maybe *I* am the God. Either way, you serve no purpose here."

47

Kimberley's eyes began to fade to a dull white glow, and dark black swirls began to emerge at her feet before slowly creeping up her legs.

Shots from the shotgun and the modified pistols rang out as Kristin and Kathryn began firing at Monarch repeatedly. He loosened his grip slightly, but within seconds, the wounds had healed. Kristin noticed the mass beneath his shirt began to glow golden, and she knew what it was. Whether Monarch was drawing power from the amulet, or simply using it to strengthen his healing, the fact that it was in his possession was not good.

The dark swirls of fog had reached Kimberley's chest, her entire lower body now gone, and she knew this was it. She managed to tilt her head downwards to look at her friends. She had not known them for long, but they had shown her what a family could be, even through the problems that had disrupted it recently. She was glad she experienced it before she died. She closed her eyes and waited.

But death didn't come.

The ground rumbled beneath Kristin's feet, and Kathryn staggered back. As she glanced behind her, she saw Annie, floating at least fifteen feet off the ground, completely enveloped in a blue flame, sparks shooting away from her in every direction. She looked up at Monarch, her eyes a deep indigo. As he looked at her, his smile began to fade, and the points on his teeth receded slightly.

"What the…" was all he managed.

Annie threw her arms forward and all of the light and the energy and power she had conjured surged forward and blew the rest of the church wall out, sending shockwaves through the rest of the building. The bell in the tower broke free and cascaded down through the structure, shattering the altar as it landed. The blue barrage struck Monarch with an almighty force. His grip loosened on Kimberley, who fell from the sky, her form reassembling as she did so until she landed fully formed in an open

wooden cart, crushing it. Monarch, was propelled through the General
Store, out the other side and through two houses, before crashing through
a barn roof and landing on an upturned pitchfork. His screams of pain
echoed across the valley, and the people who had not yet abandoned
Crossroads were cowering in their homes, terrified for their lives, and
wondering what they had signed up for.

Annie slowly lowered herself to the ground, and as she opened her eyes,
all evidence of her power faded. Kimberley dragged herself out of the
wreckage of the cart and staggered over to her.

"I mean, I'm very grateful, but holy shit what was that?" she asked
between laboured breaths.

Annie was visibly tired from the effort of manifesting whatever defence
she had just directed at their enemy, but she did muster a smile.

"That… was the Montana Special."

Kristin patted her on the back smiling, before the sound of splintering
wood reminded them that they were not done here. As they ran towards
the barn, Kathryn asked Annie another question.

"What is he, Annie? A wraith or a demon, or something else?"

Annie, struggling to catch her breath, gave her reply.

"I have a theory, but I'd need to check it. But if he is what I think he is,
then we are in very deep trouble."

The quadruplet arrived at the barn in time to see Monarch rip the
pitchfork from his side, and watched the wounds heal, the amulet glowing
beneath him once more. He looked at the team and noticed Kristin's gaze.
He touched the amulet with his right hand and smiled.

"This really is quite an impressive trinket. I could have done with this two centuries ago."

Kristin now took a stand at the front of the group.

"Where is Grace, Monarch? What have you done with her?"

Monarch laughed again, and then shrugged his shoulders.

"She is gone. Where? Who knows. Lost in time, or space. Or both. Either way, you're never getting her back."

Annie was distracted by the mention of time and space. It was her understanding that these doorways, although mythical until now, only lead to other parts of the world or other realms. She was unaware they may lead to other times.

"That amulet doesn't belong to you," she said defiantly.

Her appearance made Monarch perk up some more.

"Now you, are a curious thing. Strong. Pure of heart. You're not like these others. I wonder if they know just how powerful you truly are."

Kristin, Kimberley and Kathryn all exchanged looks, and then watched the exchanges back and forth as if watching a tennis match as Monarch side stepped one way, and Annie the other.

"I gave you a demonstration of my power. Do you need another?"

Kimberley raised an eyebrow at the sassiness she had not previously seen in her friend.

"I was unaware any of you had made it into this realm. I believed I was the only one to break the barrier. I see I was wrong."

The rest of the team were now more confused than they had ever been. What was Monarch talking about when he said, 'any of you'? Was Annie hiding something? What realm had he come from? Right now, this exchange was getting them nowhere.

Kathryn moved to speak, but noticed a thin green line appear just behind Monarch. Barely visible at first, it began to glow brighter, and trace upwards before making a sharp ninety degree turn right, and then moments later another in a downwards direction, until it resembled the outline of a door. A quick glance to her left confirmed that Kimberley had seen it to. Annie must have noticed it as she was looking right at Monarch, but her gaze did not alter.

The air began to tingle with some unseen force. Monarch's eyes began to burn golden, and blue fire began to swirl around Annie's feet once more. The power was building, and it was almost touchable. Kristin primed her shotgun and launched forward towards Monarch, fed up of waiting for something to happen, but as she fired, he thrust his right arm out, and a string of golden thread whipped the gun from her hands, and a second from his left hand wrapped around her torso.

As he pulled her towards him, Kimberley thrust herself forwards, scattering purple mist and dust around as she did so, and Kathryn ran full pelt. As they all came together, Annie unleashed another violent blast of blue energy at Monarch, sending him spiralling backwards. As he did so, he threw out several golden threads, each grabbing one of the team, Annie included, and the force of Annie's initial blast sent all five of them cascading through the green door.

As they disappeared, so did the gateway, and within seconds, everything was silent.

51

7

The light was so bright it was as if it were sharpened blades attempting to pierce the eyes of anyone who chose to gaze upon it. This, however, was not a golden sun but a white ball of intense light hovering in the sky like a giant Christmas bauble. No dips, or flares on its surface. A perfectly smooth ball of white.

The only other immediate sound was that of water lapping at the edge of the wooden structure that Kathryn now found herself in. The spinning took a while to dissipate, but as it did so, she was able to open her eyes more, and attempt to take in her surroundings. As she rolled onto her side from her back, she noticed one peculiar thing. Her clothing had changed. Trying to remember the events leading to her arriving here, she recalled a battle with Monarch and then being thrown off her feet... then nothing.

One thing she was sure of, was that she had been wearing dark blue jeans and a leather jacket. Now, however, she was wearing khaki combat trousers and a white vest top. Examining the alterations further, she found a holster strapped to her left thigh containing a .45 and a second smaller one on her belt containing a rather sharp dagger.

She tried to stand, but the motion of the water and her still unfocused head sent her crashing back down to the bottom of the small row boat she found herself in. Taking a second or two to re-establish her bearings, she moved onto her knees and looked around. She was floating in a small boat made of darkened wood, no oars, and she appeared to be in the middle of the ocean.

There were no signs of land, or any civilisation. Neither were there any other boats in the vicinity. The eeriest part of this, however, was the lack of any wind or breeze. The water was moving, but there was no breeze to create the waves. No birds in the sky. No planes, and no signs of any fish or other marine life. Then more details came back to Kathryn. The doorway. She remembered the green doorway appear behind Monarch, and that he entangled them all with some kind of energy. They must have gone through it. But where was she? And where was everybody else?

"Hello!" she shouted.

No response. No echo. Nothing.

"HELLO!" she bawled even louder.

For a moment, nothing. Then Kathryn thought she could hear a faint coughing noise. She shouted again, and the coughing sounded a little closer. Scanning the water, she spotted a thin piece of driftwood floating roughly a hundred yards away. Clinging on to the wood, was Annie.

"Annie!" Kathryn shouted, but Annie couldn't find her voice. "Hang on! I'm coming!"

Kathryn searched the bottom of the boat for anything she could use as an oar, but finding nothing, she kicked the top slat of wood until it splintered away, ripped it from the top of the boat and started using it to paddle closer to her friend.

Annie's eyes were not focussing well, and there were no signs of any blue energy surrounding her. The arrival here had apparently subdued her abilities. A few minutes later, she felt herself being hauled up, and after lying on her back for a few moments, she opened her eyes to see Kathryn looking back at her.

"Nice outfit," she said with a thin smile. "Been to the *Tomb Raider* store?"

Kathryn chuckled, relieved to see Annie was still herself. She too was in a different costume. Her red sundress had been replaced by black jeans and a black blouse. Her hair was also different. It too was now black, but had a streak of electric blue running down the left side at the front.

53

"Speak for yourself *Evanescence*."

Annie examined her new look, and found herself raising her eyebrows and nodding in approval.

"Actually, this is pretty good," she said.

"Okay, so we have new looks and we're floating in an endless ocean with a giant lightbulb. Where are we Annie?"

While she waited for her colleagues' reply, Kathryn continued to scan the horizon. Annie meanwhile, was attempting to theorise as to their location.

"Well, we are definitely in a different realm. This is *not* Earth. The energy is different."

Kathryn turned around and looked at her.

"You can tell that?" she asked, surprised.

Annie laughed.

"You did see how much energy I produced back there right? I can almost smell that this isn't right. Impressed?"

"Yeah, actually."

Annie reached up, and took Kathryn's hand and they both stood together, once again scanning for any signs of life. Annie closed her eyes and mumbled words under her breath, and then opened them before letting out a sigh.

"Well, wherever this is, something here is inhibiting my ability to conjure anything. I'm effectively switched off."

"That's not good. I hope if that yellow eyed bastard is here somewhere, the same has happened to him. What the hell is he by the way?"

Annie steadied herself as the boat rocked, but appeared to delay answering the question, by asking another.

"Hey, what's that over there?"

She was pointing behind them, where a dark grey cloud had appeared over the water. The eerie sight had materialised from nowhere, and the ball of light illuminating the sky was still hovering above them, but this phenomenon appeared to be moving independently. Noting Annie had once again not answered her question, she squinted her eyes attempting to focus on what was headed their way.

"I dunno, but whatever it is, it's getting bigger and coming this way."

The two of them dropped to the bottom of the boat and Kathryn reached for her makeshift oar, handing it to Annie before breaking the matching piece of wood from the other side of the boat for herself. The two of them began paddling as hard as they could, but the mist was approaching, and with it came an ever increasing rumbling. Something was inside the cloud.

Suddenly a deafening foghorn sounded, so loud it forced both women to drop their oars and cover their ears. The boat began to vibrate violently, and as they turned to look behind them, an enormous vessel began to emerge from the fog. As they watched on, Kathryn realised there was no way they were going to escape the path of the ship in time, and lunged at Annie, sending them both over the side and into the ocean. They both kicked their legs as fast as their bodies would allow, just clearing the danger zone as the ship's bow crushed their row boat into kindling.

The currents from the ship swirled around them both dragging them under the waves several times. However, when they popped back up and were able to remain there, they noticed the ship itself had not created a backwash or any other waves. Annie then noticed something else.

The ship had blood dripping from the railings on the deck.

This fact had not gone unnoticed by Kathryn, but her attention was captured by something else. With Annie still preoccupied, Kathryn shot forwards and began kicking her legs towards the side of the vessel, heading for a rope ladder hanging from those very same railings. Annie waited for a moment, until she saw what Kathryn was aiming for.

Clinging on to the bottom of the ladder, was Kristin.

Reaching her wife, Kathryn was relieved to see that Kristin was conscious and clinging to the ladder of her own free will. She reached out a hand and Kathryn grabbed on, and wrapped her arm around her, and the two of them each held a rung. Annie grabbed Kathryn's hand, and they both lifted Kristin up so she could get a foothold on the ladder. She climbed up five rungs, before gesturing to the other two to follow.

"Hey, Kris, wait."

Annie pointed her towards the blood covered railings, but was not prepared for her reply.

"I know. It's Kimberley. She did it."

Kristin, also sporting a more military look with black combat trousers and a navy t-shirt, along with an array of knives, continued to climb up the ladder, stopping just short of the deck. Kathryn was not happy with the explanation given to her and tugged Kristin's leg.

"What the hell do you mean, Kimberley did it?" she whispered loudly.

Kristin drew one of the daggers from her belt and clutched it tightly, before sliding up onto the deck on her belly. Kathryn looked down at

Annie, who shrugged her shoulders in reply, and the two of them began climbing until they too were lying on the deck. Following on Kristin's lead, they all gradually rose to their feet and the scene before them was unveiled.

The deck was an older style light wood, railings that were unbloodied were metal, painted ice white. The actual deck area appeared to be that of a luxury cruise liner. But the light wood soon turned into something more gruesome. Vast puddles of dark red blood covered the wood from the railings right across to the other side of the walkway, and streaks ran down the inside of the windows directly in front of them.

"Kris, I need some info here."

Kristin paused and held her hand out for patience. She sighed and turned to face her wife. It was at this point that Kathryn noticed a large tear in the front of Kristin's shirt, and a clear slash across her stomach through the gap.

"Jesus, what happened?" she exclaimed.

Kristin held a hand up for silence, and her face turned to anger.

"What happened, is that I've been stuck here fighting an unhinged pain wraith and smoke demons for two fucking weeks alone! That's what's happened! Nice of you to show up and tag along!"

Two weeks? How is that possible? Wait, smoke demons? All of these thoughts running through Kathryn's mind were clashing against one another, but Annie remained calm. She seemed to accept the information as if it had been expected. Kathryn was not about to let it go this time.

"Okay, somebody please tell me what the hell is going on here!"

Annie held up her hands in defeat, and Kristin gestured to move across to a sheltered alcove near the steps up to the bridge. When all three were inside, Annie offered her explanation.

"Okay, so if I'm correct, Monarch is a Yellow Demon. They are an ethereal creature that once existed in the Land Beyond. They inhabited the bodies of mortal men who were harbouring more ambitious goals and wanted to take over the kingdom for themselves. The Demons unleashed the most unhinged and purest evil of thoughts and possibilities within each of them. They tore through the land and slaughtered anyone who stood in their way. They were only defeated when the warriors within the realm managed to imprison them in a micro-prison where they could never escape. Obviously Monarch did."

Both Kathryn and Kristin stood looking at Annie, open mouthed, in pure disbelief of what they were hearing. Fables, and legends and mystical powers of some fantasy land.

"What the actual fuck are you talking about?" Kathryn blurted out. "And how can you possibly know that? That doesn't come from books, at least not the kind of books on *our* planet."

"Kathryn, please…"

"And why do I get the feeling you're holding out on something about who *you* are too!"

"I'm just trying to…"

"I don't give a shit what you're trying to do Annie, I want the truth right now!"

"ENOUGH!"

Kristin bellowed at her wife, and pushed her away.

"Annie, just tell her about the doorways and Kimberley. That's all we need to know for now."

Kathryn now realised that perhaps she was the one who had only just arrived, and that Annie and Kristin had been together for a while before she turned up.

"The doorways don't have guardians anymore, so when they're used, they disappear. The way we came through isn't our way back. Kimberley's energy amplified whatever was causing the doorways to appear in Wealdstone, and now we are here, whatever this place is, it nullifies abilities. So now, Kimberley is mortal, but with centuries of painful memories playing out inside her head, driving her slowly mad."

Kathryn now slightly calmer was beginning to take information in more readily, but she had not forgotten the revelation of Monarch's supposed origins. Annie volunteered more information.

"I got here first, landed in a lifeboat. Kristin arrived a day later, fell straight into the sea beside me, and we found a ship. Nineteenth century design. There was nobody on board, but it seemed to drive itself along. Then we came upon floating wreckage of a plane. Nobody inside it, but then we heard a scream. There was a second plane and sat on the top was Kimberley, head in her hands, pulling at her hair. We tried to get her on board but she fought us all the way. She tore her way through that ship until she managed to blow it up. I fell into the water and managed to climb onto that piece of wreckage you found me on. Obviously I drifted for longer than I thought. I lost sight of Kristin and Kimberley. Then eventually, you found me."

Kathryn nodded, and looked over at her wife, who was doing everything possible not to look at her. Without any suggestion from Kathryn, she completed the story.

"I followed Kim as best as I could. She was swimming from wreckage to wreckage and then I caught sight of this ship. I heard screams, and I saw some sort of… creatures running around on the deck practically tearing people apart. They were like swirls of smoke, but sentient. Then out of that smoke, I saw her. Kimberley was screaming and taking down whoever was left. This was some sort of cruise ship. And it used to have a crew. The smoke creatures started the attack, but Kimberley took out the rest."

The horror that had been described to Kathryn was almost unbelievable. Had they not been through the scenarios they had, she would have said impossible. But her thought process was then interrupted by a loud feral growl coming from an open doorway just ahead.

"Never thought I'd say this again," said Kristin, "but let's go hunt us a pain wraith."

8

The taste of the salt caused his throat to gag until he began choking on the sea water. Eyes still closed, he felt as though his hands had been tied. It was only when his consciousness began to strengthen that he realised, that his left hand was planted on a solid surface. Twisting his fingers, Monarch realised it was sand. Another wave lapped at his face, and he coughed and spluttered as the water washed down his throat once more.

Finally opening his eyes, the sun burned into his mind. Something was not right. He felt, somehow, weaker. It was as if his very soul had been removed from within him. Where was he? What had happened?

The doorway.

He remembered being pulled through a doorway. That had not been any part of his plan. He had fought too hard to be in control of them, it had never been his intention to cross one. Not again. But this place was different. He had not seen this realm before. The beach led up a small incline at the top of which he could see a collection of trees and what appeared to be a house or hut of some kind. But the image was not clear. Monarch rubbed his palms over his eyes and squinted, but it wasn't his vision. Everything was clear until the border at the top of the hill. The images appeared to be waving like heat rays in extreme weather.

He pulled himself upright, the sand shifting beneath his feet. He placed a hand on his chest, and it was at this point, he noticed his clothing had altered. He was wearing a much more modern outfit with jeans and a black t-shirt. He also noticed something else. The amulet was gone. Monarch gritted his teeth as he realised it must've happened as he was hit before falling through the doorway. His vision was now clear, and he was taking in his surroundings. What he couldn't come to terms with was how he felt… mortal. His mind was his own, but his strength was gone. He reached out his right hand in an effort to conjure something, but nothing happened. His eyes were a normal deep shade of green. There was no evidence that he was anything other than a normal man, washed up on a beach.

He began to climb up the sandy incline towards this invisible barrier, and the closer he got to it, the more he felt like he was being watched. He span around but saw nobody. A faint rumble in the sand caused him to shift his footing, but again, nothing emerged. Then he began to hear muffled shouting, and he realised it was coming from behind the barrier. Confused, Monarch again squinted his eyes, but saw nothing on the other side.

Another low rumble behind him caused him to spin around for a second time, but this time, something was different. The sky began to darken slightly, and a cloud emerged seemingly out of nowhere. The foggy mass began to swirl in an unusual way. It was almost as if the cloud was *alive*. Again, Monarch heard the shouting from behind him, but did not turn away. The swirling grey mass began to move down towards the beach, and within it, lightning bolts flashed red, but the accompanying sound was not of thunder, but of an animal. A loud roar came from the swirling mass as it wound its way towards Monarch. As it once again dawned on him that his abilities had left him, the shouting intensified, and he finally turned and began sprinting towards the barrier. As he did so, the fog picked up speed, and roared once more.

Monarch stumbled but reached the energy barrier. He stopped just short of it and turned back to see the fog morph into a circular mouth, the mist shaping itself into razor sharp teeth. For the first time in over two hundred years, Monarch felt fear. He had no defences. As he froze on the spot and prepared for his doom, he felt something within him. There was a sense of relief. A calming within him. Something began to re-emerge from his inner most core. Something he had not felt for millennia.

He felt *human*.

The rage and the anger that had dwelled within him for so very long began to diminish. His shoulders began to relax, and he even felt himself begin to form a smile on his lips. As he opened his eyes to see this incredible behemoth about to devour him, he took a deep breath and sighed.

"I'm me again."

Suddenly, two hands grabbed hold of Monarch from behind, and yanked him through the energy barrier backwards until he emerged on the other side collapsed onto his back, looking up at the sky, now clear once more, the giant ball of light hanging in the air. All evidence of the darker skies had vanished. Three heads emerged looking down at him. For a moment, he was taken over by confusion, but after a few seconds, he began to feel his strength returning. He experienced a surge of energy coursing through his veins like water running down a drainpipe after a torrential storm. The calm and peaceful moment of just a few seconds ago was now a distant memory. As the yellow glow returned to his eyes, he leapt up from the ground, and took in an enormous lung full of air.

The people surrounding him took a defensive leap backwards, and watched on as Monarch calmed his breathing and stood straight up. As he turned to face them, his eyes had softened to a more golden hue, and his face appeared more normal. He looked around and was slightly taken aback at what he saw. There were ten homes constructed in a line under the shade of six trees. But these homes were not made of normal construction materials, or even of twigs and leaves as you may perhaps expect on a deserted island. They were made of mostly metal scraps.

The nearest house to Monarch was also the largest structure, and had several markings on the walls and doorframes. He moved closer to get a better look as the apparent inhabitants looked on. He read some of the markings with great intrigue.

USS Cyclops.

A naval vessel perhaps? Monarch was not overly familiar with human history, but he was aware of US Naval vessels adopting similar names.

This part of the structure appeared to be very old by human terms. Decades, if not a hundred years old perhaps. Rust was visible along the rivet points. A second piece on the front of the building appeared to have come from a different structure altogether.

Eastern Caribbean Airways.

A commercial airliner. It appeared much more recent an addition than the first few pieces from the *Cyclops*. One final named piece formed the door to the house.

Witchcraft.

Another boat, perhaps? Or an ironic commentary on the abilities which were seemingly coming back to Monarch the longer he remained within this secluded settlement. In a way it reminded him of Crossroads. Contained within its own little bubble, designed to keep people out. He strolled along the line of houses, allowed to wander by the crowd of people now watching. He saw that every home was of different design and size, but all appeared to be built from wreckage or components of ships, or planes. Except the final dwelling. Something was very different about this one.

The house itself was a triangular shape, like the others, but this one was lying flat on its back rather than pointing upwards, the wider base forming the front of the dwelling and the point at the far back. The edges, however, were rounded and not sharp, and there appeared to be a circular tube sat on top, reminiscent of an engine. But not of this world's design.

The final structure which caught his eye was not that of a house or shelter. It was of a bright shiny metal fence, constructed beneath the shade of the farthest tree from the camp. The silver shine was quite striking, despite it being well weathered, and the fence came to an opening where it then morphed into a gateway with an arch above it, hammered out from the same reflective metal. A propeller sat in the middle of the archway, and Monarch could see that there were smaller structures sticking out of the ground.

He stopped at the entrance to this little garden. The propeller sat over another marking. The marking read *NR16020*. Directly in front of him was the largest of what he now recognised were gravestones. Etched into the metal was a short paragraph, followed by a name.

'Never interrupt someone doing what you said couldn't be done. Amelia Earhart.'

"She was the first. But there have been many others."

A voice from behind Monarch, startled him. He looked over his shoulder, but what he saw was not a conventional man. This individual appeared to be adorned with crystal. No, not crystal. Diamonds. He resembled a rock based creature he had once seen in his home long ago, but more intricately designed.

"Of all designs, apparently," he replied.

The diamond-skinned man nodded, gazing at the ground.

"This is a place of damnation for not just the human world, but others as well."

"What is this place?" Monarch asked.

"The humans had a name for it, and the rest of us adopted it the same. They call it The Triangle."

"Triangle?"

"On Earth, there is an area of their oceans known as the Bermuda Triangle. It is a place where vessels and aircraft often mysteriously

65

disappear. On Deltaria, we call it Varnok. Whatever the name for it, a place exists in every realm. This is where you end up."

Monarch listened intently. As his powers began to return to him, he was assessing how he could make use of this place. He decided it would be to his benefit to extract as much information as he could.

"What about that creature out there?" he asked, pointing to where he had come through the barrier.

"That was just one of them. We call them the Shrike. They feast on those in the Triangle."

Monarch raised an eyebrow.

"Friendly creatures."

The Deltarian man shook his head.

"You do not seem to understand my yellow-eyed friend. This is not a realm for life to thrive. The Triangle is not simply a random occurrence on Earth. It is the joint purgatory for every realm in existence. Humans believe the Bermuda Triangle to be located on their planet, but it is merely a doorway to this place. This is a feeding ground for the Shrike. Nothing more."

The Deltarian was now joined by a human female, mid-thirties with long red hair, and a human male, mid-sixties wearing leather gloves. The woman introduced herself and the man.

"My name is Francine. I was on a Turkish Airlines flight in 2017. We hit turbulence and I blacked out. Next thing I knew, I was here on the beach, and the plane was nowhere in sight. This here is Fred Noonan. He was Ms. Earhart's co-pilot when they crashed here."

Monarch wasn't particularly interested in the intricacies of the other's arrival. What he was interested in was how long they had been here.

"When did you arrive here?"

Fred Noonan chortled to himself.

"How long indeed."

Monarch looked at Francine, who elaborated.

"Well, Fred crashed here in 1937. I woke up here in 2017. Our Deltarian friend here crashed his ship in 2207. But the thing is, while Fred has been here a long time, I've only been here two weeks, and Ces'An has been here four."

Not for the first time, Monarch showed a look of confusion. The Deltarian, he now knew was called Ces'An continued the explanation.

"This place exists in all of time and space, throughout history in every realm. Time has no meaning here. You can crash your starship in the 23rd century and arrive here one day, to be joined by someone from the 18th century a month later. Time and energy are suspended here. You probably noticed your abilities diminished outside of the bubble. I presume from your eyes you are not human either."

Monarch began to smile, but prevented himself from grinning and revealing himself too early.

"Not quite."

"That is why we created this bubble using the technology from Ces'An's vessel," said Francine. "It allows us to protect ourselves from the Shrike, age as nature intended, and for those of us with extra abilities, we can be free to use them."

It made sense to Monarch that whatever monsters occupied this Triangle, were clearly a superior life-form. They trap creatures and other species, use some kind of dampening field to make them helpless and then devour them without issue. He admired the Shrike for their ingenuity. Why travel to the supermarket when you can get your food delivered.

"I didn't go through the Bermuda Triangle on Earth, I was thrown through what we call a Guardian Gateway. They are interlinked portals to other times and realms and universes. Without the guardians, once passed through, the gateway closes permanently. You wouldn't happen to know of the existence of one here?"

Each of the settlers exchanged looks before Fred volunteered his contribution. He walked past Monarch until he reached the other edge of the bubble, and simply pointed. Monarch and the others wandered over to join him.

"That is the only way out of the Triangle."

Monarch's initial smile faded somewhat. Fred was pointing at a large dark swirling mass hovering over the ocean. Beneath them was an oblong shaped gap in the water. With glowing green edges.

"Has anyone ever made it through? Well, no, I suppose not if it's still there."

Fred walked away, and Monarch followed him with his eyes. As Fred stopped and turned back towards him, he seemed to be filled with rage.

"Of course nobody has escaped! The Shrike will rip you limb from limb, eat your raw flesh and spit out the parts they don't want!"

Francine offered an apology to Monarch.

"I'm sorry, Fred hasn't been the same since Amelia died. None of us have really. She was the first to pass away here. That's the only time I've ever seen the Shrike react, almost in *pain*. Whenever they bring somebody here and they die in the bubble, they seem to weaken."

Monarch's eyebrows raised again.

"Is that so?" he asked.

Francine nodded. Ces'An continued.

"They utilise their energy to pull people and their vessels through. When they don't consume the energy and they lose it, they hurt."

Fred returned to the conversation, this time with a more puzzled face having thought about something Monarch had said.

"These doorways… you said they're Guardian Gateways? What happened to these… Guardians?"

Monarch turned to look back at the Shrike circling the doorway. His smile began to widen beyond the limits of his mouth and his eyes began to burn like yellow fire. He didn't answer.

Fred began to exhibit signs of discomfort at the fact that Monarch now appeared to be ignoring them. Francine shared his confusion. Monarch's back appeared to grow broader and tense. Ces'An too sensed something was wrong. Fred asked again.

"I said, what happened to the Guardians?"

Monarch slowly turned to face them, his mouth now wide apart, teeth at their maximum points, and he hovered above the ground slightly. As the drool began to drip from the edges of his smile, he gave his reply.

"I killed them."

9

Right about now, Kathryn wished she had a flashlight. There were brief shimmers on the white gloss walls from the artificial-looking sun, but beyond that, images were consumed by their own shadows. Kristin led the trio, with Annie at the back, feeling much more vulnerable without her magic. Perhaps it was an advantage to just be normal, Kathryn thought. They had needed to train themselves in martial arts, and defence methods, and weapons training, but they had no abilities to be taken away. Despite their situation, she found some comfort in that.

Another low growl came from directly ahead, and as Kristin moved slightly left to press her arm against the wall, she thought she saw movement in the darkness ahead. More questions plagued Kathryn's mind than answers, and she still had so many more. But this was not the time. Their friend was in trouble, and the ever deepening rift between her and her wife would have to remain for the time being.

"Where did all these clothes and weapons come from?" she asked as quietly as she could.

"We're in another realm, Kat." Annie was now growing tired of being the narrator. "This is how we would look if this was *our* realm. In this place, we'd look like this."

Kathryn raised her eyebrows in acceptance, and tilted her head to one side. She was far from displeased with her outfit and accessories.

"Maybe I'll dress like this when we get home. I kinda dig it."

Despite her anger towards her wife, Kristin couldn't help but smile to herself. Roleplay was something Kathryn had previously been reluctant to try at home. Perhaps all was not lost after all.

A loud crash came from the other side of a door up ahead, and Kristin held her hand up for the group to stop. Kathryn checked her gun, and found it missing just one bullet. Kristin did the same. Just two left. Her two week adventure had taken its toll, and she felt obligated to go for a blade instead. There was no telling how long they would be here, and her brief encounter with the Shrike had left her pining for more ammunition.

Kristin took a deep breath, and raising her military style boot, kicked the door open, rushing in and angling to the left to allow the others to enter the room alongside her. Immediately, Kimberley charged Annie, shoulder barging her in the chest, her fairly slender frame launched off the ground, slamming into the nearest wall with a thud, and falling to the floor in a heap. Kristin tried to circle round the back as Kimberley veered towards Kathryn, but sensing the presence behind her, she snapped round and her eyes locked with Kristin.

"Come on Kim, this isn't you. You know us."

For a moment, there was a hint of recognition in her eyes, but she seemed so lost. The pain was carved into her face. All the centuries of death and pain, and all of the lives she had before were all constantly running through her mind like a slideshow of agony. Kristin's voice seemed like a distant call on the wind. Fire burned through her entire body, and she needed to cleanse it, extinguish it. The only way her now mortal body could do that was to lash out in the hopes of ripping it away from her. Unfortunately for Kristin, that meant she was vastly outranked in battle. Kimberley may not have had her abilities, but the rage and pain gave her excessive strength.

Before Kristin had chance to react to Kimberley's advance, the former wraith had grabbed her arm, twisted it back and grabbed hold of her knife. One swift thrust and the blade was plunged into Kristin's side, and she fell to the floor, letting out a scream of agony as she did so. Without even looking in her direction, Kimberley launched the blade directly at Kathryn, with it missing her head by a mere inch and embedding itself in the wooden trim on the wall.

Kristin could feel she was now losing a fair bit of blood, and looking over at Annie in the corner, she could see that her friend still had not regained consciousness. This was not exactly how she had planned to go out.

With nowhere to go, and no help left, Kathryn hunched down and prepared for Kimberley's attack. The two ran at each other, and as they collided, they crashed to the floor, rolling over one another until they hit the opposite wall and came apart. Kathryn scrambled to get to her feet, but just half way to being upright, Kimberley launched the same shoulder barge she had employed on Annie, and Kathryn exploded through a wooden door, beyond which was daylight. The brightness burned into Kristin's eyes, and as Kathryn landed on a narrow balcony outside, she too couldn't see. Luckily, this also had a brief effect on Kimberley, and Kathryn was able to pull herself up with the railings.

Inside, Kristin had regained her vision and began dragging herself along the floor towards Annie, who was still not moving. She could feel sweat beginning to build up on her forehead, which was not a good sign. Her skin was now clammy, and she knew she was not in good shape. Still she attempted to rouse Annie.

Kathryn propped herself up against the outside of the ship as Kimberley shook her head trying to adjust to the brightness. When she did, she turned and locked her eyes on Kathryn. Within a second, she had her hands wrapped around her throat, her teeth gritted tightly and she began screaming in agony, despite being the one inflicting the damage. Kathryn slowly began to drift away.

Suddenly, the ship impacted upon something with such force, Kimberley was thrown over the balcony and out of sight, Kathryn followed, but managed to cling on to the railings, and inside the room, Kristin and Annie's bodies were thrown from one side of the room to the other. The loud groaning from the ship's engines was deafening as the ship came to a halt. They were still trying to drive the vessel forward, but the ship did not move.

Kathryn did everything she could to pull herself back up and over the railings, and collapsed onto her back on the wooden deck. After a moment to catch her breath back, rubbing her throat with her hands to soothe it from her attempted choking, she looked up and saw that they had apparently beached on an island. It was only at this point, that she remembered the other two were still inside.

"Kris? Annie?" she called, but got no answer.

She made her way back into the room, which now illuminated by daylight she could see had been a private cabin. All of the furniture was smashed in a corner either by the impact or by Kimberley previously. On the furthest wall underneath a broken rectangular mirror, was a long streak of blood, which led down to the floor and an unconscious Kristin, lying in a small puddle of her own blood.

"Kristin!"

Kathryn ran over, and knelt down beside her wife. Her skin was pale, and her shirt was soaked in blood from the knife wound Kimberley had inflicted. She ripped off the bottom part of that shirt to inspect it, but it was not a good image. Kimberley had not simply stabbed Kristin, she had plunged the knife in, and twisted it so there was a jagged hole in her side. Kristin began to stir slightly, and her eyes flickered.

"Hey, there you are," Kathryn said as calmly as she could, tears forming in her eyes. "I was worried about you for a minute."

Kristin smiled.

"Hey, I'm the only one who does anything properly round here, you think I'd leave you in charge?"

Kathryn smiled at the comment, but also felt slightly offended that Kristin had now confirmed her status as new leader. Nevertheless, she had to try and stem the bleeding somehow, and that was not going to be easy. Kristin glanced at the doorway.

"Where are we?" she asked.

"I don't know. We crashed into some island or beach or something."

"Kimberley?"

Kathryn simply shook her head.

"Annie?" Kristin asked, again looking at the doorway.

"I don't know, I haven't checked her out yet, but I'm pretty sure she's just knocked out."

Kristin shook her head.

"No, Annie. She's gone."

Kathryn looked around the cabin, and her wife was right. Annie was nowhere to be seen. She gently lowered Kristin back to the floor, and then walked back out on to the balcony. Looking around, she could see what appeared to be some kind of settlement on the beach. Or at least what used to be a settlement. There was a lot of rubble, and smoke coming from some of the former houses. But something wasn't quite right. The image of the settlement was somehow distorted. It was almost as if there was a wavy film between them and the location. And then she saw her. Annie was standing inside the bubble, arms reaching out to her side, and blue strands of energy beginning to wrap themselves around her body.

"Kris, we have to go!"

Kathryn ran back inside, and quickly picked her wife up in her arms. She staggered slightly getting up, and let out a large gust of air.

"Jesus, Kris. How many doughnuts have you been eating lately?" she said in jest.

But she didn't get a reply. Kristin was now fully unconscious and not moving. She was still breathing, but it was shallow. Kathryn lumbered forwards as quickly as she could, taking care not to slip or trip as she made her way back down the corridor and up the stairs to the deck. Remembering that the part of the ship they had just been was still hovering over the water, she carried on moving towards the bow of the ship. Had this not been a nightmare scenario, she could see herself enjoying a nice pina colada on a sun lounger on this deck, floating through the Caribbean. Snapping herself back to reality, she shook her head clear, and pushed on.

The closest she could get to the actual bow was the final two lifeboat storage racks. Slipping Kristin into one of the boats, and climbing in next to her, she reached up and detached the rope from the safety catch and began lowering the boat down. Half way down the side of the ship, Kathryn noticed that Annie was no longer alone. Kimberley was collapsed on the sand at her feet, not moving, but also beginning to show signs of their abilities returning, with a few flickers of purple lightning emanating from her fingertips.

Moments later, the lifeboat landed with a thud on the sand, and Kathryn climbed out, struggling to lift Kristin out, and they both fell onto the wet sand. Rather than try and pick her up again, Kathryn grabbed both of her forearms, and began dragging her backwards along the sand towards the translucent barrier. As they reached it, Kathryn turned and saw Annie gesturing towards her, and shouting, but she could not hear the words. She held up her hand and waved it through what felt like treacle, but on the other side was warm air. Deciding it must be safe, she pulled Kristin through, and once more collapsed onto the sand from exhaustion.

"Kat, move!" Annie shouted.

75

Kathryn looked up to see Annie preparing to charge towards her, energy now swirling around her friend in all shades of blue, her hair waving through the air as if it were underwater. Kathryn dived to the side, and Annie unleashed a barrage of energy beams, and as Kathryn turned to look behind her, swirls of black smoke were penetrating the barrier, growling and morphing into giant mouths.

Each blow knocked one of them back, but they kept coming. Then she felt a hand on her shoulder. Looking around, she saw Kimberley holding out a hand of help. Smiling at recognising her friend once more, she accepted the lift and they both ran towards Kristin, and dragged her away from the edge of the barrier. The translucent effect was becoming clearer and clearer as each new monster began to push through. Kimberley left Kathryn and Kristin together and joined Annie in pushing them back. Kathryn watched on in awe as both Annie and Kimberley directed a large beam of energy towards each other, and simultaneously threw it towards the creatures. In an incredible explosion of blue, violet and black, the creatures dissipated into thin air, a distant scream all that remained.

Annie fell to her knees, exhausted from her efforts, and all traces of her powers gone. She reached into her pocket, and pulled out something, before handing it to Kimberley. She ran over to Kristin, and Kathryn watched as she placed the amulet around Kristin's neck. It took over a minute before the device began to glow, and relief permeated the air as Kristin's skin began to return to its normal colouring. Annie joined the group, and she too was relieved.

"So do you wanna tell me what *this* place is, Annie? Or should I just ignore it and move on?"

Annie took a deep breath, before taking a look around.

"I actually don't know. But whatever is keeping this bubble going, is creating a dampening field on the effects of this realm. Good thing too, because without it, we'd be lunch."

Kathryn thought about the twisted creatures they had just seen.

"What the hell were those things?"

Although the question was directed at Annie, it was Kimberley who answered.

"They're called The Shrike."

Now it was Annie's turn to look surprised.

"And this? This is what you on Earth would call the Bermuda Triangle."

While under normal circumstances, Annie and Kathryn would laugh that comment away, these weren't normal circumstances. They therefore allowed her to continue.

"The Bermuda Triangle is simply an amplified doorway, much like the one we fell through. It takes people to another realm. But it doesn't just exist on Earth. Every realm or world, or universe has a gateway to this place. This is where the Shrike live."

Kristin was now awake enough to join in the conversation.

"And what exactly are The Shrike?" she asked, coughing after getting her question out.

"They are a sub-species of wraith. They used to patrol a place called The Horizon. A point in space and time where those who enter it would find themselves transported back to their most desired place or time. Every time somebody would reach it, it would diminish the phenomena's lifespan. So the pain wraiths and the other wraiths in neighbouring realms created the Shrike to patrol it."

Annie waved her hands about in protest.

77

"Woah, woah. So you're telling me there are *other* wraiths?"

Kathryn and Kristin exchanged looks too of uncertainty and concern.

"Yes, obviously. You humans have been sighting wraiths on Earth for millennia. There aren't just pain wraiths you know. Anyway, when The Shrike got tired of patrolling such power and not being able to utilise it, they joined together and used the Horizon to create their own realm. Then they created invisible doorways for people to fall through... and then they consume them."

Kristin gulped.

"Consume... you mean eat?"

Kimberley nodded.

"To keep the doorways open, they expend a lot of energy, so they lure people or species, or whoever into the Triangle, and then consume them which replenishes their energy and gives them an extra boost."

"Guys?"

Kristin had now moved away from the others, and was looking around the decimated settlement they had found themselves in. She was stood over the body of a large humanoid mass, but they clearly were not human. The others wandered over and while Kathryn and Annie were shocked at the image before them, Kimberley simply emitted sadness.

"Deltarian."

"I'm sorry?" Kristin asked.

"He's a Deltarian. They're a species on the far side of your galaxy. They were always admired by the pain wraiths for their approach to loyalty and efficiency when it came to taking action. It takes a lot to kill one of these guys."

Annie's voice cut through the air.

"There's more over here."

As the team walked along the edge of the camp, they saw dozens of bodies. Some looked like they had been torn apart by wild animals, others as if they had been burnt. But they were all dead.

Kathryn was thinking it but Kristin was the one who spoke it aloud.

"Monarch."

Kimberley and Annie nodded in unison.

"He's the only thing powerful enough to take down this place, and defeat the Shrike. Whatever he is, he is far more powerful than either me or Annie."

Annie shrunk back slightly, and once again her secrecy was called into question, but this time by Kristin.

"Annie, this is some next level shit. We nearly didn't make it out of this and if we are going to survive, then we need to know everything. And I mean everything."

Annie looked at each of the group in turn, and then sat down in the sand, crossed her legs and closed her eyes. The blue strands of energy they group now associated with their friend, began to swirl around them all until they were completely encapsulated in a dome of symbols and as they stared in disbelief, images began to appear. Annie began to describe what they were seeing.

"My mother, Ariella, was a pain wraith as you know. She met my father after her first battle with Jasmine, and they ended up having me as a result of their marriage."

An image appeared before them of Arthur and Ariella coming out of a church, confetti being thrown everywhere, and smiles on both of their faces.

"No child born of a pain wraith and a human had ever exhibited any form of powers or abilities, as Kimberley can confirm. But what my mother didn't know, and what I never knew, was that my father… was not human."

The images changed to show a world of great beauty. Forests teeming with life, a beautiful waterfall surrounded by a selection of small houses.

"My father was an entity known as a Blue Spirit. He was born in another realm, known as the Land Beyond. It gets its name from the belief that it is the final realm in existence before the void. It's actual name is unknown."

Again the images morphed until they depicted a battle. Rather unsettlingly, the image showed a familiar figure.

"My father was on the front line when the Yellow Demons emerged from their confinement when they were first discovered. The Blue Spirits and the White Falcons were the only creatures powerful enough to subdue them and lock them away. Unfortunately, as they were sealed into their tomb for what they believed would be eternity, one of them managed to briefly influence my father's mind."

A yellow mist rose up into the air, and plunged into Arthur's chest.

"My father was strong, but his mind was weakened by this attack. While he managed to return the final demon to the confinement, his mind had been altered by the experience. He found himself lusting after the same

80

power the Yellow Demons had been looking for. He began to lose his mind. In his crazed state, my father almost killed two of the White Falcons."

As the imagery before the group altered again, it depicted a scene of Arthur on his knees at the front of a castle, in glowing chains, some kind of royalty standing over him with a staff made of silver.

"The King of Beyond knew that my father had been influenced beyond his own control and that his actions were not his own. However, the damage had been done. The demon in question had now moved into another host, and vanished. My father was banished from the Land Beyond, and cast out of the realm through the doorway guarded by the Green Dragon, one of the guardians of the doorways between realms."

Another change and this time, the group were clearly looking at Wealdstone in the mid nineties. While the story appeared to be more or less complete, Kathryn had a question.

"What happened to Monarch? Did anyone track him down?"

Annie sighed, and the visions altered again.

"Monarch was a rarity. A creature that could outwit and defeat the White Falcons. They were a group of warriors who were tasked with guarding the realm, from the skies and the ground, as well as the border between Beyond and the Void. As for his whereabouts, there's no documentation."

Kimberley nodded as all of the imagery disappeared.

"That is why he is so powerful. These Yellow Demons did not corrupt mortal men, they were already seeking power. He fed on their desires."

Annie nodded.

"I only found out about the existence of the Land Beyond when I was thrown back to Victorian England as a teenager, and I met another Blue Spirit. She had sought refuge in our realm when the war between the Demons and Spirits erupted. She told me all about my father and that was when I started exploring magic. While he had not been stripped of his abilities, he had chosen to never use them again as his own form of punishment. But I felt that maybe there was some kind of power within me. So I started to explore that, and then when I went to Montana, I began developing my powers into what you see now."

Kathryn smiled.

"So you're a Blue Spirit?" she asked, smirking that they may finally have an advantage.

"Technically, I'm a hybrid Blue Spirit, Pain Wraith," she replied.

Kimberley raised eyebrows.

"My powers have developed beyond those of the Blue Spirits, so I'm guessing that Pain Wraith and Blue Spirit DNA is pretty potent."

Smiles spread across all of the women on the beach. However this didn't last very long, when they remembered where they were, and that they were surrounded by slaughtered people. Then a new question emerged.

"So, how do we get out of here?" asked Kristin.

The group looked around, but it was Annie who spotted it. She ran across the sand until the view of the doorway in the ocean came into view. Swirling above it was a dark mass of dissipated cloud. There was no life within the mass, and the doorway was warping.

"The Shrike?" she asked.

"All dead," replied Kimberley.

82

"But the doorway is still there," replied Kathryn. "Can we not just get through there?"

Annie stared at the doorway intently. It was no longer a coherent shape, wasn't glowing green and was definitely getting smaller.

"It is still active, but barely. In it's current state, we may not all end up in the same place, or time."

Hesitation in the group did not last long. Kristin dusted herself off, and turned to address the others.

"If we don't try, then we will never get home."

The others were in agreement, and together, they exited the bubble, retrieved the lifeboat from the shore, and climbed into it, Kathryn and Kimberley rowing them towards the whirlpool which encompassed the doorway.

"Here we go!" shouted Annie.

The current took hold, and the boat was sucked into a vortex of water. The doorway twisted into a spiral, and then back to a rectangle, just long enough for the boat to be sucked through. As the group vanished into the darkness, the doorway vanished, and the whirlpool of water was gone.

10

"This isn't funny."

"I wasn't laughing!"

"You were 100% taking the piss."

"I wasn't!"

"This is literally my worst nightmare."

Kristin was now huddled back against the wall of the hotel room they had materialised in, looking out of the window at anything she could focus on to ignore the content of said room. Despite her clothes more or less returning to normal, Kristin felt very out of place as this particular hotel room was filled… with clowns.

Much to Kimberley's delight, her colleague was sweating profusely, and gripping the wallpaper so hard it was now starting to peel away. The clock above her told them it was ten a.m. They weren't sure where Kathryn and Annie had ended up, but at least they appeared to be on Earth.

"You know, this place would be good for kids parties," Kimberley tried to alleviate the tension.

"Kids HATE clowns, Kim. Nobody actually likes them. They're scary and creepy and should be outlawed!"

Kimberley laughed again and walked over to the dresser which housed several leaflets and flyers about the area and things to do. Her smile evaporated when she discovered where they were.

"Uh, Kris?" she started. "We're in Frankland Hill."

That caught her attention.

"That's six hours from Wealdstone."

"I know. The question is, is it *our* Wealdstone?"

Kristin thought for a moment, and the thinking distracted her from the numerous clown pictures, models, ornaments and wallpaper.

"If the others came through here too, then they'll head for home, right?"

Kimberley nodded.

"Yeah, that makes sense. I mean that's what I'd do."

"Well then, let's head for Wealdstone and see what we find."

The two of them left the hotel room, and after dodging numerous life-sized clown statues along the corridor, they made it to the elevator. It did occur to them, that despite this being the middle of the day, they hadn't seen anyone, and it was remarkably quiet. Nevertheless, the lift arrived and they descended to the ground floor, where again, they found nobody present.

"You'd think a hotel would have reception staff or porters or somebody around in the middle of the day," Kristin mentioned.

"Something isn't right here. The energy is off."

Something was unsettling Kimberley but she couldn't put her finger on it. What she did want to do was get out of this hotel. Even she was now getting creeped out by the number of clown motifs. Once they reached the parking lot, they realised it wasn't just the hotel that was seemingly abandoned. It was the whole of Frankland Hill. There were cars in the car

85

park, but no owners, and all of them had a thin layer of dust. Clearly they hadn't moved in a while.

"Okay, I think it's safe to say that we aren't in our own Frankland Hill," Kimberley suggested.

"Which means this Wealdstone, won't be our Wealdstone," Kristin suggested.

Kimberley nodded.

"No, but we are still gonna need to get there. This place looks like it too a beating a long time ago. We don't know how to find or navigate these doorways, but getting to Wealdstone is our best chance right now."

Kimberley made a valid point. Kristin opened the door to the nearest car, and predictably found no keys inside. She turned and looked at Kimberley.

"Think you've still got your powers?" she asked.

"Only one way to find out."

Kimberley flicked her wrist towards the car's ignition, and a jet of purple lightning shot through the hole normally occupied by the key. The car coughed into life, and they both smiled.

"Still got it," Kimberley said as she strolled towards the driver's seat.

"Excuse me, where do you think you're going?" asked Kristin.

"I started the car, I'm driving it," answered Kimberley.

Kristin shook her head and waggled her finger.

"There's no way you're trying to kill me and then driving me six hours down the highway."

Kimberley felt a tinge of sadness at the thought that she nearly killed one of her friends, but grateful that it was being mentioned in jest. Kristin sensed she may have mentioned it too soon, and tried to create more levity.

"But in these extra ordinary circumstances, I'll wave the 'driver chooses the music, shotgun shuts their cakehole' rule."

Kimberley smiled and jumped into the passenger seat and moments later they turned onto the highway and disappeared into the distance, leaving a trail of dust behind them.

11

The dust was so thick, Kathryn thought she was going to choke to death. There was no sign of Kristin, Kimberley or Annie anywhere, and she felt like she had landed on her back. Pulling herself upright using debris around her, she realised she was in familiar surroundings. Lying all around her feet were smashed up TV sets and radio equipment. In fact, as her eyes settled in front of her, she noticed that she was in the electrical outlet downtown. That was until she noticed the entire front of the shop was missing. As her mind began to settle down, she began to feel intensely bad vibes. Something about this scenario rang familiar and she had the feeling it wasn't a good memory. She began to crunch her way through wreckage and stepped out of the storefront.

And that's when she saw it.

She was standing in the aftermath of Jasmine's attack on Wealdstone a few years earlier. Most of the high street was still rubble, Sisko's was blown apart, and there were not many signs of life other than a few birds overhead. It was eerie being back here. Home but not as she knew it. She began to wander down the middle of the ruined street, instinctively back towards where the mansion had been. As she walked past the smashed hardware store, she remembered Scarlett working there, and her chest tightened a little. They had lost a lot in such a short space of time. And it had all had a serious effect on the team.

She paused while she reflected on all the people they had lost. She thought about Jack. All the recent developments and her changing behaviour made her question if she made the right choice staying with Kristin. While she could not deny how much she loved her wife, she had to admit their relationship had never been perfect. There were always arguments. Almost daily. While it could be said that Kristin had become much more distant and hostile over the past three years, she had to admit her part of the downturn in their marriage. Kristin wasn't the one who almost slept with her ex. But now was not the time. She was alone and she needed to figure out what to do next.

But before she could think about that, she heard movement from the old pharmacy. Noting that her outfit had returned to it's usual design, she was pleased to discover her guns and ammo were also in their usual place in her jacket. Drawing her modified silver gun, she aimed it at the rubble and began to edge forward. More noises, and she saw some of the bricks move and fall down the edge of a small heap. She cocked the gun, and crouched slightly, trying to get a better look. She paused at the base of the pile and waited.

"Fucking shoes. Seriously, like I would ever wear these damn things!"

Kathryn raised an eyebrow at the sound of cursing coming from the darkness. But the voice sounded familiar.

"Annie?" she called into the hole.

"Kat? Is that you?" came the reply.

Kathryn lowered her gun.

"Yeah it's me, how did you get in there?"

Annie's head popped up in the gap as she clambered through the hole. Kathryn then realised why she was cursing so much. Her sensible flat shoes had been replaced by stiletto heels with a very steep angle. Unlike Kathryn, however, Annie had retained the look from the Triangle realm.

"How come you get to keep the cool look, and I go back to casual vampire slayer?" she asked, reaching out a hand to help her down to the street level.

"I know this place is as decimated as it was after Jasmine, but the first thing I'm doing is going into the boutique and stealing some shoes!"

Annie had not previously shown much frustration, and Kathryn couldn't recall her ever swearing before. But she had to admit that she kind of liked it.

After switching her shoes, Annie emerged back onto the street and looked around. She had not seen the immediate aftermath last time. Her grandmother had taken her out early on in the battle when her powers were still very limited. However, even she could sense this was not their Wealdstone.

"I know I missed most of the battle, but this isn't quite right is it?" she asked.

Kathryn looked around, more carefully this time. Annie was right. Things were not quite the same as they had been. The differences were subtle, but they were numerous. The car that Grace had been thrown against was now a full sized bus. The broken Sisko's sign was not the illuminated card design they knew, but a neon sign. And the hill that led up to the mansion curved to the left instead of the right.

"So are we back in time, or are we in an alternate Wealdstone?" she asked.

Annie closed her eyes and conjured a ball of energy in her hands. But the energy she created wasn't blue. It was purple. She opened her eyes and looked at Kathryn.

"Definitely an alternate universe."

Kathryn was more than impressed. She had only ever heard of alternate universes in science fiction novels. She was now less worried and more intrigued as to what else was different.

"I wonder where the others ended up," she said.

"Hopefully they're here somewhere. The question is, where is everyone else?" replied Annie.

"Where indeed," came a deep booming voice from behind them.

They spun around just in time to see a bolt of yellow lightning strike Annie in the middle of the chest and send her flying back down the street, coming to rest against the bus. Kathryn dived out of the way behind a discarded dumpster as Monarch shot another blast towards her.

"Oh come, I'm just as curious as you are as to where we are. Do you not want to come out and chat?"

His distorted grin was the widest Annie had seen it so far, and he was elevated six feet from the floor. What she hadn't expected, was for what happened next. Across the street where Kathryn had hidden, the dumpster exploded outwards and sent shards of metal at Monarch, who was clearly not expecting it, and he was pummelled to the floor. To Annie's shock and amazement, Kathryn was now glowing bright blue, and hovering in mid-air herself.

"Woah!" exclaimed Annie.

Kathryn turned to look at her, with her own eyes bulging and gave an exasperated reply.

"I know! What the hell!"

Monarch, now furious he had been sideswiped by an attack, had picked himself up and was now bounding down the street towards them, his energy firing all rubble and vehicles out of the way, smashing any remaining structures with the force. Annie and Kathryn exchanged a hurried look, and both thrust their arms forward towards him. The street was illuminated by blue and purple beams of energy, Monarch bounding left and right avoiding the streams as he got closer.

Kathryn leaned left and diverted a blast into his left shoulder, which altered his course and he was pushed down into the gap in the pharmacy wall where Annie had materialised.

Kathryn returned to the ground and ran over to Annie, who was still in shock at what she had just witnessed.

"So apparently, you're a Blue Spirit in this universe," she said, still unable to fully comprehend it.

"I don't even know how I did it. The whole thing just came to me instinctively," she replied, staring at her now normal hands.

"Either way," began Annie, "we need to get out of here."

Kathryn nodded and the two began running towards the top of the street. If their old mansion was still here, maybe there were weapons there that could help them. As they reached the bottom of the hill, the pharmacy ruins exploded with an earth shattering eruption, bricks and mortar flying in all directions, and Monarch let out a deafening roar as he flew out of the rubble, landing with a thud on the street which cracked the pavement in a ten foot radius. Annie and Kathryn stopped and turned round, preparing to defend themselves from another attack.

The town clock struck four p.m. and began to ring loudly. Monarch threw out his left arm and a bolt of yellow lightning blew the tower apart, silencing the clock, the faces now shattered crumbling to the ground. Thrusting his arms forward, he sent several lightning bolts at them, but they managed to dodge out of the way. As Monarch reached the intersection, he stopped and ribbons of golden energy wrapped themselves around a fragmented piece of one of the clock faces, and raised it in the air. Suddenly the sound of a car engine came into earshot, and as Monarch moved to release the shard of marble, a car ploughed into his side, and wiped him off the street. The car span out as Monarch's body flew into the woodlands, caught a pile of bricks, and flipped.

As the car rolled down the street, the front end hit a parking meter, and the car came to rest on it's side, the dust slowly settling on top of it.

Annie and Kathryn sprinted over to the wreckage, constantly looking out for any signs of Monarch. As they reached the wreck, the driver's door flew open, surrounded by a stream of purple fog, and a hand reached out. Annie and Kathryn expected the worst, but were relieved to see Kimberley's head pop up. She gave them a smile.

"Better late than never, right?"

She clambered out of the car, and sat on the top of the upended vehicle, turning and reaching back into the car. Moments later, Kristin emerged and the two of them slid down to the street.

"So, what's up with you guys?" she asked, smiling.

Kathryn felt the need to run over and embrace her wife, but something stopped her. She wasn't sure what it was, but it felt like she *should* do it, rather than *wanting* to do it. She stood back while Annie gave them hugs instead. It didn't go unnoticed by Kristin, but thankfully, Annie distracted her with the revelation that Kathryn was a Blue Spirit.

"What? How is that possible?" she enquired.

"I guess in this universe, whichever universe it is, Kathryn is a Blue Spirit, and my Pain Wraith side is the dominant one."

Kimberley chimed in.

"Well I'm just glad I'm still me."

Kathryn nodded.

"Unfortunately so is Monarch."

93

They all turned to look into the woodland, but saw nothing. Edging closer, Kristin drew her weapon, and Kathryn adopted the unusual pose of preparing to launch energy from her bare hands. As they reached the edge of the ditch that merged into the woods, they saw where Monarch had landed, but he was gone.

"So now what do we do?" asked Kathryn, lowering her hands. "We're in an alternate universe with a madman demon on the loose."

"We need to find the mansion, see if there is anything there, and then try and figure out our next move," suggested Kimberley.

"Agreed."

Kristin and Annie spoke in unison. They exchanged looks and smiled at each other. Kristin too had noticed that Annie was more ballsy in this universe, and they walked alongside each other as they all headed up the hill to where their mansion should be. Kathryn didn't remember the hill being so steep, and it felt wrong to veer off to the opposite direction once at the top. But sure enough as they entered the grounds, the house was still standing.

"I guess in this universe, Desmond didn't blow it up."

The words from Annie were a little curt, and didn't sound quite right coming out of her mouth, but the others chose to ignore it and they continued up the main driveway towards the house. However, as Annie placed one foot inside the outer wall of the main entrance, a gunshot ran out, and a bullet struck the gravel where she was standing, sending her toppling backwards, and pieces of aggregate everywhere. The others scattered as more shots rang out, and Kristin returned fire, blindly, a couple of bullets striking the stone walls of the house, another shattering a window.

Annie scrambled back beside one of the walls alongside Kimberley. They both mumbled to each other and between gunfire, both leaned over the wall and sent a blast of energy directly at the source of the fire, which happened to be one of the balconies over looking the entrance. Their combined force blew the balcony apart, and the gunman was sent spiralling in the air, and landed with a heavy thud on top of a jeep, crushing the roof, and shattering all the windows.

All four women then advanced towards him, but as they did so, the front door swung open and two women emerged, each holding a rifle.

"Don't fucking move!" screamed one of the women.

They all stopped in their tracks. Annie, Kimberley and Kristin were looking at the woman holding the bigger rifle. Kathryn however, was standing over the man, now coming round from the impact. The entirety of the last three years was now rushing back before her eyes as she realised she was looking down at Jack.

The woman holding the rifle was now slowly lowering it, and staring intently at Kristin.

"No. It can't be."

Kristin was equally in shock. She had no words. Staring back at her, was Daniella.

"I thought I'd lost you!" Daniella exclaimed.

She threw the rifle to the floor, sprinted over to Kristin, and embraced her passionately, kissing her with such a force that Kristin couldn't catch her breath. She knew it was wrong, but Kristin began to kiss her back, before she gently pushed her away. Staring into Daniella's eyes, something was different. The shock of seeing her friend alive once more, considering the last time she had laid eyes on her, she had been literally torn apart, was now mired with confusion at the greeting she had just received.

Trying to formulate a response, Kristin could only manage a sentence.

95

"Daniella, I'm… I'm not who you think I am."

Slightly confused at her response, Daniella placed her hand on Kristin's left temple, and brushed her hair away from her face.

"I think I know my own wife, Kristin."

12

The whole situation had been incredibly surreal for everyone. Inside the mansion, they were all now sat around a large maple wood round table, and sat in the middle of the antique was a familiar looking knife. Annie remained fixed on the Elder blade, and in her mind was replaying all of the horrific events of the last time she saw it. Kimberley was keeping her distance in the far corner, but not simply because of the presence of the blade diminishing her power.

Jack was slouched in a leather chair with an ice pack on his head, sporting a split lip and a cut above his right eyebrow. While he was not paying much attention to Kimberley, she on the other hand was paying a lot of attention to him. And so was Kathryn. All of the feelings and thoughts she had been having for the past three years that she thought were filed away following his death, were now running free in her head. She was finding it very hard not to say anything just yet.

Everyone, however, was focussed at least a little on the fact that Daniella was not only alive in this reality, but was apparently married to Kristin, who still had not processed the initial kiss the two had shared.

"So how exactly did all this play out in your reality?" asked Annie, managing to break her gaze from the knife that killed not only her mother, but her grandmother.

Daniella walked past her, glass of scotch in one hand, rifle in the other. She leaned the weapon against a nearby bookcase, and sat down in the chair directly opposite Kristin, her eyes longing and tinged with sadness.

"We had the year from hell," she began. "One night, a tear opened up in the sky, and a huge purple bolt of lightning blasted out of it, and deposited something right in the middle of town. Me and Kris…"

Daniella trailed off for a moment, and again looked at Kristin, tears filling her eyes. She downed the glass of scotch, and wiped away the tears before continuing.

"We drove down to investigate, and found something out of a *Marvel* movie. Some witch or demon woman was firing blasts of pure energy into every building she could find. Vaporising people. Women, children, men, everybody. Every bolt was a deadly one. We were no match. Jack and Kathryn… *our* Kathryn tried to conjure up some protective barrier around the mansion, but it didn't work. She broke through pretty quick.

By the time me and my Kris had pulled ourselves out of the rubble of some store fronts and helped a few people to safety, Ariella had already made her way into the mansion."

That name made everybody perk up.

"Ariella destroyed the town?" asked Kimberley.

Jack joined in the conversation, throwing the ice pack on the table.

"Ariella. She was a pain wraith. She had lost her mother on Earth. She left their realm to start a new life on Earth with somebody she loved, but he had left her for another woman, and Jasmine had taken her own life."

Another shiver amongst the team. They were fully aware of the level of devastation and death both Jasmine and Ariella were capable of. In any reality. Sensing they may be drawing similarities, Daniella continued the story.

"When Ariella learned humans were to blame for Jasmine's death, she broke free of her realm and came to Earth to wipe us out. Centuries of being subjected to pain and torture had driven her mad, and we had nothing that could stop it. She phased in and out of existence over the course of six or seven months, unable to maintain a physical form. It gave us time to get as many people out of Wealdstone as possible. But the final time she reappeared, she sealed the town. Anyone crossing the city limits out of Wealdstone turned to dust. Over time, the barrier has weakened at certain points on the other side. Occasionally we get burning birds fly through. I see you managed to drive through. In nearly all places, the wall is impenetrable. You must be lucky."

Kimberley stared at the elder blade once again, and it caught Daniella's attention. Her next comment was directed directly at her apprehension.

"Or maybe had somebody… unique with you."

Kathryn's constant stares had now drawn Jack's attention. He took over the story again, but this time directed the words directly at Kathryn.

"Her first visit to the mansion looking for the Elder blade cost Kathryn her life. She blasted me through a wall to safety and took the full brunt of Ariella's attack. There was nothing left of her by the time I came round."

The leading commonality in this tale seemed to be that both Jack and Daniella were mourning the loss of their separate partners. Now the arrival of duplicates of those people was beginning to dominate the energy in the room. Grief was clearly overwhelming their minds and thought processes. While Daniella and Jack both knew these were not *their* partners, in a sense they also *were*. But the person who was not expecting to have feelings of any kind other than jealousy at the fact Jack was suddenly back in their lives, was Kristin.

Whether it was being in an alternate universe and effectively taking the place of the Kristin that existed there, or whether the chasm between her and her wife had grown to an irreversible point, she found herself still unable to move past that initial kiss with Daniella. She hung on her every word.

"We lost Kathryn, Duncan and Grace that first week. We all wanted to leave, but we knew we couldn't. Wealdstone was where Ariella appeared to be drawn to, or stuck, so we had to stay and fight her. Over the next five and a half months, we would get an advantage, then we'd be pushed back. Kathryn was our secret weapon, being a Blue Spirit, and we'd lost her right at the start. Kristin... she began to dabble in dark magic. She said the only way we could defeat Ariella was by playing dirty. I warned her against it, but she wouldn't listen."

Daniella stood up and walked over to the side table under the nearest window, and poured herself another scotch. Sensing she wouldn't be able to continue, Jack took over once more, still fixated on Kathryn. This time, Kristin noticed, but didn't feel the burning jealousy she expected. She almost felt comfort. Why, she couldn't tell. But perhaps her answer lay in that defined lack of jealousy.

"Kristin headed down to the high street to try and lure Ariella out of the Realm of Screams by conjuring her mother's spirit in a spell that she failed to keep control over. It lured Ariella back as she had intended, but the spell backfired, and Kristin was injured. She'd gone alone, no backup, no real plan. And Ariella killed her."

The room fell silent. Only the faint ticking of a clock on the far wall was audible. Annie looked back at the blade on the table, and wondered if it was inhibiting her new abilities as a pain wraith. Not wanting to bring any more bad memories into the room, she decided not to try.

It was at this point that the younger woman who had drawn a weapon on them upon their arrival came into the room. She surveyed the scene before her, said nothing and then walked into the kitchen. Daniella followed her path with a vacant stare and then addressed the room.

"That's Max. You have to forgive her. Your friend Monarch cut out her tongue."

"I'm sorry?" Kristin asked.

"You see, during one of our final battles with Ariella, we managed to regain control of the Elder Blade. But we never got to use it. Monarch

100

dropped from the sky like some great golden superhero, landed smack bang in the middle of Main Street. Even made the road surface ripple like a wave for an entire mile in either direction. He literally walked towards Ariella, and with one flick of his wrist, he tore her apart. It wasn't even an effort to him. Pulled her apart like cotton candy, and sent her black foggy ass back up to the hell she came from."

Kathryn decided to stop gazing at Jack and volunteered a question.

"Wait, so how long has Monarch been here?" she asked.

"Two years."

That piece of information was the most shattering of all.

"Two years?" asked Kimberley. "How is that possible?"

"How the fuck should I know?" Daniella retorted violently, slamming her glass down on the table. "He shows up, blows apart the demon we've been trying to kill for the better part of a year, and while we were thinking he was our saviour, he just carried on right where she left off!"

"You lost more people?" Annie asked.

Daniella's head snapped around to face her.

"We lost everybody."

"I'm so sorry," Kristin said apologetically. "In our Wealdstone, it was Jasmine who came to attack us. And she killed a lot of our friends. And Monarch has taken our Grace. So we know how you feel."

Daniella swiped her glass off the table in anger, and it smashed across the floor.

101

"NO! You don't know how it feels! We *started* losing friends, wives, husbands, but when Monarch came, we lost EVERYBODY else! Don't you dare tell me you know how I feel."

She looked once more around the room, before storming off across the floor and up the stairs out of view.

"Daniella?" Jack called after her.

Kristin held up her hand.

"It's okay, I'll go after her."

Kathryn watched as Kristin disappeared up the stairs, her wife only looking back towards her briefly, as she rounded the top of the stairs and headed down the west wing.

"I'm sorry about that," Jack offered. "She's had it harder than the rest of us. She lost her wife, her niece, her brother and her best friend. And she kind of adopted Max, so everything that happens to her, she blames on herself."

Kathryn had gotten over the strangeness of seeing Max as a woman rather than a nerdy teenage boy, but Jack was different to how she knew him. He was more weathered. His voice was older. He had been through a lot more than her version of Jack. And then it dawned on her that Kimberley was standing behind her. She hadn't even thought how strange this must be for her. She had tried to break out of her realm since she was taken from him, only to find he was dead. And now here he was. She must be feeling very similar to how she was.

"How long were you and your Kathryn together?" she asked, hoping not to seem insensitive to either him, or her friend.

Jack looked at her, and her only. He didn't even acknowledge Kimberley's existence.

102

"Five years. She moved away from here a long time ago. Ended up being a nurse in San Francisco."

The parodies of their own lives just kept coming. Kimberley audibly inhaled deeply, which briefly caught Jack's attention, but only for a moment. He continued.

"We were hunting a pack of vampires, nothing like we had ever seen. They could walk in daylight, were immune to garlic and silver. Daniella and Kristin were out of town hunting a wendigo, and I needed help. She came back and she never left. I was actually going to propose to her the week Ariella arrived."

Jack looked down at the floor, and Kathryn instinctively placed her hand on his thigh, and he responded by placing his on top of hers. Kimberley began to breath faster as her anger and sadness began to overwhelm her. It was quite lucky for everybody else in the room that the Elder blade was present and restricting her abilities. She stormed off outside, slamming the door behind her. Jack was unsure what he had done.

"What's with your friend?" he asked.

Kathryn smiled.

"In our reality, you two were engaged. She's a pain wraith, and it was you in San Francisco, and she was the nurse. When the pain wraith mafia came down to find our version of Jasmine, they killed her in a case of mistaken identity, and by the time she broke free of her realm… you were dead."

Jack looked at the door for a moment, trying to process the possibility of being with someone else.

"And you, Kathryn? What about you?"

Kathryn looked up at the ceiling and tried to keep her gaze away from Jack at all costs as she spoke.

"Uh, me and you dated in college, it didn't work out and we moved apart. There was a summer after you graduated from the police academy where you came back for your father's funeral, where we kind of rekindled our romance for a month or so, but then you went back to San Francisco, and I didn't see you again, until the week you died."

"I was a cop?" he asked.

Kathryn looked at him and chuckled.

"Yeah. You were apparently the precinct record holder for the shooting range in every category. You certainly showed it when I needed you. Blew a possessed guy right between the eyes from three hundred yards away."

Jack raised his eyebrows.

"Really? That's a pretty good shot!"

The two of them giggled. Expecting that they had completely forgotten she even existed, Annie got up and went outside to find Kimberley. Neither Jack nor Kathryn noticed. What he did notice however, was Kathryn's wedding ring.

"I'm guessing you found someone in the end though?" he said as he gestured towards the wedding band.

Kathryn looked at it and the smile faded and she let out a long sigh.

"Yeah. I married Kristin."

Jack's eyebrows once again raised.

104

"Oh, wow. Cool. And how's that going?"

Kathryn gave him a stern look before replying.

"It was going fine. Was. When we met, everything was just fun and we got on so well, and I fell for her like I'd never done before. But then everything started changing. The more we got into this kind of work, the further we drifted, and then the whole 'nearly' moment in the mansion more or less put the nail in the coffin."

Jack knew he probably shouldn't ask, but he pressed anyway, curiosity getting the better of him.

"Nearly moment?"

Kathryn looked into his eyes, and spoke to him straight.

"A me and you 'nearly' moment."

"Ah."

"Yeah. Very nearly."

"And she found out about it?"

Kathryn nodded and then gestured to the drinks table, still dripping with the spilled scotch from Daniella's upturned glass.

"Started having a lot more of that than I should do, and blurted it out in the middle of Sisko's in front of everybody including Kimberley. Not my finest hour."

Jack started giggling, which seemed to annoy Kathryn initially. She gave him a light smack on the knee.

"It's not funny, my marriage is all but over! Then again, when I think about it, maybe it never really started. Everything went downwards when we got married. Even ended up getting very nearly killed on our honeymoon. I do love her though, Jack. At least... I did. I'm not so sure anymore. For me or her."

Jack reciprocated the earlier gesture Kathryn had made, and placed his hand on her knee.

"My Kathryn used to say if you're truly happy with someone, you don't need to analyse everything. If you're analysing moments and actions, then maybe you aren't as happy as you thought you were."

Kathryn nodded, and then as often is the case, her mind reverted to the whole discussion around Monarch.

"Changing the subject completely, you said Monarch has been here for two years?"

Jack nodded.

"Yeah, give or take."

"Why hasn't he left? He's surely looking for a doorway out of here, so why is he still here?"

Jack held his hands wide suggesting an obvious reason, before realising he wasn't talking to *his* Kathryn.

"When he killed Ariella, she disappeared, but the barrier she put in place didn't. Nobody can enter and nobody can leave. It's why we're stuck here."

"But if he killed a pain wraith with a flick of the wrist, surely he could break down the barrier?"

"That's what we thought, but no. He's tried many times, but hasn't managed it. He keeps isolated near the city limits. He's been digging for the last year looking for something."

Kathryn's eyes bulged.

"Digging? For what?"

Jack shrugged his shoulders.

"I dunno. But he rarely comes into town anymore. Not since he paid a visit to Max. He wanted information."

Kathryn was now very animated.

"What kind of information?" she asked, getting her face very close to his.

"He wanted to know where someplace called Crossroads was."

"I knew it!" she exclaimed and jumped from her seat.

"What is it?" Jack asked, also now standing.

Kathryn rushed outside where she found Kimberley and Annie sharing hushed conversation. Kimberley gave her a look of dissatisfaction, but Kathryn chose to ignore it. Too much was at stake here.

"Monarch IS trying to get to Crossroads! But it's buried! It was never restored in this reality, so he's having to excavate it himself! If he finds the settlement, he's probably going to find the doorways!"

That would not be good news. If they were going to find a way back to their own reality, they needed to find those doorways first. They would need to act fast.

13

The house was much like she remembered it. Strolling past what used to be Grace's room, Kristin had a moment of reflection. With everything going on with Monarch and moving through different realms and now realities and universes, Grace's fate had somewhat wandered to the back of her mind. Each time she realised this, a flood of guilt would move forward and bury her feelings for Kathryn. It seemed she may no longer be capable of focussing on one person at a time. It was either one or the other. She knew more than anyone that she had thrown herself into the supernatural investigation work at full throttle.

Her business at the shopping district, although mostly rebuilt, was no longer a priority and had left most of that side of things to the running of a chairman. In truth, she had led a fairly sheltered and boring life up until she moved to Wealdstone. Setting up a financial advisor business as someone who was a successful entrepreneur, had felt like her dream at the time. Then she started hearing whispers about Wealdstone and its past. From there, she met Kathryn, and they were both enveloped in that world from then on.

The realisation of her need to put her work front and centre now confirmed to Kristin, that she wasn't capable of a marriage. She couldn't devote herself to it in the way Kathryn or any other woman deserved. She partially blamed herself for creating such distance between them, but in truth, the two of them had been thrown together and they had tried to make the best of things.

And now here she was, standing in an alternate universe version of her former office, essentially, about to walk into a room with a formerly dead friend who she admired greatly, who just happened to be her wife in this reality. That hadn't been in the job description when she signed up.

Kristin could hear the gentle sobbing coming from Daniella's room, but the room in question struck a nerve with her too. This had been her and

Kathryn's room when they'd been waiting for their own house to be renovated. As she swung the door open, slowly, she saw Daniella sat on the seat in front of the window. She looked up at Kristin briefly, and smiled as she caught her breath, and then looked outside.

"You always loved this view," offered Kristin. "That is to say, our Daniella did. She fought to have this room, but me and Kat sort of muscled our way in. She used to come in here when we were away and just sit in the window."

Daniella nodded.

"My Kristin always liked it too. She used to enjoy watching the deer bound through the trees and drink over by the stream. Saw a werewolf here once. Just briefly. Always wondered what it would be like to have that power."

Kristin sat down next to her, and looked directly into her blue eyes, confused slightly.

"You mean, you don't know?" she asked surprised.

Daniella was the one now looking confused.

"What do you mean?" she asked.

"Well, our Daniella *was* a werewolf."

Alternate Daniella laughed out loud in disbelief.

"Me? Seriously? How did I manage to do that?"

Kristin took a deep breath.

"Well, you were married to Duncan, Grace was your daughter, and one summer Duncan was working such long hours that you had an affair with your neighbour, who happened to be a werewolf."

Daniella was slightly repulsed at the suggestion she and Duncan had been in any form of relationship.

"Duncan? And me? Duncan was my brother! And Grace was my younger sister! Eww. Just… no thanks."

Kristin couldn't help but laugh at the incredible differences stepping through one doorway could produce.

"So the only person in your Wealdstone with any sort of extra abilities was Kathryn?" she asked.

Daniella looked down at the floor as she spoke.

"Not… exactly."

Kristin reached her hand down and took Daniella's in her palm.

"Go on."

Daniella's shoulders immediately eased their tension, and she looked back up at her face.

"There was Scarlett."

Kristin was taken aback a little both at the fact that there was also a Scarlett here, but also at the fact she hadn't even thought about the possibility. Here comes that guilt again, she thought to herself.

"She was a friend of Duncan's. He worked with her all the way from college at Fairmont through to us starting this whole thing. Every job he did, she moved to the same employer. They were thick as thieves. Actually thought they were gonna get together."

"But they didn't?"

"No. She was more interested in… other areas."

Kristin looked slightly confused for a moment, but Daniella's raised eyebrows delivered the suggestive 'if you know what I mean' look. A smirk of recognition from Kristin, and she carried on.

"Anyway, she started to exhibit strange behaviour just before Ariella arrived. Going missing for days at a time, not speaking to people for months. Then one day she showed up claiming that she wasn't who she used to be and something within her had changed."

Kristin felt almost refreshed at not having heard this kind of mirror story before. Nothing like this had happened with anyone in their reality, and she was hanging on Daniella's every word.

"I asked her what she meant, and my Kristin tried to spend more time with her, but she kept making excuses not to be around anybody, and started hiding in Jack's cabin down by the lake. When Ariella made her first attack, I ran down there to find her and she was surrounded by marble tablets, and scrolls, all covered in some form of ancient texts… and she was floating."

"Floating? Like *Scarlet Witch* at the end of *Wandavision*?"

Daniella's face went blank. Clearly their universe either didn't have *Disney+* or the life they'd lived didn't afford them binging time.

"Never mind, carry on."

Daniella returned to look out of the window and continued the tale.

"She was surrounded by swirling black smoke. It was actually moving *through* her. And her eyes. They were black as the night. When I opened the door, her head snapped around and she looked directly at me, opened her mouth, and this black smoke shot out from between her lips and hit me full in the chest, like I'd been hit by a bus. I ended up flying about thirty feet backwards into the lake. When I finally managed to clamber out, she was gone. And so were all the texts."

Kristin let out a deep breath, and shook her head in disbelief.

"What do you think she was doing?" she asked.

"Kathryn thought she had been suckered in to some of the ancient practices of a coven that we had investigated a few months prior. They were trying to raise the Devil. As you do."

Kristin nodded.

"She was the one who took them down, but started to take extra interest in what they had been doing. Being from another realm, Kathryn knew the signs of sorcery and she also had a theory that Scarlett was trying to find a way to break through the barriers to do the same."

"Why would she want to leave this realm?" Kristin asked.

"I don't know," replied Daniella. "But I'm assuming she succeeded. Because we never saw her again."

Kristin hesitated in a moment of realisation.

"And that's when *your* Kristin decided to dabble in magic to help stop Ariella?"

Daniella nodded, looking heartbroken once more.

Kristin took her other hand and squeezed it tight.

112

"You really have lost a lot haven't you?" she asked in a tender caring tone.

Daniella began to form tears at the edge of her eyes again.

"Everything. Jack and Max are all I have left, and I feel myself drifting away from them more every day."

Kristin nodded, and a little snort found its way out for which she was immediately embarrassed.

"Oh my God, I'm sorry, it's just… I feel exactly the same way. We were such a tight team, and then Jasmine arrived, and everything just fell in on itself. It's hard keeping a team together when the centre doesn't hold."

The two of them just stared into each other's eyes for what seemed like an eternity. For Daniella, it was the recognition of the woman she had loved doing what she always used to do. Comfort her and reassure her. And for Kristin, it was finally being able to relate to someone going through the same distancing issues that she was experiencing, with the added benefit of it being an old friend. Perhaps this is what Kathryn had felt with Jack. Maybe now, she could at least understand a part of the reason for what had happened.

As footsteps could be heard getting louder, approaching down the corridor, the two of them instinctively moved apart, and attempted to right themselves in their seats, as unnatural as it looked. Annie entered the room with Kathryn, both looking exasperated and out of breath.

"What's up?" asked Kristin.

"Crossroads!" Kathryn puffed out. "He's trying to find Crossroads!"

14

"The ever laborious tasks of mortal people."

Monarch had no time for undertaking such a medial task as digging dirt out of the ground. An entity of his immense power and ability should be able to raise an entire town to the ground with fairly minimal effort. And yet the activities of a lesser being had some how resulted in him not being able to utilise those abilities.

"Stuck in this hell-hole for two years with a shovel and a bunch of interfering creatures always meddling!"

It had been a very long time since Monarch had been in a situation where he was shackled in any way. Being locked up in a trans-dimensional prison was almost preferable to manual labour. The truth of the matter was that the experience in the Triangle when he was almost extracted from his host had terrified him. Unlike the Pain Wraiths, the Yellow Demons could not exist outside of a physical body. They could not conjure their own. The thought of him being lost in a limbo miniature universe had shaken him. That was a kind of fear he had not felt in over a thousand years. And despite the fact he had been in this version of Wealdstone for the last two years, it had not satiated his desire to feel powerful once more. He couldn't bear to imagine being limited in such a way again.

Another thing he had not counted on, was that not everything in this version of the town was in the same place as in *his* Wealdstone. When he first arrived, he proceeded immediately to where his Crossroads had been, only to find an abandoned gas station. Figuring it was hidden beneath, he had blown the gas station apart with his bare hands and his demonic abilities, much as he had done the buildings in the main town.

However, once the gas station was demolished, and he found nothing, he was then forced to examine other locations. He had killed everyone in or near the city library, and taken all references of the settlement in order to find where it was. Three locations searched, destroyed, and found empty, he returned to Wealdstone to extract information from Max, who he knew had worked in the local museum. He found that out by torturing another member of the *Scooby gang* this town seemed to run with. When she told him nothing, he cut out her tongue and found the information himself from more archives in city hall.

The whole process had taken three months, but finally, he had the location. That was when his real problems started. The barrier created by Ariella had used a lot of energy, and when Monarch killed her, the barrier strength intensified by a factor of a thousand. What he hadn't known at the time, was she had put a protective incantation around herself in order to wield the Elder Blade, and as he was the one to end her life, *his* powers were now restricted when in close proximity to the barrier. Which was exactly where Crossroads was buried.

For the past twenty-two months he had been forced to excavate the settlement by hand. The old-west town had been lost to the ravages of time and the weather, and in this reality had never been restored by a historical society. The fact that this may not even be where the doorway was located in this reality was not even permitted to enter his mind. The Triangle had been a fluke. He knew not every doorway would be so obvious and easily accessible.

The absolute truth of the matter was that Monarch had no more of an idea how to find and navigate these doorways than anybody else. His bold claim of slaying all of the guardians of the doorways was certainly exaggerated. And ultimately, so were his final goals.

As there was no wind inside the bubble, the digging, were it to be a genuine construction site, would have been a very simple job using machinery, with all of the dirt and sand staying where it was put. However, the lack of fuel for the machinery available in town because of the bubble meant he had only been able to extract the top half of the church and two of the stores before switching to the old fashioned method.

"Maybe I should have dragged that witch over here to use her fancy blue swirls of light on this forsaken place."

Monarch chuckled to himself for a moment. Talking to himself was another thing he hadn't done for a very long time. He slammed the shovel into the ground again, and an audible clunk echoed around the shaft he had dug. He leant down to wipe away the loose sediment, to find the handle to the church door. He smiled as he ran his fingers over the smooth brass ring of the handle. He may not have had full use of his powers, but he was still a strong man, and with a swift kick of his boot, the door caved in, and the soil beneath his feet flowed through the doorway into the church, carrying Monarch with him.

He threw out his hands, and enough energy came from his fingertips to steady him, and prevent him from falling flat onto the rotten floor before fizzling out. Monarch coughed as dust fell all around him, and then started to catch his breath as his eyes adjusted to the surroundings.

It was not quite as he remembered it, but despite the different location of Crossroads, he was hopeful that everything within the settlement itself was the same design. He walked along the aisle between the broken pews, crunching dirt and glass from the broken windows beneath his feet. As he reached the altar, he felt like he was being watched. Reaching for one of the candles, he blew the dust from the top of it, and managed just enough power to create a spark to light the wick.

"You know, it's not nice to spy on people."

His voice was amplified around the walls of the church, echoing slightly.

"Well in fairness, you probably shouldn't be here."

The reply came from the same doorway he had fallen through moments before. The difference was that the female now gliding down into the church in a circle of black smoke seemed to be in full control of her abilities.

"I have… personal interest in Crossroads. You however, I don't know."

This was the first instance where Monarch had encountered someone he felt could either be useful or a worthy adversary. He had not yet made up his mind.

"But I know who you are… Monarch."

This woman was nothing like he had ever seen, either in this realm, or his own. She seemed human, but her presence, and her aura seemed to be something of great age and power. He decided it would be unwise to challenge her at this time, and if he was honest, his curiosity got the better of him.

"Well you seem to have me at a disadvantage Miss…?"

"Scarlett."

"Ah, Miss. Scarlett. Now I know who you are, would you mind enlightening me as to how you know who I am?"

Scarlett landed gently on the dirt floor, the smoke retracting into her body, and her eyes returning to their normal shade of hazel. The clouds above the church parted, and more light filtered in through the broken roof.

"I have visited your realm. Among many others. I have heard of the Yellow Demon who managed to break free of his confinement not once, but twice. And then also managed to escape to the human world. That is quite a feat."

117

Monarch was now feeling like a bit of a celebrity, but he was still very cautious, and kept his back to the small doorway he had been heading towards.

"I'm a very determined man, Miss Scarlett."

Scarlett smiled.

"Indeed, you are. However, you have something I need. Something I have been searching for."

Monarch's smile disappeared from his face as Scarlett reached out a hand, and a tunnel of dark smoke emerged from her palm surged forward, and wrapped itself around his body. He struggled against the restraints as he was lifted from the floor, and moved to the side. Scarlett walked past him, her eyes never leaving the destination, not even to glance at him as she moved past him. He was doing his best to create a worthy performance, but even he was a little afraid his plan was beginning to unravel slightly.

"Who *are* you!?" he shouted, but he already knew the answer. This was simply to keep up appearances.

It was then that she stopped and turned to face him.

"I… am the Phantom Wraith."

The Phantom Wraith had previously been a myth people in Beyond had been told as children to frighten them into bed. And now, not only was she real, but she was inhabiting a human body. There was no time for Monarch to question her directly, as more black smoke wrapped around his throat and covered his mouth.

"You have something that I want. Something I *need*. The key to breaking the barrier between realms."

Monarch mumbled beneath the smoke, and Scarlett swiped a finger, clearing his mouth for him to speak.

"But if you have travelled to other realms, why do you need it?"

Scarlett placed a hand on the cold, damp surface of the smaller door at the back of the altar. Monarch knew she would find nothing in there. It was all part of his plan. Scarlett glanced back at him, and smiled a smile that stretched almost as wide as his own, black liquid pouring from her mouth.

"Wouldn't you like to know."

15

Jack had been stockpiling for over a year, expecting that at some point a large scale confrontation with Monarch was coming. His cabin was now his haven and his armoury. Opening a large door hidden under the rug by the bed, he lowered himself into the floor and pulled a suspended light switch, illuminating a more modest *Bat Cave* with weapons on every wall, what looked like an advanced chemistry set, and crates of ammunition lining the edge of the room all along the floor.

As he slipped a small case of silver bullets into his duffel bag, he heard a knock at the door to the cabin. Confused slightly, thinking everyone was up at the mansion preparing to leave for Crossroads, he climbed up the small staircase into the main cabin and closed the hatch behind him. Through the small window in the door, Jack could see Kimberley's face, looking slightly forlorn and he reached for the handle, opening the door.

"Hey," he said. "What's up?"

Kimberley said nothing. Her eyes darted back and forth as she looked at the man she had loved and that she had been torn away from and all of the feelings and memories were running in front of her eyes even more intensely than some of the painful memories of her ethereal youth. Again, Jack asked her if she was okay.

Again, she said nothing. Suddenly, her shoulders tensed, a small flicker of purple energy left her fingertips, and she leapt forward, gripping Jack's arms and kissed him passionately. Jack was taken aback by the suddenness of the kiss and attempted to push her back.

"Woah, hey, what…"

But Kimberley was insistent. She pushed him back into the cabin, slamming the door closed with her left hand and using her enhanced strength, driven by her intense emotions, continued to advance them towards the bed.

Without allowing Jack a second to compose himself, or try a second attempt at stopping this, she lifted up her blue t-shirt, and tossed it behind her. As she discarded her shirt, Jack couldn't help but notice the way the light shone on the intricate white lace pattern of her bra. It was delicate and alluring, just like Kimberley herself. But none of this made sense to him. He may have been captivated by her beauty, but he was in no way committing himself to this. He did not want this.

Kimberley moved in closer, her hands roaming over Jack's body as she whispered in his ear.

"Remember me, please! I love you."

She was trying to convince him to give in to her desires and succumb to her advances. Her sensibilities had gone out of the window, and her intense emotions were dominating her actions. But as much as Jack was tempted, he knew that it was not the right thing to do. He didn't even know Kimberley, only what the others had told him about her. He steeled himself, and as Kimberley moved her hands towards his belt buckle, he gripped her wrists and pulled away.

Kimberley looked up at him, disappointment etched on her face. She had hoped that he would give in to the passion she felt between them, but as she slowed and took a breath, she began to realise where she was and what she was doing.

"Kimberley, look. Please stop this. I know that in your reality, we were close, really close. But in my reality, we never met. This is just really not appropriate, and not the time. I don't feel about you that way. The way I feel about…"

"Kathryn."

121

She finished his sentence before he could even get the rest of his words out.

He nodded, and looked at the floor as he turned away from her and straightened a lamp on a table that had been knocked during Kimberley's advances. He straightened up and looked back over to Kimberley, and she in turn stared back at him. She reluctantly began to understand. Jack didn't love her. He didn't even know her. She suddenly became very aware that she was not fully dressed, and leaned down to pick up her shirt. As she pulled the shirt back over her head, she could feel the weight of the situation bearing down on her. She had come to Jack hoping for something more, but instead, she was leaving with a sense of unfulfilled desire. This was not her Jack, and she would find no comfort here.

With one last look at Jack, Kimberley turned and walked out of the cabin, her mind racing with questions and doubts about what could have been. But the most dangerous thought racing through her mind as she left him standing staring through the open doorway, was if there were doorways to other realities as well as other realms, maybe she could find one where Jack *did* love her. As she felt the imagery of that possibility develop in her mind, her eyes flashed bright purple, and sparkles of lightning once again came from her fingertips. An almost angry look came over her face, and she clenched her fists.

As Jack watched, she disappeared into the trees, and he was left wondering just what the hell had happened.

16

The journey to Crossroads was completed in silence.

The truck barrelled down the road, kicking up the dust, but the only noise came from the tyres on the road surface. There was an unspoken tension between everybody. Kathryn and Jack kept exchanging looks, which did not go unnoticed by Kristin, but her own feelings towards Daniella were now developing into something she wasn't sure of. Kimberley was sat in the truck bed with Annie, and she was rolling a ball of violet energy between her hands, eyes fixed on the land behind them, not looking at anyone, not saying a word. Annie was feeling like the left out one of the group. She was easily the second most powerful, and in this reality shared Kimberley's abilities, but for some reason, she felt the weakest at this point.

The break in the deafening quiet came when Daniella banged her fist on the glass to alert them to the fact that Crossroads had come into view. She pulled over to the side of the road, and all seven of them attempted to take in what they were seeing.

The top half of the church was now sticking up out of the ground, along with what looked like an old General Store, and a crumbling house. The scene was somewhat familiar to Kristin, Kathryn, Annie and Kimberley, having seen the full settlement in their own reality. But for Daniella, Max and Jack, this was very surreal.

However, the real confusion came from the emanating black smoke which was surrounding the church, swirling in and out of the broken windows.

"Oh no," Daniella sighed.

Kristin looked over to her. Daniella's story was still fresh in her mind.

"Scarlett?" she asked.

Daniella nodded, and put the truck into drive before slamming her foot on the pedal. The vehicle accelerated very quickly, and Daniella gripped the wheel so tightly that her knuckles almost glowed white. Kathryn, however, was not about to let that name drop go without saying anything.

"Woah, woah, woah, back up. Scarlett? Little, innocent Scarlett?"

Daniella, slightly aggrieved at this suggestion, gave a curt reply.

"Not so innocent in *our* reality, actually."

Kathryn held up her hands in apology, but still nibbled away at Daniella's temper.

"So, is she the same as our Scarlett was, but enhanced? What is it?"

Daniella slammed on the brakes so hard, that Kimberley actually slid along the truck bed, and up over the tailgate, slamming onto the road surface.

"Scarlett, whatever she is, whatever she has become, is no longer human. And she is certainly not innocent or defenceless. I don't give a fuck about your realm, or reality or wherever the fuck you come from. You are NOT my friend, and you don't have the first clue about what is happening in THIS Wealdstone. So either roll with it, or get the fuck out of my truck!"

Everybody in the cab was now looking at Daniella, eyes wide with surprise. What she didn't expect was Kathryn to start smiling at her.

"I've missed that hard-ass attitude."

Kristin began to smile too, as she knew exactly what Kathryn was talking about, and if anything, it drew her to Daniella even more. They had been best friends for a long time, and now those feelings were only deepening.

124

However, all of these thoughts and exchanges were disrupted by the sound of thunder above them, and a whoosh from behind the truck. As they watched, both Kimberley and Annie flew past them, high in the air, pointed like two purple arrows at Crossroads.

"Holy shit."

Jack's surprised exclamation was accompanied by a whack to the back of the head, as Daniella once again floored it, and he forgot he wasn't wearing a seatbelt. Unlike their version of Crossroads, this one had the river much closer to the settlement, and as the truck got closer, the ground began to rumble, and they saw distortions appearing alongside the edge of the water.

"What is that?" Jack asked, still rubbing the back of his head.

Kathryn squinted, and following the line of emerging green lines, realised she was correct in what she was about to say.

"Doorways. And lots of them."

Another crack of thunder above them echoed across the empty land surrounding the settlement, and they realised that the clouds of smoke around the church had grown bigger, and although already black, seemed to darken further. However, while they were now approaching the church at speed, Daniella was not slowing down.

"Uh, Dani?" Jack asked.

"Yeah?" she replied.

"The brakes?"

Daniella pushed her foot harder into the floor. Above them, Annie and Kimberley crashed down through the roof of the church.

125

"We don't need brakes. God will stop us."

She turned slightly and grinned at Jack, but he didn't feel amused or comforted, and immediately began reaching for a seatbelt. Kathryn and Kristin exchanged glances too, and as they got within ten feet of the semi-exposed church doors, they took a deep breath and put their heads down between their legs, Max doing the same.

The truck ploughed through the rotten wooden doors, the roof of the truck also tearing through the wooden wall above them. Daniella had not expected the church floor to be so far below their entry point, and as the truck careered through the air, and plummeted downwards, her smirk vanished, and genuine fear replaced it. The nose of the Chevy hit the floor first, but due to the practically dissolved nature of the floor itself, it dug into the soil beneath. The rear of the truck raised up into the air, and the entire vehicle flipped, the back end crashing down onto the pews on the left side splintering wood and glass everywhere.

The truck came to rest upside down, the metal groaning as it did so. However, the noises and thunder continued. As Kristin and a wounded Kathryn clambered out of the passenger window, they could see flashes of purple, and more clouds of black. But no sign of yellow. Daniella freed herself from her seatbelt, and reached for a knife, slicing through Jack's, and her and Max helped him out the back window of the truck.

"What is she?" Kathryn asked, wiping the blood from her forehead.

"I don't know, but whatever she is, she is powerful," replied Daniella.

The lack of yellow energy strands was not missed by Jack, and he asked the more troubling question.

"More to the point, where the hell is Monarch?"

Nobody answered, they simply looked at each other. Kathryn, however, felt her fingers begin to tingle, and she remembered that in this reality,

126

she had abilities. Taking a deep breath, she looked at Jack, turned towards the battle ensuing in front of them, and ran forwards, using bolts of blue lightning to take greater leaps in distance.

Kimberley and Annie directed large energy beams towards each other, and threw them jointly in the direction of Scarlett, who was now floating above the altar, but her dark clouds seemed to absorb them, before swiping them aside with her own blows. Annie broke through the exposed wall, rolling along the dirt before coming to rest, groaning in pain. Kimberley dodged several blows leaping through the air on steps made of her energy, and attempted to strike from above. Scarlett opened her mouth wide, her eyes now swirling black, and a solid fist of smoke erupted, and hit Kimberley square in the jaw with such force, she flew through the only undamaged part of the roof, briefly hung in the air, and fell back down at a slight angle, and as she fell, her body was impaled on the steeple of the church.

Kimberley's screams of agony, drew a wry smile from Scarlett's twisted face. The base of the steeple cracked, the integrity of the roof now completely lost, and as the remainder began to collapse in on itself, Kathryn diverted her attack to try and protect the rest of the group from the falling debris. A blue shield appeared above them, and they watched as Kimberley's impaled body bounced off the shield, and slid down to the ground outside of the church, not far from Annie.

It was at this point that Max drew a small dagger from a holster on her back, and as she charged forward, the blade unfolded several times until it became a full sized sword. She leapt, and placed a foot on top of one of the still intact pews, and leapt, sword raised above her head. As she did so, Annie flicked a bolt of energy towards her, and it engulfed the sword, almost endowing it with a flame. Scarlett fired a shot towards Max, but she twisted in the air, rather impressively to the others, and sliced the blade through the black fog, cutting through it like a knife through butter. Scarlett seemed to wince from this, almost as if she had actually experienced pain, and her attacks lessened in intensity.

127

Max landed on the floor, almost in a gymnastics pose, the tip of the sword resting delicately on the ground. Impressed by her dynamic martial arts skills, Jack and Kristin now ran forward, firing a barrage of silver bullets into the remaining fog, Daniella focussing her fire on Scarlett herself.

Kathryn lowered her shield, and began directing her own lightning bolts at Scarlett, hoping a combined attack would make the difference. Max began swinging her sword through the tentacles of smoke as if dismembering a giant octopus. This seemed to be the only thing actually causing Scarlett to weaken, as the bullets were hitting some kind of invisible shielding, and simply falling to the floor. The co-ordinated attack was beginning to frustrate Scarlett, and as Kimberley and Annie were still out of the picture, she decided to strike a decisive blow.

As Max sliced through another arm of black smoke, she raised the blade above her head and leapt once more, ready to plunge it into Scarlett's actual body, but she was ready. A thick arm of smoke erupted from Scarlett's body, smashed Jack, Daniella and Kristin out of the way, wrapped itself around one of the broken pews, and retracted like a leash. The sharpened wood cut through Max with such force and speed that it wasn't immediately evident anything was wrong. After a second or two, Max's hands released the blade and it clattered to the floor. As Daniella looked up, Max's eyes began to roll, and the top half of her body began to slide away from the lower half.

Scarlett retracted all of her smoke arms, and leapt through the remaining parts of the roof out of sight. Daniella didn't move. She just sat there on the floor, mouth agape, unable to speak or process what she had just seen. The others all rushed towards Max, except Annie, who was now helping Kimberley manifest away from the spire spike.

"Oh fuck, stay with us Max, just…"

Jack didn't know where to put his hands, there was so much blood and Max was literally in two halves. Somehow, she was still partially conscious, and she looked past the group around her to Daniella. Max

128

gestured towards her friend and Daniella found the strength to get up and jog towards her. Annie and Kimberley limped into the church and saw what had happened. With a gentle twist of her left wrist, Annie send a purple puff of smoke towards Max, and as it entered her mouth, it formed a new tongue, allowing her to speak. While joining somebody back together was beyond her knowledge, Kimberley attempted it.

"Come on, this should work! Why won't it work?"

Annie placed a hand on Kimberley's arm and lowered it gently, signalling it was hopeless. And then she remembered.

"Oh my God, I forgot!" she exclaimed.

Annie started rummaging through her pockets frantically, until her hand came to rest on the amulet. Pulling it out of her pocket, she smiled, and shot forwards to hang it around Max's neck. During all of this nobody noticed that they were still not fully alone. The pews behind them that were left in tact began to move, as Monarch lumbered his way towards them from the back of the church behind the wreckage of the truck.

Max's eyes began to flicker, and as she spoke for the first time in almost a year, she directed it to Daniella.

"Thanks for being a Mum to me."

She let out her final breath, and her eyes rolled away into the back of her head. The amulet was not glowing as it usually did.

"Why isn't this working?" asked Annie, examining it. "It should be working!"

But it didn't. The amulet did not glow, and Max was not healed. She was gone.

"Why won't it work?" Annie screamed once more.

129

The answer came from behind them.

"It can't work here."

The group span around, weapons drawn, Daniella still crying at the gruesome sight laid before her by someone she once considered a friend. Monarch was leaning against the dislodged bumper of the truck which was now several feet from the vehicle itself, his hand covering his left side, and visibly covered in blood.

"Give me one God damn reason why I shouldn't shoot you right now!"

Kristin was now charging towards Monarch, barrel aimed squarely between his eyes. But he didn't budge.

"Try it and see what happens," was his reply.

She pressed the gun against his head, and without hesitation, she pulled the trigger. The gunshot echoed around the devastated church, but the bullet hung in the air for a few seconds, before clattering to the ground. Monarch grinned, and with his free hand, swiped the back of it into Kristin with a hefty force, sending her clattering to the floor.

"Just because I'm injured, don't for one second expect me not to kill any of you if I get the chance."

Kimberley stood tall, trying to put the gruesome image of Max's body out of her mind. Annie leaned over and removed her jacket, laying it over Max.

"So what happened to you? I thought these yellow demons were meant to be superior to us mere pain wraiths?"

The bravado in her voice came not from her confidence, but her pent up aggression, and the potential for a way out of here.

130

"Brave words from such a small being, trying to attack what she doesn't understand."

Kathryn chimed in.

"So why don't you explain it to us mere mortals? Because right now, you're not in as good a shape as that truck behind you."

Jack couldn't help but smile, even in the face of such horror around him.

"You have no idea what she is, do you? Even you, Blue Spirit?"

Monarch directed his gaze at Annie.

"No, I don't know."

Monarch chuckled to himself.

"Well allow me to enlighten you. Your swirly black smoking friend is a Phantom Wraith."

Immediately, Kimberley held her hands up to her mouth in shock. Her eyes depicted true fear, and she was frozen on the spot. Annie placed her hand on her arm once more to try and calm her.

"Phantom Wraith?" she asked Kimberley.

Kimberley nodded, and blinked away a barrage of tears.

"Phantom Wraiths are… were… born from death. They exist to blanket the universe in darkness. They are the purest form of evil."

Kristin wandered over to Daniella, who was now tuning into the conversation, whilst at all times keeping an eye on Monarch. He may not have been the one to kill Max, but he certainly caused the situation which

131

led to it. She demanded more information from Kimberley, but she couldn't form it, so their other enemy volunteered in a much more jovial tone than Jack cared for.

"Simply put, when you mortal beings die, some of you come back as ghosts, some of you come back as zombies if you're really lucky. But the most evil souls, killers, butchers, the very crème de la crème of humanity? Their souls travel to the void, where they mingle together and become stronger. They are the demons you encounter in your possessions and hauntings. And do you know what the funniest part of all this is? You create them!"

Monarch laughed out loud, and Kristin lunged towards him, but Kathryn pulled her back. As she did so, Kristin yanked her arm free and shot Kathryn a very stern look. Something she hadn't seen from her wife before.

"Oh please, these wounds are only temporary. Give me a few minutes and I'll be back to the Monarch you know and love."

"I'm sure I could conjure something to prevent that," Annie offered.

"You wish," came his reply. "You see, when your little ghost hunters, or priests or whatever idiots you people use exorcise a house or a person from a demon, where do you think they go?"

Nobody spoke. Monarch's eyes flicked at each of them in turn, awaiting a response, but enjoying the fact that he was holding the room.

"Nobody? Well let me tell you! They return to the void, where the continue to merge together in the space between realms, becoming stronger and stronger, until they are conjured up by one of your teenage fools messing with things they don't understand, and they consume them."

Daniella, slightly calmer moved closer.

"Consume them? How?"

Monarch rolled his eyes.

"Let me ask you something. Did you know who that was before she became all floaty and deadly?"

Daniella nodded.

"Yes, she was my brother's best friend."

Monarch tilted his head.

"And I presume you people have been hunting down spirits and demons and the like for quite some time? Come across any satanists, or cults?"

Again, Daniella nodded.

"Do you really think that there is a Devil? A heaven? A hell? There is NOTHING! Nothing but the void! These fools are conjuring the darkest and most powerful beings in existence, and if they come through? Your world will be turned to ash."

Kathryn shoved past Kristin, still irked about her wife's attitude towards her.

"So why doesn't she like you? Clearly she's not your biggest fan."

Monarch sniggered again as he straightened himself up.

"I am the most powerful thing you could ever imagine. Your pathetic little pain wraiths? Nothing to me. I've slaughtered my share over the centuries."

Then his face changed to a more resigned look.

133

"But a Phantom Wraith is literally made up of death and misery and are older than your world stretching back to the dawn of time. They are the greatest enemy any of us will ever face, and the only things I've ever known to physically harm an entity like myself."

Monarch began to stagger forwards towards the altar where Max's body was lying. Jack shot him a question before anyone tried to attack him.

"So what was she doing here? If she's broken free of this void, what does she want with you?"

Monarch chuckled again.

"Because I broke free from my prison not once, but twice, and then broke free of Beyond. And I used something to help me do that. She was under the impression that I kept it here, but it wasn't something tangible that helped me out of Beyond."

Kimberley found her voice once more.

"And what was that?"

Monarch stretched upwards, his bones cracking back into place, but giving no answer. A rumbling came from outside, and the ground began to vibrate. It felt like the beginnings of an earthquake, but the sky began to change colour. Monarch began to giggle and the others watched as the protective shield around the town that Ariella had strengthened with her death began to crack. Each boom was like a hammer striking a nail, and with each one, Monarch laughed louder.

The group gradually backed away from the altar, and once Monarch was laughing so loud that Annie had to cover her ears, he turned to face them and showed his wound was gone.

"Distraction."

A blast of golden lightning shot from six different points in his chest, and struck each of the team in the chest with a whip-like effect. Daniella took the hardest hit, getting a slash across her right side. The hit was a powerful one, even taking Kimberley and Annie down to the ground.

"You see, I didn't break free of my realm alone. I had help. But I spread a rumour. A fable if you will, that there was a crystal. A powerful trinket that allowed me to break free without crossing the Guardians. I knew I may need an upper hand one day, so I allowed this Phantom Wraith to smash her way through the realms, killing the guardians and weakening the doorways themselves. And here we are!"

Jack managed to claw himself back to his feet, but Monarch sent a web of energy towards him and threw him to the back of the church. He leaned down to Max's body, and grabbed the amulet, tearing the cord around her neck. Immediately, the amulet began to glow.

"You see, your Phantom Wraith is the only creature powerful enough to break down this energy barrier that meddlesome Pain Wraith erected. With every hit she lands, I get stronger. But I had to get her here. So I made sure when I saw her at your little cabin last year, to encourage her to follow me. She didn't leave because of you crashing a seance," he said pointing at Daniella. "She left to chase me. I never back myself into corners. The truth of the matter is this. While she has her own goals, and good luck to her, the extra energy she brings combined with yours," he said pointing at Kimberley, "have opened up more doorways than I possibly could've hoped for. And now I have this amulet back, nothing can stop me. It may not work for you outside of its own realm, but I can use it to harness my energy. An exquisite weapon."

Monarch took one last look at them, before bounding up into the sky with a blast of golden smoke. Everybody ran outside and saw Monarch land near the water's edge and start walking towards the doorways, which now numbered twelve. Scarlett in the meantime, was still hammering at the energy barrier, confused as to why the little trinket she had stolen from

Monarch's hiding place in the church wasn't amplifying her powers. When she saw him approaching a gateway, and that he had some of his powers back, she snarled, and erupted into a column of darkness, charging through the air towards him.

"Well, time for me to go!" he shouted, breaking into a sprint.

Kimberley, Annie and Kathryn were now using their powers to take larger leaps towards them, Kathryn holding the sword Max had wielded. She saw Scarlett screaming towards Monarch, and feared the gateways may close should the two come together. Below them, Daniella, Jack and Kristin were sprinting, Jack sporting a rather nasty gash above his left eye.

Without aiming, Kathryn pulled her arm back, and launched the sword forwards. It spiralled vertically through the air, and as it began to lose momentum, both Kimberley and Annie shot their energy forwards to propel it further. The blade sliced through the cloud that Scarlett had become, cutting a great swathe down the middle, and sending her off at an angle in two pieces and each half of the cloud was sucked through a different doorway.

Monarch briefly looked back, and grinned. He stopped near to one of the remaining doorways, and lifted himself off the ground. He closed his eyes and his face transformed into the wide grimaced, glowing eyed monster they had seen before. He roared as he launched everything he had towards the group on the ground, deliberately targeting the weaker members of the team. But Kimberley would not let anything happen to Jack. Even if he was not her Jack. She turned and shot into the path of the beam, and fired her own at the ground in front of the group, knocking them off course and all into the river.

Kathryn and Annie watched on in horror as Kimberley took the full force of Monarch's available power, and she was blasted through a fourth doorway. As she vanished, she appeared to begin to disintegrate. In a second she was gone. And so was the doorway. It was at this point that

Monarch turned his attention to the remaining eight. He blasted his powers at each one in turn, decimating it, each causing a ripple in the atmosphere, knocking Kathryn and Annie back with each shockwave. There now remained only one.

As he turned to walk through it, he paused and looked back at Annie.

"I'll see you at home."

And with that he walked through the doorway, and it closed leaving them no way out of the alternate Wealdstone, and two team members down.

17

As the dejected team trundled their way up the driveway of the mansion, nobody really spoke apart from Jack. They were all soaking wet from their dunking in the river, and were growing increasingly colder now that night had begun to fall, and without the energy barrier, the wind had returned with a vengeance. It felt like a storm was beginning to roll in. Jack and Daniella had forgotten just how chilling the breeze could be, especially at night. He felt like something needed to be said to break the tension.

"We can form an action plan in the morning. Right now, we all need rest."

Jack's words were heard, but not acknowledged by Daniella and Kristin. They walked closely together away from the rest of the group, Daniella still feeling the effects of losing yet another member of their family. They had been forced to leave Max's body in the church with no transport to bring her back, but vowed to gather her the next morning and give her a proper burial. Kristin had held her hand most of the way back from Crossroads, and Kathryn watched as they entered the house together, before pausing at the door, turning to Jack.

"I don't know what's going to happen now. I normally have some kind of sense for a way around everything, but I just feel… lost."

While her words suggested that she was talking about the loss of the gateways, Kimberley and Max, Jack wondered if there was a deeper meaning to them. He glanced through the open doorway to see Daniella and Kristin walking towards the stairs, still holding hands. He secretly hoped that this was all happening for a reason, and his attraction to Kathryn could become more, finally.

Jack pulled her in for a hug. The immediate comfort she felt in that moment could not be described. It was as if she was sitting in front of a warm log fire, and all of her worries began to fade into the background. This is where she wanted to be. Held by someone who cared for her, and who would comfort her. She had been missing that over the last couple of years, in part due to the presence of the man she was now embracing. But also, in part to the lack of emotional depth in her and Kristin's marriage. The more she thought about it, the more she came to realise that while they loved each other, they weren't close. They never shared discussions about how they were feeling, or their hobbies, or even things as mundane as what their favourite animal was. Everything was either work or sex. There was nothing else to it. The last five years had been an experiment which was rapidly failing.

After a couple of minutes, Jack realised he was enjoying the moment a little too much, and feared Kristin may be watching, and worried how she might react given what Kathryn had told him that morning. He wanted more than anything to stay with Kathryn, but he slowly pulled them apart, and looked at her. Her eyes were fixed on his, and he could see her anguish at moving away from him. The cold also began to take hold of her and she started to shiver. Kathryn leaned towards his face, and gently placed a kiss on his lips. The only niggling doubt about Jack's feelings in this moment were that he was concerned he was projecting his love for his Kathryn onto this one. But the more he tried to analyse himself, the more nonsensical those thoughts became. As Kathryn backed away, and turned to go inside, Jack took several steps back, watching her go into the house, before turning around and heading down the path towards the lakeside cabin.

In the meantime, Kristin had helped Daniella up the stairs and along the corridor towards her room. She was sporting a slight limp as one would expect from being catapulted through the air several times. The wound she had suffered on her side had worried Kristin initially, but in the artificial bedroom light, it didn't look as bad as she had first feared. A few surgical strips and a quick clean would be all that was required. Kristin helped Daniella through the door, and pushed it most of the way closed for some privacy. She too was now beginning to shiver. The heat in the mansion was not particularly high, something Jack had put down to

139

dwindling fuel reserves. At least with the energy barrier gone, that may not be a problem for much longer.

"How are you doing?" she asked Daniella.

"I'd always considered her a daughter, but she'd never said it to me before."

Daniella felt a new tear slide down her cheek, and she looked up at Kristin's face.

"You know my Kristin and I knew Max from when she was a teenager. She came to work in the shopping district and ended up being the manager of the movie theatre before she was eighteen. Reliable, caring and hard-working. Me and Kristin used to joke that we'd love a daughter like that someday."

Another tear fell, and Kristin reached her hands up to cup Daniella's face gently in her palms.

"Hey, I'm here. It's okay. She loved you, and you can keep hold of that fact forever."

Daniella nodded, and blinked away a few more tears, before sniffling and shuddering from the cold.

"I know. Hey, I'm freezing, I dunno about you. I need a hot shower and a change of clothes."

Kristin nodded in agreement, and walked over to the dresser in the corner.

"Any chance you have some clothes to fit me?" she asked without thinking.

Daniella glanced towards her.

"Sorry," Kristin apologised. "Do you mind?"

Daniella shook her head.

"Go ahead, I think you'll find them an excellent match for you."

The pair shared a brief but joyous giggle. Small mercies given what they'd been through. While not as much attention was being paid to the loss of Kimberley, the fact was that both parties had lost a valuable member of the team. Kristin opened the top drawer and found a set of pyjamas with a penguin emblem on the left breast of the shirt, and a penguin motif running down the trouser legs. She chuckled to herself that even in an alternate reality, she had still loved penguins. That wasn't something she had ever shared with Kathryn. It just didn't seem the sort of thing she would be interested in.

As Kristin turned around, she saw Daniella removing her soggy shirt, throwing it across the room into the laundry basket. Her eyes fell upon Daniella's breasts and noticed how the light pink material clung to her chest. She gathered her thoughts enough to make a jest at the successful aiming of the shirt into the basket.

"Nice shot," she said.

Daniella turned around and smiled at her. She couldn't help but notice Kristin's stares were no longer aimed at her eyes. She wandered towards her, and stopped next to the dresser.

"You know, when I lost Kristin, I fell into a dark place, and I don't think I ever came out of it. In fact, I'm pretty sure I started digging further into it. But when I saw you, I just…"

Kristin leaned into Daniella, and placed a gentle kiss on her lips. The feeling was a warm and familiar one for both of them. Kristin felt a connection. Something different than she had with Kathryn. As she moved to pull away, Daniella moved to follow her, and returned the kiss

141

this time with more intensity and passion, placing her hand on Kristin's face.

Despite Kristin having initiated the move, Daniella could sense a slight hesitation in her body language and decided to take things slower. She moved back for a moment, just to see, but Kristin this time matched her movement, leaned over, and pressed a kiss that soon deepened into something much more passionate. Daniella reached down to the hem of Kristin's vest top and lifted it up, breaking the kiss just long enough to slip it off. Daniella leaned in to kiss her again, her hands trailing down over the deep burgundy lace covering Kristin's chest, and down to the waistband of her pants. She unbuttoned them, pulling the zipper down slowly as Kristin's breath quickened. The trousers fell to the floor, Kristin stepping out of them, and Daniella took a breath and tried to take in the sight now before her.

Kristin's underwear was made of delicate, sheer lace with intricate patterns, and the deep burgundy colour triggered a memory in Daniella's mind of her and *her* Kristin's first Valentine's together. Contrasting against Kristin's burgundy was the soft, pale pink of Daniella's attire. Once they had both paused and ran their eyes over each other, contemplating what they were about to do, Daniella moved her hands along to Kristin's thighs, rubbing them gently as she leaned in for another kiss. The passion intensified as Daniella's hands moved higher, caressing Kristin's skin as she went.

As Daniella reached behind Kristin's back to undo her bra, the delicate garment falling to the floor, Kristin began drawing Daniella towards the bed. They began exploring each other's bodies with a sense of tenderness, Kristin discovering new sensations that she had never felt before, and Daniella feeling like she had come home.

Daniella moved to roll on top of Kristin, and removed her bra, before the two of them continued to kiss deeply and passionately. As they moved together, wrapped in each other's arms, there was a sense of peace and belonging that had eluded them both for far too long.

A sniffle came from the doorway that went unnoticed by the two of them, now too involved in each other's embrace to notice. Several tears began to fall down Kathryn's cheeks as she watched the start of what had eluded her so far. The ending. The concrete evidence that their marriage was over. As she moved away from the door and walked a few paces down the corridor, she felt an overwhelming sadness, tinged with anger. In her mind she wanted to smash things, and scream, but then a moment of clarity. She began to feel like she had been gifted a way out. The relationship wasn't working and hadn't been working for a long time. While this is not how Kathryn wanted or expected things to end, that end had now come. There was almost a relief that she had not been the one to have to make that final leap.

And then Kathryn looked up, and her mind began to race. She wiped her face, and marched down the corridor as the sounds of moaning began to filter through the door of the bedroom. She blocked them out, her mind focussed on her new destination. Every step she took cleared her mind just that little bit more. She bounded down the stairs, two at a time, and wrenched open the front door, passing a freshly showered Annie on the way.

"Kat?" she asked.

But she gave no reply, simply slamming the door shut behind her, Annie moving into the kitchen to pour herself a drink. In truth she had no desire to start a conversation, but the concern for her colleagues and friends was a constant for her. It seemed as though some of them, however, had forgotten how to reciprocate that. Annie, despite her new found abilities, had begun to feel like she was being pushed out. The bonds that existed between the others had been there for a long while, and she had been one of the newer additions to the team.

Kimberley on the other hand, showed her nothing but love. She had latched onto Annie and they had become best friends. When Annie had moved to Montana, she had asked Kimberley to go with her. But by that

143

point, Kathryn and Kristin had started dragging her into missions and investigations more and more, and their bond had weakened.

She looked in the fridge, the cold from the motor causing her arms to shiver into goosebumps, droplets of shower water still dripping from her hair. The towel wasn't much comfort either. Annie suspected they were made of tracing paper because there was no softness or thickness to the cloth.

"Milk, or beer?" she said aloud to herself. "Thank God I'm lactose intolerant."

She grabbed three beers, and slammed the fridge shut, shuffling her way into the lobby and towards the seating area by the bookcases, where they had been gathered together just that very morning. In the distance, she could hear what sounded like gentle moaning, slowly getting louder, but she was too disinterested in what everybody else was doing. Nobody seemed to care where she was or what she was up to, so she began to adopt the same approach. She looked out of the window as she twisted the first beer open, and saw the spots of rain begin to fall. It was poignant how the weather seemed to reflect her mood. She drank the first beer within sixty seconds, and twisted open the second. She had never thought when she first came to Wealdstone with her father that she would have turned into a beer-swilling supernatural crimefighter. She sometimes missed the days of sitting down with a good book and learning something wonderful about the world.

But the truth was, the world was seeming less and less wonderful to Annie with each passing day. Even her abilities, whatever realm they were in, were no longer giving her comfort. She was the only one who now truly felt alone. This was illustrated by what was happening upstairs, and what was about to happen down by the lake.

Kathryn was now blindly charging down the track towards the lake, her wet hair whipping in the wind, and covering her face. She furiously brushed it back as she crunched through the leaves in the near darkness.

144

She saw the lights of the cabin through the gap in the curtains and walked even faster.

When she reached the porch of the cabin, she hammered on the door with her closed fist several times. Jack opened the door slowly, still unsure what to expect on the other side, especially after the encounter with Kimberley on the morning. When he saw Kathryn, he relaxed almost immediately. She looked at his topless body, her chest heaving as she tried to catch her breath both from the charge down the hill, and the way she was feeling.

"Hey, what's up? I was just about to take a shower."

Jack could see the anger and frustration etched on her face. Without saying a word, she stormed in, slamming the door closed behind her, walked up to Jack, pushed him back against the refrigerator and began to kiss him hard. Everything on top of the fridge cascaded down either side, bouncing off the floor and either breaking or rolling away.

This time, Jack felt like he didn't need to fight it. Something was different. They did move apart briefly, but it was for just a second. The tension between them was palpable. As their eyes locked, Jack knew that something must have happened, but he also felt that Kathryn needed him right now. And he needed her.

He wrapped his arms around her, pulling her close to him. He could feel her heart beating rapidly against his chest as she kissed him deeply. The softness of her lips, the sweetness of her breath, and the way she tasted made his heart race with desire. Jack moved Kathryn backwards until they slammed up against the opposite wall. Jack moved his hands down Kathryn's chest, and began unzipping her shirt, letting it fall to the ground. Their hands explored each other's bodies as they continued to kiss. Kathryn's fingers fumbled with Jack's belt, tugging it free and tossing it aside. She then reached for the button of his pants, slowly unzipping them as Jack kicked them off.

145

As Jack ran his hands down her back, Kathryn let out a soft moan, signalling her need for more. He moved his hands to her belt, pulled it open and slid Kathryn's jeans down to the floor. Jack gently lifted her up onto his waist, and carried her over to the kitchen counter, and continued to kiss her as he removed her bra and threw it on the ground. Kathryn reached down and began to slide Jack's boxers away. As he delicately kissed her breasts, and ran his hands down her back once more, he gripped the edge of her panties, and yanked them from under her, kissing her thigh as he did so.

Kathryn never thought she would feel Jack's touch again, but she now felt free. Seeing Daniella and Kristin had given her that. As Jack moved his lips over Kathryn's hips and down between her legs, she arched her back, her damp hair clinging to the granite surface. She closed her eyes tight and lost herself in the moment. This was what she had been searching for with Kristin. The ability to completely lose each other in the other person. She had never had that. She loved Kristin, but she had rarely *felt* loved. Jack moved his lips back up over her breasts and met her kiss once more, before moving away slightly to catch his breath.

The sight of Kathryn's body beneath him, exposed and vulnerable, made Jack's heart skip a beat. Kathryn smiled at him and ran her hand along his cheek. He moved his face in response and intensified his grip on her waist. Without a word, Jack moved inside her, the moans becoming more intense with each passing moment. Kathryn felt her nails running down Jack's back, and moments later, he lifted her off the counter, still holding her tight, and carried her over to the bed. Kathryn forced his shoulders down onto the sheets, and sat upright, moving her hips in rhythm to his, sweeping her hair back as she rocked. Jack's hands moved over her breasts, squeezing them gently as they rose and fell.

The rain began to fall heavier outside, and the wind whipped it against the windows, seemingly intensifying with each minute that passed. Jack rolled on top of Kathryn and their bodies entwined once more in a passionate embrace. In that moment, nothing else mattered. As the rain

146

pounded on the roof of the cabin, the world fell away as they lost themselves in each other's arms.

And up in the main house, Annie had fallen asleep on the sofa, all three beers gone, and upstairs Daniella was lying under the sheets, slowly falling asleep. Kristin was standing in the window, staring down towards the cabin, the dim light from the lamp shining off her body. She watched through a gap in one of the curtains as her wife and Jack came to climax, and moved under the covers, continuing to kiss and staring into each other's eyes.

There were no tears in Kristin's eyes, and the only hint of regret at what she had done was that she hadn't sat down with Kathryn and discussed that they should end their marriage before it ever got to this. But she knew that neither of them were happy, and after seeing what she had from that top floor window, she let herself form a slight smile. She had found comfort in Daniella, and Kathryn had found her comfort in Jack. She took one last look at the cabin and spoke quietly to herself.

"Maybe now we can both be happy."

18

"What do you mean there might be another doorway?"

Jack was now leaning forward in his seat waiting for Annie's reply. He had not had much time to process the new information that had been gathered that morning. It had been somewhat of a cat and mouse game so far between him and Kathryn, and Kristin and Daniella. Whilst Kathryn and Kristin had not said a word to each other so far, he had been debriefed by Daniella, before returning his own story of the events of the previous night. Unfortunately, he didn't get the impression that it was something Daniella intended to pursue, and from Kristin's body language, he was wondering if she had picked up on those vibes.

But right now, he needed to focus. They all did. Because Annie had discovered information that had not been available to them in their own reality.

"Okay, so in our reality, I learned everything I know from texts that were available, and from a fellow blue spirit who helped me understand my heritage. But this isn't our reality. And some of the shit that you have here is off the charts."

Kathryn spoke up, deliberately avoiding making eye contact with either Daniella or Kristin.

"So what have you found? Because I'm pretty sure I was there when Monarch somehow destabilised all the other doorways and blew us into the river."

Annie held up her hand for patience. There were other details she needed to cover before she got to that point. But it was Daniella who interjected first.

"Do you guys always have these big sit down meetings with big reveals and answers?"

Kathryn looked at her wife for the first time, and the two of them shared a knowing smile. They did indeed do this often, and as they thought about it, more than they had perhaps realised.

"Yeah. Usually clears up a lot of the plan."

Annie cleared her throat, and the others apologised for interrupting and sat back down in their chairs.

"Okay, so the texts that Scarlett was harbouring disappeared with her, right?"

Daniella nodded.

"But not the ones Kristin was examining."

Daniella looked over at this version of Kristin instinctively, before giving a look of apology and turning away again. A slight pain went through Kristin's chest at the thought that perhaps she may not be what Daniella wanted her to be. Annie continued.

"I woke up this morning in the early hours, I don't normally drink, and it caused an… effect."

Giggling rippled through the room.

"Anyways, when I came out of the bathroom, I noticed an air pocket behind one of the bookcases, and voila! There was a room behind it."

Daniella looked surprised. Clearly she did not know this house as well as she thought she did.

"I pushed it open and inside was a series of books and scrolls. There were even notebooks where Kristin… *your* Kristin, had posited theories, including one on how to expel a supernatural entity to another realm."

That had caught their attention. All four people were now fully alert and sat up straight in their chairs.

"She made reference to an anchor object. Something that a person or entity may have on their person, which belonged to where they came from. Something that could be enchanted to drag them back to their own realm."

And it was at this point that Kristin's light bulb in her mind illuminated the full hundred watts.

"The amulet!" she blurted out.

Annie nodded, while the others remained confused. Kristin elaborated.

"Monarch took the amulet from Grace originally, right? Then Annie took it back before we went through the doorways. But what did he say in the church?"

Kathryn thought for a moment, and then replied.

"It won't work here."

"Exactly," said Annie. "It won't work here. Because it is outside of its own realm."

Daniella didn't follow.

"But wasn't that amulet created in your realm? Not Monarch's?"

Annie nodded.

"That's why he said he would see us at home. He's hoping that he can find some way of enchanting the amulet in whatever realm he has now gone to, in order to pull himself back to *his* Crossroads."

Jack now joined the conversation again.

"But he isn't from your realm. Surely home, meant this Beyond place. And he spoke it to you, isn't that where you're from?"

Annie took a deep breath, and then reached behind her and opened a large old leather bound book, and slammed it down onto the table in front of everyone.

"I believe he's trying to bring Beyond to him."

The book's pages were yellowed and worn, some sporting light burn marks at the edges. However, the text and images depicted clearly showed what was some kind of battle occurring between the Yellow Demons and the Blue Spirits.

"We knew there had been conflicts, but even the spirit that I spoke to was unaware of these events. There was a full on war in Beyond, and the demons were driven out of their mortal hosts and imprisoned in their pocket universes."

Daniella sighed loudly.

"We already knew that."

Annie shot her a look that was far more stern compared to what Kathryn and Kristin were used to.

"No. We knew that during an attempted possession, they were forced back, and that at least one, Monarch, broke free for a second time. What we didn't know, was that this wasn't the second time. It was the third."

Jack leaned forward and ran his hands over his face mumbling between his fingers.

"Ah shit, this ain't gonna be good is it?"

"Well yes and no," replied Annie, turning the page. "The Yellow Demons were powerful creatures, they wanted to rule over everything, which is why they tended to be sought out by power hungry mortals. When they first escaped, and the war took over, they attempted to devise a way to leave their realm. However, what this book tells us, is that when that failed, the few demons who escaped initial capture, began slaughtering the guardians of the gateways."

Kristin piped up.

"The guardians were the ones who kept the doors open, and guarded against their usage?"

Annie nodded.

"Yes. Without the guardians, the doors either closed during the battles, or vanish once somebody goes through them. Which is why we haven't been able to essentially go back the way we came."

Daniella stood up and walked over to the drinks trolley, which thanks to the last few nights, was now in desperate need of a restock. Despite the fact that it was only nine-thirty in the morning, she poured herself a large brandy.

"Why would they need to kill the guardians if they didn't intend to cross the doorways?" she asked, before downing the entire contents of the glass.

Kathryn looked down at the floor, her mind racing with a thousand terrible scenarios.

"Because they weren't trying to escape. They were trying to formulate a bigger plan. A failsafe for if they ever managed to break free again. That's why Monarch led Scarlett on a wild goose chase around the realms. The guardians were too difficult to kill, so he had her finishing them off."

Annie turned another page, which showed not a historical document, but a prophecy.

"The blue spirits believe they were trying to find a way of uniting all of the doorways together, and dragging the realm with them. The action would likely result in the loss of many of those realms, and the ones which survived would be greatly weakened…"

"…and ripe for conquering."

Jack finished the sentence as the reality of the whole situation began to dawn on them all. But Annie wasn't done.

"We thought it was Kimberley's abundance of energy from her existence as a pain wraith which amplified these doorways to converge in such a way. But it wasn't. That was just the top up."

She reached behind her and pulled out a rolled up blueprint. As she spread it out against the wall behind her, pinning the corners into the plaster, she stepped back to reveal a place they all recognised.

"Crossroads, whatever reality or universe it exists in, sits on top of a huge geothermal and mineral rich mixture. The energy from both combined, have gradually been drawing the doorways from other parts of the world, from the other parts of our universe, towards a centre. Crossroads is that centre. Kimberley's energy simply pushed those doorways to begin opening. And in this reality, there were two pain wraiths."

Kristin now stood up.

"That's why so many doorways opened up here."

153

Annie nodded once again.

"We had no idea when we were studying these doorways in Montana, that they were not only linked to other realms, but other times, and realities as well. Crossroads is a beacon."

Daniella put down her glass and moved forward a few paces.

"And Monarch is going to drag all of them together until they implode, free the yellow demons, and rule them himself."

Annie sat down on the arm of Kristin's chair.

"Exactly."

The room fell silent for what seemed like an eternity, before anyone else spoke. The revelation of what was actually going on came as a relief to most but also tinged with a familiar sense of defeatism. It was Daniella who broke the silence in the end.

"You said there was another doorway. When you mentioned about the amulet being an anchor object. Do you mean that we can use the same method to get you back to your reality, without needing an actual doorway?"

Annie winced slightly, as if she had been stuck with a pin.

"Yes, and no."

Jack rolled his eyes.

"Do you ever give a straight answer?" he asked, now exasperated from the ups and downs of all the drama.

Kristin translated for him.

154

"Yes, we can use the same technique to get back to our reality. But no, we don't have any items with us. Hey wait, why don't we just go to your Kathryn's version of the museum and use the trinkets in there?"

Daniella shook her head.

"She didn't open one here."

Annie interjected.

"It wouldn't matter anyway. Those objects could be completely identical, and they still wouldn't work because although they were perhaps even found in the same places, they were this reality's version of those places. You'd end up not going anywhere. And the amulet was the only thing any of us had from our reality."

Kathryn cleared her throat, before standing up.

"Not exactly."

She reached into her jacket, and from the left hand pocket, withdrew a long battered piece of metal. A blade which had rusted severely, but still maintained its sharpness.

"What is that?" asked Jack.

Kristin knew exactly what it was.

"The bayonet you found at the Somme."

Kathryn nodded.

"I found it when I was looking for artifacts from famous battle sights. I figured perhaps there were things that had never been recovered, and they would have some spiritual energy to them. When I found it, I saw

155

someone. A soldier. It was like he was looking at me, and I knew in my mind that it was his. It's only half the length that it used to be, it's in pretty bad shape. But every time we are in a scrape, I feel like that soldier is there. Watching over me. So I never put it in the museum. I kept it on me. And since our clothes are the only things that have changed as we've moved between realms, it never left me."

The room again fell silent. This was their answer. Their anchor object. Everyone began to feel a renewed sense of hope, except for Annie, who looked like she was trying to work out a very difficult maths problem in her head.

"Erm… it might work, and it might not."

Jack chuckled sarcastically.

"Again with those ever so clear answers, Annie."

She shot him another one of those stern looks, and he backed off and sat down again.

"Where you found that bayonet may have been in our reality, but it is an object from an earlier point in time."

Kristin threw her hands down to her side.

"So does that mean if we can pull of this miraculous spell and it pulls us back home, it's going to be in France in the middle of a war?"

Annie shrugged her shoulders.

"It might, it might not."

The group returned to their dejected ways, and slumped down in their seats. It was then, that Jack thought about what Annie had told them.

"So if that bayonet would take us back to the early nineteen-hundreds into a war zone, does that mean the amulet would take Monarch back to the point of its creation? Well it's not made by *Apple* is it? That must be centuries old."

For the first time, Annie jumped up with a sense of optimism and a smile spread across her face.

"Jack, you're a genius!"

She ran over and kissed him on the forehead before grabbing her jacket off the coat stand and opening the front door. As she disappeared outside, the others looked at each other, shrugged their shoulders, and followed her out.

"Hey Annie, where are we going?" Jack called after her.

She stopped in her tracks, and reached into her hair. She lifted up several strands, before she extracted something from it.

"We're going to see a very old friend!" she said holding a hairclip in her hand.

Nobody had the slightest clue why she was brandishing the hair clip at them, until Kathryn noticed what was dangling from it. It was the ringer from a bell. Jack noticed she had begun to decipher whatever was going on, which given the amount of information they had been assimilating that morning, was highly impressive.

"What is it," he asked her.

Kathryn smiled.

"The amulet was created by a coven of witches in Victorian England. It's not as old as you think, simply created using far older materials and

157

incantations, but the actual form of the amulet is Victorian period. And so is that bell."

Annie now pointing to the bell on her hair clip, explained.

"I fell between the cracks in time in our Wealdstone, and ended up in Victorian London. That's where Desmond and I found the coven and put a stop to them. If that's where Monarch has gone, that's where we need to go. When I first went back in time, a cart crashed in front of me and the little bell flew off and I kicked it down the street. I picked it up and attached it to my hair clip, and it's been with me ever since."

Daniella raised her eyebrows. Clearly their counterparts had led a far more interesting life than they had.

"And exactly how do we travel to the past without a doorway?" she asked.

Annie replaced the clip in her hair, and began to swirl her hands around in front of her. The violet ribbons of energy began to emerge from her fingertips, and her eyes darted back and forth, and as they did so, the usually destructive wisps of purple began to condense and form words. Within seconds they were all looking at a projected image of the book they had just left in the house. Jack gave a very impressed look, nodding in acceptance.

Annie dropped her arms and the images vanished, a smile on her face, she began to look around.

"The place in your reality with the most amount of energy, is back at Crossroads, so we need to get there fast. Which means we need transport, preferably still intact."

Her eyes scanned the bottom of the hill, past several crushed or flipped cars and trucks, until they came to rest on something that despite its size, had somehow remained untouched.

158

Annie turned and looked at the group who had followed her down the driveway and directed them to where she was looking.

"So, anyone know how to hot-wire a bus?"

19

"What you said back there, about Monarch. What did you mean?"

Jack was trying to get along with Annie more because if he was honest, he was in awe of her powers, and he knew that she was close to Kathryn. Daniella had been the one to hot-wire the bus and was now driving it back towards Crossroads. The previous journey had been silent and fraught with anger and tension. This one was different. Kathryn was loading weaponry in the middle of the bus, directly opposite Kristin and Annie and Jack were at the back reading through the pages of the book. Jack had decided as cool as Annie's projections were, it couldn't hurt to have the original as a backup.

"Which part?" Annie replied.

"The part about existing inside of mortals. Do you mean that Monarch isn't the man, but the thing inside him?"

Annie nodded.

"Yellow demons cannot exist without a host body. They're corporeal. Pain wraiths can utilise their immense energy to manifest their own physical form, or choose to inhabit a body. Yellow demons can't do that. Without a host body, they would just float away into nothingness. That's why it's so easy to imprison them. They don't want to dissipate, so there's an element of defeat that they embrace when they're captured."

Jack thought about this for a minute. He had no problem taking out a violent and murderous entity, whatever form that took. He had learnt the hard way, as had Daniella, that sometimes you had to go to extremes to save people. But this was troubling him more than one would expect.

"So this host body, they're still in there?"

"Yeah. Their consciousness is sort of pushed o the back of the room and locked behind a sort of plexiglass barrier. When a pain wraith inhabits a host, that person's consciousness is destroyed. But Yellow demons share the body, simply becoming the dominant presence."

Jack nodded.

"So we're killing an innocent man. If we actually manage to get near, that is."

Annie put the book down, and looked Jack in the eyes.

"That innocent man tracked down the demons. The only people drawn to do that are men hellbent on power or desperate for some kind of revenge. As much as it may be hard to hear, they know what they're getting into when they go looking for evil."

"And they can't be redeemed? Separated?"

Annie had in fact been researching that very possibility, but had been reluctant to share that information with the rest of the group out of fear of being shot down. She sensed there was already a build up of conflict and deception in the group, without adding that into the mix. She wasn't entirely sure she could trust Jack either. So she decided to find out.

"So when are you going to tell me what happened between you and Kat?" she asked.

The question completely threw Jack off. He had not expected such a change in direction. But he did have to admit that the events of the previous night were very much on his mind. The fact that Kathryn and Kristin had not had chance to talk to each other yet made the situation even heavier.

"What gave it away?" he asked.

161

"The fact that she bolted out of the mansion last night. And the fact you don't know how curtains work."

Jack blushed slightly. He had built the cabin up from a dilapidated shed and put the curtain poles up himself. But there was a notch in the rail that stopped the curtains fully closing. He had decided to leave it, so he could look out at night from his bed across the lake. It was a view his Kathryn had always loved. Now of course, it was exposing what should have been a very private moment and the embarrassment was flooding in.

"I don't really know what happened. She just flew in, and it was like something had happened and she'd just... I dunno... cracked under pressure. But it felt so right."

Annie nodded, and glanced towards them, still ignoring each other.

"They've not been right for a long time. To be honest, I've only known them for around four years, and I've watched them go from happy to practically polar opposites. And in the middle of all that... was you."

Jack looked down. Kathryn had told him all about her 'nearly' moment with his counterpart.

"You know I wondered if I was just missing my Kathryn so much that I'd tricked myself into substituting your Kathryn for mine. But the more time I spend with her, the more I notice the differences. The slightly quirky things she does that my Kathryn never did. And I just feel comfortable with her. It's like coming home to an old friend, but... more. You know?"

Annie smiled. She looked at him and with all sincerity gave him a frank answer.

"She loves you. Whatever reality or universe you're from, she's always loved you. Kristin was something new for her. It brought her out of her shell, it was her first relationship with a woman, and I think they just sort of got caught up in everything. I'm not sure there was any substance to it to be honest."

Jack could understand that. He had been involved with someone a long time ago that he came to realise was just a matter of circumstances. He looked over his shoulder at Kathryn, and it was as if she sensed him looking at her. She lifted her head, and smiled at him. And he felt it. She did love him. He found himself smiling back at her.

"See? Told you."

Annie smirked as she returned to reading the text. She figured she could trust Jack now. He had confided in her, and so she would return the favour.

"This incantation is what I've been looking over. To save the man behind Monarch."

Jack's smile faded, and his eyes widened. Annie was thinking along the same lines as him. He wondered if the others were too. Thinking specifically of Daniella, he rather doubted it.

"So you gave me shit, but you're thinking exactly the same?"

Annie shrugged her shoulders.

"Hey, if we don't at least give them a chance, we're no better than them right?"

Jack smiled at Annie, and she began to show him the details of the separation process. Meanwhile, Kristin had been staring at the floor for most of the journey, and she knew it wasn't travel sickness that was making her feel ill. It was the avoidance of talking to her wife. She didn't know what they were going to be walking into and if anything happened to her before she had spoken to Kathryn, she would never forgive herself.

She put her gun down on the seat and looked up at Kathryn, who she was surprised to see was already looking at her.

"Kat, we need to talk."

Kathryn placed her weapon on the seat in the same manner, and let a long breath escape her lips.

"I know."

Kristin had the whole conversation mapped out in her brain but she was finding it hard to formulate the words, and found herself stuttering. The more she fumbled the words, the more she got frustrated. Kathryn sensed she was having difficulty and she also felt the need to just get everything out.

"I saw you last night. With Daniella."

Kristin stopped and just let out a deep sigh.

"And I saw you with Jack."

The two of them looked at each other for a minute or two, and gradually both of them began to form smiles. It was Kathryn who spoke first.

"Why did we put ourselves through this? Why did we let it go on for so long?"

Kristin shook her head.

"I don't know. I thought I was happy. I thought I had met the perfect woman. But the more I thought about it, the more I realised how little we connected… you know, outside of the bedroom."

Kathryn laughed. It was true, there was never any problem there. But it was always either work related, or business related. And the war with Jasmine had all but ended any closeness they had.

"You gave me so much, Kris. You introduced me to this whole other world. I've had so many adventures with you. I've faced challenges I would have shied away from. I owe you a lot. But I never felt like I was loved. Did you?"

Kristin thought about it for a moment.

"Yeah. I did. I felt like you loved me, and I was the one not giving it back. I got too consumed in this whole world of demons and vampires and hauntings, and never stopped to think that it wasn't all your fault. I was driving us apart as much as you. Perhaps more."

She looked at Jack, now consumed by the book Annie had discovered.

"He makes you happy, doesn't he?"

Kathryn smiled in his direction. She nodded.

"Yeah. He always did, but it was me that pushed him away all those years ago. Then I found him again, and lost him. I just don't think I can do that again."

Kathryn then looked towards Daniella, who had been completely oblivious to any of the conversations going on.

"What about her? Not as exciting as werewolf Daniella, right?" she asked, smirking as she said it.

Kristin laughed louder than she had intended, and raised a hand to her mouth to try and stem the noise.

"She's the same as me. She's lost a lot, and she's just looking for someone who understands her. I think we can make it work. The question is, do you think they will come with us?"

Kathryn shrugged her shoulders.

"I really don't know. I hope so. But then I think to myself, am I just his substitute, or is this real?"

Kristin nodded. She understood, but she felt something different with Daniella. She felt like they were attracted to each other because of their individual histories rather than being a substitute.

"I mean, I don't think we can do this without them. We've lost Kim and Grace. God I keep forgetting about Grace."

Kathryn looked down at the floor. She was also ashamed with how often she had forgotten about her niece. That was the whole reason they were in this mess in the first place, trying to track her down.

"They've lost more. They lost everyone. We still have each other. We started as friends, I hope we can stay friends."

Kristin started twirling her wedding ring around her finger, before sliding it off and handing it to Kathryn.

"You bought them. Keep it. As a reminder of all the good times we had. Just in case."

Kathryn pushed it around in her palm for a minute, before taking off a necklace she was wearing, and undoing the clasp. She slid the chain through the middle of the ring, and put the necklace back over her head.

"Maybe I'll put it in the museum when we get home."

166

The two of them laughed. For the first time since they were first dating, they were both feeling happy. Despite the awful situation they were embroiled in, a huge weight had been lifted from both of their shoulders. They both had someone more suited to them that they wanted to be with. They both acknowledged what had gone wrong, and that they hadn't been suited as a couple. And now they were free. Kathryn leaned in and put her arms around Kristin. They shared perhaps the most loving hug they had shared. As they parted, they looked each other in the eyes, and shared a final tender kiss. The bus jerked to a stop, and they broke apart a little quicker than they may have intended.

"We're here."

Daniella's voice was serious and returned everyone to the present. They had quite a task ahead of them. Jack and Annie walked down from the back of the bus, joining Kathryn and Kristin.

"We ready?" asked Jack.

Kristin looked at Kathryn and nodded.

"Let's do this."

20

Being unconscious was a very unusual feeling for Monarch. Even in the rare times his physical host had been rendered out of action, his own consciousness had remained active. But this was different. As he opened his eyes, he felt groggy and dazed. Confusion occupied his every thought. He felt his hands move to either temple and he squeezed his head to try and steady his vision. But there was nothing to see. There was only darkness. He had known choosing a random doorway to go through was risky, but he had dealt with all of it so far.

He stopped trying to stand, and instead ran his hands along the ground. Smooth. Cold. Definitely man made. As his eyes focussed, they began to emit a low golden glow, and he was able to make out some outlines of objects within the room. He could hear a faint voice and as his eyes moved across the outline of a large metal door, he realised the voices were coming from beyond that threshold.

"What I wouldn't give for some lights," he mumbled aloud to himself.

As if by magic, the room illuminated, and the sharpness of the light forced Monarch to cower down and cover his face. As his eyes once again adjusted to his surroundings, he began to realise that he was most definitely in a facility of some kind. But the air was off. He felt as though the room was moving somehow, despite the fact he was standing still. Still unsure of how the room had come to life, he thought for a moment.

"Open the door," he said.

The door parted with a whisper, almost silently, revealing a long corridor lit up with a red glow from above pulsing lights, at the end of which appeared to be a small set of steps. Still unsure about where he was, he attempted to conjure something. The corridor's red glow was transformed into a dark orange as Monarch discovered his abilities were indeed fully functional. But bearing in mind he needed somewhere stable to enact his plan, he proceeded with caution. The voices got louder the closer he got to the staircase, and to his surprise, he found himself standing next to a window.

But there was no light coming through this window.

Monarch found himself looking at his own reflection, beyond which was an entire galaxy of stars. This supernatural being was not one to be mesmerised, but the fact that he was somehow in space astounded him. He had never considered that the doorways traversed the stars as well as times and realms. And then, in the far right of his view, a turquoise glow began to appear, in which the Earth grew larger.

The voices were getting closer, and against his usual nature, Monarch hid in the doorway of a locked room opposite.

"You cannot just take one, Torath. Do you not understand that if this fails…"

"It will not fail! The Resurrection chamber is almost complete, and I have tested it myself. The first humans I gathered were most useful."

Monarch wanted to take a look at the people having the argument, but he remained still for now.

"You say they were useful. The first or second time that they went mad? This delusion you programmed into their minds destroyed them! And where are they now? And what about these Deltarians pursuing you? You are drawing unwanted attention to our work. Questions are being asked about our second outpost on Deltaria."

"The second outpost will not be needed. I can handle Lu'Thar. The Decimator vessel has entered the system. I must collect the specimen."

"Torath, if this doesn't work…"

"Computer, end communications."

An audible beep sounded and the two voices became the one. The man named Torath was now stomping around in the room. Monarch could wait no longer. He emerged from his hiding place and slowly walked up the steps and entered what he could only describe as a command centre. There were consoles around the edge of the room in a circle, and above them was one wall of glass, with a view of the Earth from above. What really threw him was the appearance of Torath.

"Goodness me," he exclaimed without thinking about where he was.

Torath span around, his bright blonde hair slowly turning to a deep burgundy, his eyes glowing brightly.

"Who the hell are you, and how did you get aboard my ship?"

Torath's loud voice was matched by his seven-foot frame and imposing posture. This did not intimidate Monarch, it merely intrigued him.

"What exactly are you?" he asked, ignoring the outrage on Torath's face.

"What am I? What are you?!"

Monarch's patience was beginning to waver, and his intrigue had lessened. He thrust his right arm forwards, and a golden ribbon swirled around the room, until it came into contact with Torath, when it split into four, each wrapping around one of his limbs and lifting him into the air.

"I am what humans call a demon. I'll ask you again, my blue skinned friend. What are you?"

Torath was stunned at this mystical power being demonstrated before his eyes. Nevertheless, his mission was now in jeopardy and so he replied to the questions being asked of him.

170

"My name is Torath. I am Captain of the Saxon vessel Trinity."

Monarch raised his eyebrows a little.

"So that would make you a Saxon? An alien in laments terms. And why are you orbiting Earth like this?"

After delaying his answer slightly, and being reminded of his position by the tightening of the magical ropes around him, he yielded.

"The humans are about to be destroyed by a heavily armed vessel. I am here to save one of them."

Monarch raised his eyebrows again. His curiosity was once more at its peak.

"Just one? How curious. And this… vessel you speak of. How do you know it is coming to destroy them?"

Torath gritted his teeth slightly.

"Because I sent them."

"Curious."

Monarch strolled around the control room, taking in everything he saw. Dials, buttons, touch screen panels. He was accumulating knowledge as fast as he could absorb it.

"This… ship of yours is quite impressive. Tell me, is it capable of taking me down to the surface?"

Torath now sported a look of confusion.

"The surface? But it is about to be obliterated. Are you not here to stop me?"

171

Monarch gave a hearty belly laugh, which took both him and Torath by surprise.

"Stop you? Oh no my dear fellow. I couldn't give a damn about the humans. They're far too meddlesome. I'm only here because several of them meddled in my affairs. Oh by the way, what year is this? I presume I'm now in the future, given the fact I'm on a spaceship. Or do you prefer starship?"

"I… don't really have a preference. And it's 2151. Where are you from?"

Monarch smirked as he tapped a few controls on the nearest console to Torath.

"It's more of a time *and* place as opposed to one or the other. As you've probably guessed I am not a creature of your realm. A mystical doorway brought me here, and I was hoping for some peace and quiet while I work on a little project. But I suppose I'll have to deal with you first instead."

Torath attempted to see what he was doing but couldn't make out which controls he was pushing. He didn't have to wait long for his answer. With a flick of his wrist, the yellow strand of energy holding Torath's right arm branched into two, the second now acting as a gag across his mouth. Monarch then attempted to solidify his advantage.

"Computer, can you translate these controls into English?"

"*Affirmative. Making translation now.*"

Monarch's grin widened almost to its maximum point as the controls were translated from pictorial symbols into words he recognised.

"Ah, that's better."

He tapped in a message and selected the destination. It was followed by a beep of recognition, and a message that read 'co-ordinates sent.'

Torath struggled and mumbled against his restraints, but to no avail. Monarch continued to interrogate the ship.

"Computer, tell me. How far away is this Decimator vessel?"

"The vessel will reach Earth in approximately twenty minutes."

"Hmm. Computer, am I able to be transported to the surface?"

More angry mumbles from Torath drew a sigh from Monarch.

"Why don't you take a nap my giant friend?"

The ropes of energy wrapped around Torath retracted allowing him to land on his feet, before combining into one thick rope which slammed into his chest and sent him careering into the control panel on the farthest wall. It erupted in a shower of sparks and broken class, and Torath himself fell to the floor, landing with a heavy thump, where he remained.

"Much better. Now, computer if you could kindly answer my last question?"

"The teleporter is online. What is your destination?"

Where else thought Monarch? There was only one place he could guarantee a doorway would be active. Travelling through space would be too risky. Even as powerful as he was, he needed to keep as much control over the situation as possible. And with only a short time before the planet was due to be destroyed, he would have to traverse another doorway before attempting to use the anchor object. The computer prompted him again.

"Repeat, what is your destination?"

173

Monarch took one last look at the communications console, which was now glowing with the words 'Deltarian vessel incoming,' before replying.

"Wealdstone, United States."

21

"Are you sure you know what you're doing?"

Annie snapped her head around to look at Kristin, and gave her another one of those stern looks she was becoming known for in this reality. Kristin held her hands up in defeat, and strolled back over towards Daniella, who was staring at where the energy barrier used to be.

"I did wonder why people hadn't suddenly started flowing into town," she said, gesturing with her head towards the town limits.

"Yeah, ain't no getting through that," replied Kristin.

'That' was a ten foot high wall of sand, dust and debris which had obviously stacked up around the barrier while it was in place. Over time, the weather appeared to have compacted it and it would take considerable time to break it down.

"Um, listen Kris," started Daniella, shuffling her feet around. "I think we need to talk about what happened last night."

Kristin perked up and a smile began spreading across her face. Jumping the gun, she interrupted Daniella.

"It's okay. Me and Kathryn had a long talk about it on the bus. We both agreed that we should have gone our separate ways years ago. But she's found comfort with Jack, and now I have you."

Daniella's face fell and she started kicking dirt around on the floor, doing everything she could to avoid looking Kristin in the eyes. Sensing something was wrong, Kristin lost her smile immediately, and her stomach began fluttering not with butterflies, but a decidedly more unsettled movement.

"What is it?" she asked.

"Kris, listen. Last night was amazing. It was as if the last two years hadn't happened and my wife was back in my arms, and everything melted away. I felt like I was home, and nothing else mattered because you were with me again."

Kristin smiled.

"I am with you."

Daniella shook her head.

"*You're* with me. *She* isn't."

The smile faded again. Kristin took a couple steps back. Daniella completed her delivery.

"I looked at you, I kissed you, I made love to you. But it wasn't you I was thinking of. It was *my* Kristin. I got lost in the moment and swept up in the emotion. But when I woke up this morning, I realised that it was wrong. I wasn't seeing you. I was seeing her. I'm sorry."

Daniella's eyes began to tear up, and she looked at Kristin who was now completely devastated, before walking away leaving her standing there.

"But…" she began as her lip started trembling.

She never finished the sentence, and the tears began to flow. She didn't dare look back towards the others. She had taken the leap and found there was no safety net after all. Her breath quickened and she felt as if she may hyperventilate. Kristin was not used to being in situations like this. She had always been in control of everything she did, from building her business as a financial advisor, to constructing the Silverton Shopping District, and in a way leading her relationship with Kathryn. And yet here she was. She had lost everything. And all in the space of one night.

176

A loud cracking sound echoed across the sky, and Kristin jumped at the noise, her nerves completely shot. Behind her, Annie had seemingly completed the incantation in the book which should have led to relief. But the expression on her face was anything but hopeful. Kristin pushed her feelings down as far as she could manage and ran towards the others to see what was going on.

"Something's wrong!" shouted Annie, as the wind began to whip up, dust tornadoes forming all around the Crossroads site.

"What is it?" Kathryn shouted as the noises became louder and more frequent.

Annie shook her head, reading the book again, but finding no errors in the spell she had performed.

"The bayonet isn't acting as the anchor object! It's anchoring Crossroads!"

"What!?" shouted Jack. "It's using the settlement as the anchor object!?"

Annie nodded furiously, the sky was now darkening, clouds swirling above. A huge rumble started as the general store lifted into the sky, tore from its foundations, and hurtled towards them.

"RUN!" shouted Daniella.

Annie grabbed the book and the bayonet, and all of them sprinted towards the bus. Lightning flashed throughout the sky, one of the bolts striking the remaining metalwork atop the church, blowing the structure apart completely. The ground began to rumble and cracks formed in the dirt. Just ahead of them, the earth split apart forcing them all to skid to a halt. The chasm expanded rapidly, and the team were forced back.

"Oh shit."

Kathryn pointed as the bus veered upwards, the rear falling into a newly formed crack, and swallowing the bus whole. The remains of the church crashed into the river, which itself was beginning to develop into water spirals in the air.

They had nowhere to go, and the very ground they were standing on was beginning to rise.

"What is happening?" shouted Jack. "How do we stop this?"

Annie frantically flicked through the book, but as she reached the page with the incantation and began to read it in reverse in an effort to stop what was going on, a black spot appeared in the middle of the page. Annie stopped reading.

"What the fuck is that?" asked Kathryn as the spot expanded to fill the page.

"Oh no."

Annie's face twisted into an image of pure fear. She threw the book on the ground, but the booby trap had been activated.

"What is it?" asked Jack.

Annie watched as a stream of black smoke began to emerge from the book and swirl around it, lifting it into the sky.

"Scarlett."

The book exploded and tentacles of dark smoke thrust forward and slammed into Annie's chest. The impact lifted her clean off the ground, and spiralling, unconscious through the air. As the others watched, a portal opened in the sky, and Annie careered through it, before it closed behind her.

Jack looked back at the remains of the book just in time to avoid the same fate. The smoke swept past his right shoulder, but a third stream struck Kathryn and she clattered into him, the two of them sent soaring through a second newly formed portal. That closed too, and Kristin and Daniella sprinted as fast as they could. The smoke twisted and took on the form of a beast, hunting its way across the ground at speed. Kristin speared off to the right, leaving Daniella alone as she charged towards the barrier of debris.

The smoke monster directly behind her, Kristin took a sharp right and dived through the window of a nearby house, glass exploding upon impact and covering the floor inside. As she hit the floor, the cloud blasted through the side of the house, and ripped the entire building above her away. It curled around and began to home in on her again.

"Ah fuck."

The stream of fog appeared to strike the ground and almost kick out at Kristin. The sound of bones cracking was audible, and she lost consciousness immediately. Her limp body cartwheeled into a new portal, which swallowed her up before closing. That just left Daniella.

She was incredibly athletic and had managed to avoid the swipes and assaults thus far. However, her luck had now run out. The swirl which had taken out Kristin had now flanked her, and hit her side on. Her ribs caved upon impact, and as the fourth portal opened, her eyes flickered shut and she vanished along with the rest of the team.

The smoke creature immediately retracted across the ground until it returned to the book. The pages reassembled themselves, the wind died down, and the book gently closed itself. As it faded, the now gentle breeze blew the book apart as if it were made from ash.

The book was gone. And so was everyone else.

179

22

Not only was darkness consuming Kristin from the inside, but she was now surrounded in it. She wasn't sure how long she had been here. Two, maybe three days. She had kept passing in and out of consciousness. She remembered vague images of a light, and then dampness. But then nothing. She couldn't make out anything. Even her own hands were lost to her. She felt the ground and as she recalled, she was sat in a puddle of some sort.

Hunger tore through her stomach, and she cried out in pain. It was as she tensed up from this, that she jolted her shoulder which had been injured when she was hit by... what was it? She struggled to piece it together. Smoke? Fog? Images of the Shrike from the triangle realm flashed before her, but she dismissed those. No, a name was mentioned. A familiar name.

Scarlett.

Annie had failed to spot a booby trap of intricate design, and the book had taken her somewhere. It had taken them all somewhere. But where was this somewhere, and were the rest of the team in the same place? These were questions that were smashing up against the inside of her mind, along with all of the memories rushing back to her. Watching Kathryn with Jack, confiding in Daniella, her rapidly developing feelings for her being rejected. She had lost her niece, her wife and now the person she thought she could move forward with.

Fear was certainly surrounding her, but the anger alongside it was building up in her very core. For the first time, she began to feel an almost hatred. Everything around her was crumbling, and it was crumbling fast. Kristin had barely had time to breathe between each blow. She reached down to feel in her pockets, only to find no pockets there. Instead she felt bare skin.

Her hand retracted in shock. This was the first time in the day or so she had been here that she was coherent enough to notice her situation. She ran her hand along her chest and her legs. She was naked. In the dark and cold dampness. Her head snapped around, the pain from the blows she took in the fight causing her to wince.

"HELLO!" she screamed out.

There was no echo. She was not in a room, or a cave. Her lower half began to feel the cold now she was alert enough to notice it. She placed her hands in the inch or so of water and pushed herself upwards, managing to clamber to her feet. Her eyes were slowly adjusting, but in truth there was nothing to see. She moved her arms across her chest and lower body in an attempt to cover her modesty, before realising that if she couldn't see herself, then neither could anybody, or anything, else.

Gradually, she began to take small steps forward, holding out her left hand in case she approached a solid object. Again, she called out.

"HELLO!"

This time, in the distance, she heard a very low growl. It was barely audible, but it was definitely there. Instinctively, Kristin dropped to a hunched position, her eyes searching the darkness, but finding nothing.

Another growl, this time louder. It was coming *closer*.

"Whatever you are, stay the fuck away from me!" she yelled into the distance.

The growl intensified in tone and volume. Squinting, Kristin could now make out a very faint pair of glowing red eyes. Her breath quickened as she watched the eyes gain height. When they stopped rising, they were at least five feet above her eye line. Whatever this creature was, it was enormous.

181

"Stay away from me!" she screamed, more in terror than anger.

The creature lunged forwards, roared and bared glistening white teeth so bright, they illuminated in the darkness without any other form of light. Kristin didn't have time to move, the beast moved so quickly. She just felt the pain.

She looked down to see a long, black, jagged rock protruding from her stomach. She couldn't speak as she began to choke on her own blood. Her left hand felt behind her, and found the tip of the rock sticking out from her back. The blood began to trickle down her chin, and she dropped to her knees, an audible splash breaking the silence. A low guttural sound came from behind her, and as she struggled to turn her head, a slight breeze blew past her face.

As Kristin's head slid away from her body, it seemed to float to the ground rather than fall. It did not land heavily, but like a feather.

And she could *see* her body. She was fully aware of what was happening. She watched as a swirl of black and darkest red swallowed her body, twisting and turning around it before pulling it apart in one swift movement into a thousand pieces, and vanishing.

She tried to move her mouth but nothing happened. She closed her eyes tightly, and inside her mind, she screamed louder than she had ever thought possible. Her mind swayed for a moment. The feeling like she was on a ship at sea. When she opened her eyes, that was exactly where she was.

"What the…"

She ran her hands over her body, and everything was as it should be. She was in one piece, there was daylight, and she was standing on a ship. Then she realised where she was.

She was back in the triangle.

"You've got to be kidding me."

Kristin was exactly where they had started, in the same outfit, with the same weapons. But it *wasn't* the same. She heard the same growling behind her that she had just experienced. But was that a dream, or another realm? The pain had certainly been real. She reached for one of the many blades on the belt. But they were gone.

She looked down, and the belt had gone in its entirety. Looking back up, the ship was gone, and she was now standing *on* the ocean. Instinctively, she jumped, but the water didn't move beneath her. With every blink of her eyes, the scene altered, each time becoming more and more terrifying. The sky vanished and was replaced by a grey mist, the ocean around her began to rise and crash as if sentient. Each time Kristin moved, the scene around her would react and trap her where she was.

Then, all of a sudden, everything fell silent and calm. Kristin's breathing was the only sound. She felt a breath on the back of her neck, and could feel a presence behind her. She closed her eyes, steeled herself and spun around only to be faced by Kathryn. Instantly, Kristin's guard collapsed and she tried to move forward towards Kathryn. But she couldn't. Her legs were stuck in place. Above her, the grey mist morphed into the Shrike. Hundreds upon thousands of them swirled above her. One of them swooped down towards her, but jerked to the left at the last minute, rising once more, before swooping down again and flying right into Kathryn's back. Her eyes turned black.

"K...Kat?" Kristin managed to speak, but only briefly.

Kathryn's eyes narrowed, the black in her eyes now swirling with grey smoke. She reached her arms forward, her hands gripped Kristin's head, and she twisted it to the side, and up, sharply. Kristin's body dropped to the floor, and the image of Kathryn drifted away.

Mere seconds later, Kristin was once again alive and standing this time in the mansion. She was still reliving the fact that Kathryn had apparently just killed her. The image of her being torn apart was also still fresh. She had felt the pain from every part of this experience, and was still feeling it when she realised where she was.

She was in the destroyed basement, following the events of Jasmine's pre-emptive strike on the mansion. Lying in pieces before her was the dismembered body of Daniella. The scene hit harder having been in alternate Daniella's company, and after the collapse of that brief relationship. What really scared her was the fact that once again she felt she was being watched.

And then Daniella's eyes opened.

Kristin jumped back, and placed her hand over her mouth. Blood poured from Daniella's mouth down onto the concrete and rubble.

"You killed me Kristin… you don't have abilities… you aren't special… wherever you go death follows."

This was perhaps more horrifying than anything that had come before. Kristin felt like she was going to pass out from lack of oxygen. She was being torn down piece by piece. The pale white face of her friend repeated the lines over and over and suddenly stopped. Kristin felt a hand on her shoulder, and she turned to face alternate Daniella.

"And now it's your turn to die."

With one swift movement, Daniella thrust her entire right arm through Kristin's chest, bursting out of her back. Kristin's mouth was wide open, her scream trapped in her throat, her eyes wide. She glanced down and watched as Daniella pulled her arm back through her torso as quickly as it had punctured it, and saw she was holding Kristin's still beating heart.

184

Daniella looked at it briefly, Kristin trembling, losing integrity. She looked back at Kristin, her eyes turned to black, and gritting her teeth, she crushed the heart in her hand, the blood dripping and spraying over her arm and across into Kristin's face. With one final breath, Kristin fell to the floor, dead, eyes still wide open, and Daniella dissolved in the air floating away like pieces of burnt paper.

The third cycle of torture would not be the last. Kristin continued to be murdered, killed, tortured over and over again, each time feeling the pain and the agony. Sometimes it was family members, sometimes supernatural entities, sometimes a copy of herself. But the agony continued until she had experienced *thousands* of horrific deaths. There was no way out, and nobody to rescue her.

23

"Jack? Jack, wake up. WAKE UP DAMNIT!"

Kathryn delivered a hefty slap across the face to Jack and he sat bolt upright, almost headbutting her in the face. The speedy rise from the ground sent his head spinning even more than it already had been.

"Nice of you to fucking join me!"

Jack rubbed his palms over his eyes and mumbled his reply.

"Could've done with five more minutes if I'm honest. I was having a wonderful nightmare involving phantoms, demons and alternate realities."

He opened his eyes and saw exactly what Kathryn appeared so ready to get away from.

"Oh no, my mistake. It was all real."

They were in the middle of a crumbling street, cars burnt out and rubble everywhere. To the left of them was what used to be the famous Arc De Triomphe, split in two, one pillar and the arch itself on the ground, the other pillar still upstanding. And directly in front of them, was a crowd.

A crowd of zombies.

"Get your ass up, I'm not carrying you!" Kathryn shouted, yanking him by his arm.

"Alright, alright, Jesus. You sound like my…"

Jack stopped his sentence dead both from his realisation of what he was about to say, and from the look being directed at him by Kathryn. Jack

186

hobbled a few steps as he got his bearings and tried to shake off the aches from the impact of being flung through the air like a shotput, before he got some speed back into his stride.

"Where are the others?" he asked, his breathing picking up the pace.

Kathryn shook her head.

"I don't know, but I've got a feeling that booby trap was designed to split us all up. We've been here about fifteen minutes and I've seen nobody. Until the friendly neighbourhood welcoming committee showed up."

She turned to look over her shoulder and the crowd of undead had grown. Others merged from the various avenues, knocking each other down as they bumped into one another. The groaning became louder as they too picked up the pace at the smell of fresh meat.

Jack despite everything, gave a little chuckle. Kathryn glared at him.

"What the hell is so funny?"

He giggled again.

"They are literally the most stereotypical zombies I have ever seen. I mean come on! They're not even *Walking Dead* quality zombies. More like a *Scooby-Doo* level!"

"Are you seriously joking right now?"

Kathryn was now becoming more and more infuriated, but for some reason, Jack's levity continued.

"Oh please, I've seen scarier creatures in my sock drawer!"

Jack then pushed away from Kathryn, and began wobbling on his feet. If she didn't know any better, she would have sworn he was drunk.

187

"What is the matter with you?" she demanded.

Jack turned around and began walking back towards the crowd of undead.

"Jack! What the fuck are you doing?"

Jack stumbled forward, and it was then that Kathryn noticed something worrying. Jack had a very large open wound on the back of his head. It was clear that his balance was off and his mental acuity was being disrupted. He gave a brief belly laugh, before placing his hands on his head, and wincing in pain.

"Shit, something is wrong," he said, as he stopped laughing and knelt down on one knee. "Kat, I don't feel so…"

Jack collapsed, unconscious and unresponsive. Kathryn raced over to him, and tried to rouse him, but nothing she tried worked. Neither of them had any weapons in this reality, and there were no nearby objects to be used for defence. All she could do was try and drag him off the streets to somewhere more safe.

"Jack, come on. I need you to wake up!" she said as she struggled to drag him across broken tarmac. "Right now!"

Mere mumbles of laboured breath came from his mouth, but he was not going to wake up anytime soon. From in front of them, Kathryn heard more groaning. It was now almost in stereo.

"Ah shit."

Another crowd of undead began filing out ahead of them, blocking the avenue completely. Kathryn stopped, exhausted from the combination of dragging Jack, and the events leading up to it. The crowds closed around them in a circle, and there was now no escape. Kathryn desperately

188

searched for anything she could use. But she didn't even have her bayonet. That was left in the alternate Crossroads when the spell backfired.

She didn't know much about zombies from movies, they were generally the sorts she avoided. But she figured the old adage of 'go for the head' would apply. As a few moved close enough to them to be a threat, she ducked behind one, and wrenched its head to the side. The crack was loud, and the life left the beast immediately. She spotted a second moving in on Jack, and shoulder barged it to the ground. Before it could get up, she stomped her boot into its skull, and the rotten brains within spilled out onto the road surface.

Kathryn moved to intercept a third, but the creatures began snapping forward with their decrepit teeth, and she jumped back. The sound of decaying flesh slapping on exposed bone, and the smacking of saliva dripping lips made Kathryn shudder in both fear and disgust. Then it dawned on her. There was no way out of this. This was the end.

As five or six zombies reached towards her, she closed her eyes and hunched down next to Jack. But death never came. Rapid gunfire rang out around her, and the sound of bullets penetrating the torn clothing followed. She opened her eyes to see wave after wave of undead clattering to the ground, flesh and blood spattering everywhere. She swivelled her head from left to right but saw no gunman. More shots rang out, and she caught the trajectory of one. It appeared to cut through its victim in a *downward* motion.

It was only then that Kathryn looked up, and saw flashes visible from the top half of the Eiffel Tower. Being at least two kilometres away, she couldn't make out details, but the firing was definitely coming from the restaurant at the top of the tower itself.

"That must be a hell of a weapon," Kathryn said to Jack before remembering he was out of it.

The final zombie dropped to the ground, and from above it looked like a large pinwheel of death. There was no way Kathryn was going to either leave Jack, or drag him a mile or so to the tower. But she didn't need to.

As she watched, she saw a small figure move towards one of the flags still erected on the flagpoles either side of the elevator doors. To her amazement, whoever it was, lifted the flag into the air, and leapt from the balcony. Kathryn instinctively wanted to catch them, but she soon realised it had been a foolish gesture, and was glad nobody was watching.

The flag became a parachute of sorts, and the pilot, seemingly with practice, altered the course of their flight as if it was indeed a genuine parachute. The descent levelled out, and despite the distance, they landed just left of the Arc's remains, rolling as they hit the grass.

Jack began to move, and Kathryn looked down to see his eyes begin to flicker open. She failed to notice the footsteps of their saviour approaching, and as Jack opened his eyes fully, he smiled.

"Sorry, did I miss anything?" he asked.

"You could say that, yeah."

Kathryn smiled back at him, and then her senses alerted her to the figure now standing beside them. As her eyes moved up from the ground, she saw the barrel of a high calibre sniper rifle, which had been modified to include a large volume clip magazine. As her eyes continued to move up their hero to their face, she gasped in shock.

"Hey Auntie Kat."

24

"How long has she been here?"

"I don't know, I found her like this."

"Have you tried getting her attention?"

"Of course I have! I wouldn't have come to get you otherwise, would I?"

Chan had not seen a spectacle such as this in at least eighty years. In fact, he hadn't seen much Blue Spirit activities for most of his life. He had heard about them when he was younger, but never actually encountered one. Nybor on the other hand, had.

"We should try and get her somewhere safe. If anybody sees her, there are going to be questions and maybe an inquiry."

Chan leaned forwards to grab hold of Annie's arm.

"I wouldn't do that if I were you," Nybor warned him.

"What's the worst that could…"

Chan didn't complete his sentence, because the instant he touched Annie's arm, a charge of blue energy shot from her chest, and struck him in the shoulder, sending him spiralling backwards, into the thick tree trunk, falling to the ground with a thud.

"Told you," Nybor said, trying hard to conceal her amusement.

Chan climbed to his feet and stumbled back towards them, rubbing his shoulder, shaking his head in an effort to regain focus.

"You were the one who said to move her!" he said exasperatingly.

"I didn't mean literally grab her and move her. Blue Spirits have a protective aura around them when they enter these trances. It's a defence mechanism when they've been victim of a particularly powerful attack."

Nybor had been a member of the Order of the Falcon for a hundred and twenty years. She had seen the last of the Blue Spirits perish, and the tumultuous time that it created. Blue Spirits had once been the chief protectors of the realm, but the conflict with the Yellow Demons had shifted the balance of power within all the kingdoms. But the presence of Annie to her meant two things.

One : This Blue Spirit was not of this realm.

Two : Something dangerous was coming.

"So how exactly are we supposed to move her then?" asked Chan.

Nybor strode forward, her large white wings unfolding from her cloak, and she lifted her wooden staff from the ground. As she reached Annie's position, she began twirling the staff around between her two hands, getting faster and faster, until the thing was simply a blur of arctic white light. A whistling sound accompanied the movement, and as it reached maximum speed, the sound was so high pitched, Chan had to cover his ears to prevent the pain.

With one swift movement, Nybor leapt into the air, flipped backwards, and landed with great force, slamming the staff into the ground. A shockwave rippled around them for fifty feet, the breeze blowing leaves from the trees, and sending Chan back onto his backside.

The shockwave also disrupted the protective spell surrounding Annie, and she woke with a start, instinctively generating bursts of energy and firing them forwards. Nybor deflected two of the blows with her staff and very little effort. She held her hands up in peace, and Annie's breathing began to slow.

192

"I am not here to hurt you, Spirit."

Nybor leaned forward, and began to kneel down beside Annie, her wings folding back down and vanishing beneath her cloak. Chan very cautiously remained where he had fallen, but moved his body into a position where he could run if needed.

"You... you're a... oh no. I'm here aren't I?"

Annie's voice was slightly horse and her realisation of where she was, made her very uncomfortable. She recognised Nybor's appearance from texts she had been shown by the Blue Spirit she had encountered while in Victorian London.

"If you're referring to Beyond, then yes. You are."

Nybor's voice was calming and reassuring, and Annie lowered her arms in response.

"You're a white falcon, aren't you?" she asked.

Nybor nodded.

"At your service. My name is Nybor. And this is Chan."

She pointed behind her at her friend, who waved, despite still being cowered near the trees.

"You're certainly not an expected arrival, miss...?"

"Annie."

"Ah, Miss Annie. So you're not of this realm, and you certainly don't have a name from this realm. How did you get here?"

193

A look of fear began to spread across Annie's face as she remembered how she got to Beyond, and why she had encompassed herself in the protective spell.

"Well, it's… complicated."

Nybor smiled.

"You'd be surprised how many things no longer surprise me. Try me."

Annie took a deep breath.

"An incantation I was trying to use to return to my reality was spiked by a Phantom Wraith."

Nybor's smile lessened significantly, and Chan, who had begun approaching the two of them, retreated back to the edge of the trees upon hearing the name Phantom Wraith. Nybor remained at Annie's side, and placed a reassuring hand on her shoulder.

"Unfortunately, I have had dealings with a Phantom Wraith in the past. I can help you…"

Annie held up her hand to cut Nybor off mid-sentence.

"That isn't the problem, we had already dealt with her."

Confused, Nybor pushed for more detail.

"Then why the protective spell? What separated you from your realm?"

Annie looked up at her cobalt blue eyes, and spoke with apprehension.

"Monarch."

Nybor leapt back and stood upright. Faster than Annie could take a breath, the White Falcon unfurled her wings and flew directly up in the air until she was above the towering oak trees, and began circling the clearing where Annie and Chan were sat. Her staff was once again twirling, but every few feet, it shot a bolt of white lightning down to the ground, and a transparent column as wide as that from a castle, planted itself in the ground, dust funnelling up from the impact of each one. The process continued until a translucent circle of energy, anchored by these columns surrounded Annie and Chan. A twirl in the air later, Nybor swooped back down to the ground and once again, struck her staff into the ground, only this time, she left it there, and a bolt of white light fired from the top into the centre of the circle, high above them. When it reached the height of the tallest tree, it exploded like a firework, creating a shimmering white net of energy, which then fell and attached itself to each of the see-through columns. They were now encompassed in a protective forcefield of white energy.

Annie had read about the protective nature of the White Falcons, but she had never imagined seeing it for real. She was in absolute awe of the action and for a brief moment, forgot the seriousness of her situation. Nybor retracted her wings once more, and gestured for Chan to join her. She stopped in front of Annie, and took a deep breath.

"Monarch has plagued this realm for millennia. If he has escaped, then all the realms are at stake. I need you to tell me everything you know about what he has done, and what you have experienced so far."

The three of them sat in the protective circle for what seemed like hours, and Annie relayed the entire tale from the suspected cult activity, to Grace's disappearance and their first conflict with him. She explained about the doorways, and how they were collapsing. She explained how they not only led to other realms, but also alternate realities, and time periods. She described Scarlett and her involvement, and what she suspected Monarch was trying to achieve. When she had finished, Chan was sat alongside her, captivated as if he had been told the famous story of a mythical warrior. He absorbed every word. Nybor's face did not alter

195

during the entire story, offering no words until Annie had stopped. It was only then that she gave her contribution.

"The stories surrounding Monarch have been greatly distorted over the last two thousand years. Men of greed and power have always sought out the prison containing the Yellow Demons, but few have been successful. The mortal who discovered how to break the demons out of their prison, was the second son of King Tellemicus. His father was dying, and his older brother, Nata, was due to take the throne. When Nata became King, the first thing he did was strip the man of his royal titles. You see, Nata wanted to be a more benevolent king than his father, and restore prosperity to all the corners of the various kingdoms. But Monarch was against this. He felt that a king needed to rule with an iron fist, and that there should be a clean line between the royal family and the people they ruled over.

That is when he sought out the prison of the Yellow Demons. He was so desperate to get the power to take down his brother, he began recruiting like minded people to help him, with the promise of power. Between them, they killed a dozen of your kind, and were successful in freeing the Yellow Demons.

However, King Nata had gotten word of his brother's plans, and he sent the entire Order of White Falcons to stop him. My maternal grandfather was among them. He died that day, along with over thirty others. But Monarch and all of the others were stopped, and the demons were separated from their mortal hosts and returned to the prison they came from.

For three hundred years, peace ruled, until King Nata was poisoned by his wife, Lecithin. Nata's brother…"

Annie held up a hand to ask a question.

"What was Nata's brother called? You haven't said. You've either referred to him as the mortal, or Monarch's vessel. Since Monarch is the name of the demon, I'm assuming the man had a name."

Nybor sighed.

"He did. His name was Dorn. He was my father."

Annie couldn't help but gasp audibly at this revelation. Although she had just met Nybor and Chan, she felt a kindred connection with them. Although born human, Annie was developing into something else. The combination of her pain wraith and Blue Spirit parentage was coming to fruition, and along with that came these feelings of belonging. Nybor appeared wistful at Annie's reaction, and stopped her tale. She appeared to be reflecting on her past. This time it was Annie who placed a reassuring hand on her shoulder.

"Please, continue," she said.

Nybor nodded, and appeared to wipe away a tear from her eyes.

"As I was saying, Nata's wife, Lecithin, had become lovers with Dorn behind the king's back. She believed my father's feelings to be true, but it was simply him playing the long game, and as soon as Nata was dead, he left her. She was the rightful next in line to the throne, but Dorn claimed it should be him. When he was cast out of the kingdom and his plot was revealed to all, he fled before he could be imprisoned, and once again found the prison of the demons. This time, however, he freed only one. Monarch. With nobody able to stop him, Monarch raged through all five kingdoms slaughtering countless thousands. The Order was disbanded years before, with nobody wanting to continue the tradition, and the Blue Spirits were in hiding.

It was actually a friend of my grandfather who managed to imprison Monarch once again. He was a Blue Spirit named Arthur."

197

Again, Annie gasped, and her eyes widened. Her father had imprisoned Monarch. Nybor was slightly distracted by her reaction, but Annie attempted to conceal her emotions, desperate to hear the end of the story.

"P…Please continue."

Nybor raised one of her eyebrows, but nodded.

"Something went wrong. Arthur wasn't versed in the art of magic as a Blue Spirit. Beyond his natural abilities, he knew nothing. He managed to free Dorn from Monarch once more, but a tiny piece of Monarch migrated to Arthur. His behaviour became… unhinged. He retreated to the shadowlands, and did not return for nearly three decades as he battled to contain the evil within. Dorn had continued his life as an outcast, still lusting for the power of the throne, but unable to continue his quest.

One day, Arthur returned to the prison of Yellow Demons, convinced he had found a way to banish the presence of Monarch. But all it did was draw Dorn back and a fight ensued, which resulted in the freeing of all of the Yellow Demons in existence. One had slaughtered thousands. Imagine what ten thousand could do."

Annie shuddered at the thought. She also could not shake the feeling that her father was responsible. Nybor turned away from her, the memories proving painful, and attempted to complete her story.

"The Blue Spirits returned to aid the battle, led by Arthur. A new Order of White Falcons was created, and the Green Dragons came from the gateways to help return the Yellow Demons to their confinement. The war raged on for a thousand years. I was born as a result of the affair between Dorn and Lecithin. I joined the Order over a century ago to continue the legacy of my grandfather."

Annie paused for a moment and attempted to do the math in her head.

"That would make you over a thousand years old?"

198

Nybor chuckled, smiling for the first time since the story had started.

"Is that all?" she replied.

"But you look so young," Annie offered.

"You're too kind. Once you become a White Falcon, you stop ageing. Perks of the job, I guess."

Annie looked past her to Chan.

"And I suppose you're seven hundred and ninety three?" she said, tinged with humorous sarcasm.

Chan looked annoyed.

"No, I'm ninety-nine actually!"

Annie held her hands up in apology, and gestured for Nybor to continue.

"When the war was over, all of the demons were locked away for the third time. This time a powerful incantation was performed that was deemed to be unbreakable. It had been sourced from a powerful witch residing in the shadowlands. But there was a problem. The little piece of Monarch remained in Arthur. The incantation managed to trap them all. Except Monarch. But without a body to inhabit, it was assumed he floated away into the atmosphere. Now we know different."

Annie felt it important to volunteer her side of the story.

"Arthur let Monarch out of Beyond, and into the human realm. Now we know why. He was… possessed. And when Monarch left in Dorn's body, he took the remaining piece of Monarch from my father and…"

Annie was unable to stop herself before Nybor turned to look at her, having heard what she had just said. She let out a deep sigh as Nybor's deep blue eyes bore into her soul.

"Arthur was your father?"

Annie took another deep breath, and explained to Nybor and Chan her parentage and how until recently, she had been unaware of what she was. Nybor seemed to be astonished. She knew Arthur had been banished from Beyond, but did not know where he had gone, or what had become of him. It saddened her that his life had come to an end so far from his homeland, but pleased that he had been able to have a family.

"Can I ask if you have any idea about the doorways, and how to navigate them. Or why they're closing once passed through?" Annie asked, now bordering on desperation.

Nybor thought for a moment. She had a theory but wasn't sure it explained everything.

"The guardians who keep watch over the doorways here in Beyond, are the Green Dragons. At least, they were. Once a guardian dies, their gateway remains open until someone passes through it. With nobody to stand guard, there is nobody to keep it open, and it closes. I don't know if the Green Dragons guard doorways across existence, or only in Beyond, but there are only a handful left and they've become... isolated."

"Isolated?"

"They suffered heavy casualties in the war. They blamed everyone for dragging them into a conflict that had nothing to do with them, and then sealed off their doorways, dedicated to protecting them above all else."

Although slightly deflated, a thought suddenly sparked into life inside Annie's mind.

"Wait, if Monarch escaped through a doorway into the human realm, does that mean that gateway is still open?"

"Perhaps. Why?" Nybor asked.

Annie laughed out loud with relief.

"Because that gateway leads to Wealdstone! My home! And that is where Monarch is trying to get back to! We need to go!"

Nybor stepped into her path, and shook her head.

"The doorway you are referring to has not been used since that day. Getting near it is practically impossible. And even if we did…"

"Even if we did…" interrupted Chan, "the Green Dragon wouldn't let us pass. He's not one of us."

"What do you mean, not one of you?" asked Annie.

"He is human. He was thrown through the doorway by Monarch five hundred years ago in a state of madness. He was treated by the Order before being offered the chance to return to the human realm as you call it. But on the way he witnessed a family being ambushed by mercenaries. He saved their lives, and was offered the chance to take over from the Green Dragon guarding the doorway you speak of. He's been there ever since. But he has… an attitude problem."

Annie wandered around for a few minutes, trying to absorb all of the information she had been told, and the realisation of her father's past. With the threat of Monarch, the team being split into who knows how many realms, the uncertain demise of both Kimberley and Daniella, and the almost forgotten potential threat of the Phantom Wraith, Annie had started to wish she had stayed in Victorian London. Things had seemed so much simpler then. Nevertheless, she had to help her friends, and if she couldn't do that, she needed to stop Monarch and his plans to merge the realms. She knew that he was planning to make it to Victorian London using the amulet as an anchor object. How he planned to get back to present day Wealdstone was still unknown, but given that time passed much faster in Beyond than Earth, she suspected that this was similar across all the realms and he would somehow find a way back to Crossroads.

"The protective shield will fail shortly, and we will be vulnerable to interference and potential attack from those seeking the doorways. Are you sure you want to go through with this?" Nybor asked Annie, her eyes never blinking, never wavering from her gaze.

Annie looked past her to Chan, who seemed to be bouncing on his toes with excitement. She smiled and looked back at Nybor.

"Chan's one-hundred years old soon. Don't you think he should have his first adventure?"

25

PARIS, TWO YEARS AGO

Chantel sprinted as fast as her legs would carry her. She tried her very best to remain quiet, but running across a rubble laden avenue in bare feet caused the occasional yelp of pain, each time relaying her position to the crowds of undead moving in on her. She gained a good fifty yards on the horde behind her, but as she stepped on a jagged rock, she dropped her papers, digital recorder and the belt of vials she had hidden in an A4 folder.

She turned around and gathered up her work, and strapped the vials of formula around her wrist, tightening it to the point where her hand began to lose feeling. It would be worth it, she thought. This serum was too important. As she reached the base of the Eiffel Tower, she saw that the elevator was missing. Expecting it to be at the top, near the restaurant, she looked up. But it wasn't there. It was then that she noticed the two elevator cars were completely detached from their shafts and lying on the ground on opposite sides of the ticket booth.

"Merde!" she shouted aloud.

Chantel looked behind her, and her outburst of profanity had once again led the undead in her direction. She ran forwards, with a slight limp from the multiple wounds her feet had sustained in the escape from her lab, until she found herself standing in front of the now empty elevator shafts. She saw that on either side, was a ladder, somewhat enclosed in a ring of safety railings, which led all the way up to the top, stopping on multiple platforms on the way.

Knowing that there was no way she could climb up there carrying all of this research and other files, she shot into the abandoned giftshop, and grabbed a rucksack from one of the shelves. As she ran back outside, she almost sprinted directly into a zombie who was walking past the door.

She managed to stop and turn just in time, but in doing so, fell sideways onto the floor, the noise alerting the creature to turn around.

As it grabbed towards her ankle, she kicked out and delivered a strong blow to the face of the zombie, knocking it back slightly, just enough for her to get space and stand up. As it moved in for another attack, she resumed her sprint towards the shafts. Once she reached the bottom, she stuffed her notes and files into the rucksack, and knowing she would need fully functioning hands to climb the ladders, she put the vials of serum in there too. She swung the pack over her shoulder, and started her ascent.

The rusty metal rungs of the ladder dug into her already battered feet, but she couldn't stop. She had no choice. She must reach the top of the tower, whatever the cost. At first, dozens of the undead horde attempted to climb the ladder, but with no cohesion to their mission, too many tried to climb at once, and the bottom section of the ladder split away from the rest and they all tumbled back to the ground, where they simply amassed, groaning and drooling at the prospect of a fresh meal somewhere above them.

Chantel reached the first platform fairly quickly, and looking down, she felt relief and took a breather. Her feet were badly injured with several cuts and a laceration to her right heel. She had not had time to grab a medical kit, and did not think to grab some shoes from the gift shop. Above her, she heard what sounded like a whip cracking, but looking up and seeing nothing, she figured it for more creaking rusted metalwork falling away. The tower had not fared well after an electrical storm had struck the capital before the epidemic. Several lightning bolts hit the tower and destabilised the paintwork and the metal itself. Several of the scientists not working on the cure for the new strain of cancer had theorised it was interference from a space based phenomenon. The more 'spiritual' folks had suggested the invasion of energy based entities from another realm. Either way, once the undead began to rise, repairing landmarks was far from top of the list.

Four more platforms up, Chantel heard the cracking noise again and as she looked up, she saw a flash of light. There was a glimmer, a green glow three platforms up. And then it was gone. Chantel decided whatever it was, it wasn't the zombies, and so chose to proceed, but with extreme caution.

Upon reaching that platform, she saw nothing. No lights, no people. Nothing. Chantel was now so high up and so far up the tower, that she could no longer make out individual members of the late lamented below. She was exhausted and was struggling to maintain any kind of determination. It would soon be nightfall, and if she did not make it to the top of the tower and into the restaurant, she was fairly certain she would fall to her death.

Swallowing every ounce of fear, anxiety, and tiredness, she tightened the straps on the rucksack, and began climbing towards her destination. There were now only two platforms between her and salvation. With every inch of her remaining strength, she hauled herself up each rung, grunting loudly as she did so, knowing she would now not be caught by those wishing to devour her flesh below, until finally, she hauled herself through the open doorway into the Jules Verne Restaurant.

She peered around the immediate vicinity, and saw nothing, and no sign of life. Then, she collapsed on the floor, her head resting on a shredded pile of menus, and closed her eyes. The wind whistled through the broken windows, and kissed her face gently, cooling her after her immense feat to reach this point. Chantel rested for what seemed like moments, but when she opened her eyes again, it was dark, and glancing at her wristwatch, she saw that three hours had passed.

The air was now much colder than it had been in the early evening, and she looked around for a jacket or blanket of some kind. Finding a chef's coat hanging behind the bar, she swung it around her and pulled it tight. It reminded her of her lab coat, and she felt strangely comforted. She wandered back over to the rucksack and reached inside to pull out her folder, and her digital recorder. Turning on the device, she saw the battery

205

level had reduced to just fifteen percent. With no electricity, there would be no way to recharge the recorder.

"Well, I guess I had better make this count," she said aloud to herself.

She had managed to retrieve several candles from the upturned tables in the eatery and found a lighter in the chef's jacket, so created a small degree of illumination. She moved behind the bar, clearing the floor, and placing the candles around her in order to keep the wind from extinguishing the flames. As she opened her folder, she clicked record on the device and began to speak.

"5th April 2063. Probably my last entry. In the event I am lost… or eaten… may these recordings help to replicate the cure to the mutation. I have already detailed the ingredients, process and details needed to create the serum. I am hiding the research notes and the related work behind the bar in the Jules Verne Restaurant at the top of the Eiffel Tower. I have no further need of it, now I have created samples and it will remain here until discovered by other humans. If any remain besides myself.

The bacteria from the *angulum obscurum* flower has not been found in any other plant species, and I am therefore confident that my cure will work on the proposed test subjects, and we will not face any further danger of mutation. However, in order to test this, I will need to capture a member of the horde and subdue it. I am uncertain how to achieve this, and it is likely to end up in my death.

Therefore, I would like to say goodbye. I have no family or friends remaining. All I have is my work, and the test vials, which I will leave up here as detailed. The recorder I plan to leave in the cash register in the gift shop when I make my attempted capture. Please remember me for my work. But also remember me as someone who loved humanity so much, that she died for it.

I will make my attempt at capturing tomorrow around noon, and…"

Chantel was cut off by the returning sound of cracking, now coming from below her. She paused the recording, and picked up one of the candles. More cracking and a flash of green light illuminated the elevator shaft, but this time, remained. As she got closer to the doorway, which she had attempted to pull shut, and failed, the light flashed even brighter, and then was extinguished. A thud on the metal platform followed, and moments later a loud moaning noise was audible.

This, however, was not the same groans coming from the base of the tower, this sounded like an injured person. Chantel poked her head through the gap in the doors and looked down. She could just make out movement three platforms below in the glow of the moonlight. More groaning followed. It definitely appeared to be a person. Against her better judgement, Chantel called out.

"Hello?"

A groaned reply.

"Are you alright?" she called out again.

"Wh...where...where am I?" came the reply.

Chantel was rather taken aback by the English spoken reply. She had not seen or heard from anyone outside of France since her lab was overrun, and there were not many ways to travel internationally these days. Chantel did however, speak English and attempted to learn more.

"Are you ok? Are you hurt?"

More groans as the person, who Chantel could now make out was a woman, sat up and propped herself up against the railings.

"I'm fine, I think. Where am I?"

207

She was an American. All the more unlikely that she would have made it across the Atlantic unaided. But that kind of interrogation would have to wait. She needed to get the woman up to her location.

"You are on a service platform near the top of the Eiffel Tower!" she shouted down.

"What?!" the woman shouted in shock.

Suddenly she became very aware of her surroundings and began grasping for the railings, slipping her arm through them several times, causing increased panic. Chantel feared for her safety, and attempted to reassure her.

"Please do not panic! Grab hold of the rails and calm yourself. The only way up here is with the ladder. Do you think you can climb it?"

The woman shook her head.

"I… I think I can make it."

Chantel was confused.

"What do you mean make it? You mean climbing the ladder?"

She reached for the lighter in her pocket and extinguished the flame on her candle.

"I can drop this candle and lighter down to you so you can see, but you'll need to catch it, and find some way of holding it while you climb."

The woman shook her head, and steeled herself enough to let go of the railings, and crouched in the middle of the platform.

"No, I don't mean climb. I think I can jump."

208

Chantel's stomach dropped. Jump? Surely she was delusional and meant she would leap to her death. Nobody can leap *upwards* like that?

"I think you're confused! You need to climb!"

Again the woman shook her head, and looked up towards Chantel.

"Stand back!" she shouted.

Presumably on auto-pilot, Chantel moved back and slightly to the side, enough so that she could still see the young woman. To her astonishment, she leapt with such force that she reached the next platform in a single bound, clinging to the *outside* of the railings cage. Never before has Chantel seen anything like this. A second leap had the woman on the penultimate platform, and Chantel realised this was actually happening. As the woman launched herself upwards for the third and final time, Chantel flung herself backwards away from the doors, and saw a pair of hands land on the floor.

"Little help?"

Chantel gathered herself and ran back towards the doors, grabbing the woman's hands and pulling her inside, the two collapsing onto each other, before composing themselves and clambering to their feet.

"How did you…" began Chantel.

"It's a very long story."

Chantel remained speechless for a moment, and allowed the young woman to look around and take in where she was. As she spoke, Chantel had no reply ready for what she was about to hear.

"You said the Eiffel Tower? But this is *old* and *decimated*. What… where did that doorway take me? One minute I was fighting with that demon

209

Monarch, and the next I'm half way up the Eiffel Tower on the other side of the world?"

The woman span around and looked directly at Chantel.

"What day is it?"

Chantel looked puzzled, whilst also trying to assimilate the phrase 'fighting that demon' in her brain.

"Uh, it's Thursday."

The woman rolled her eyes, her full strength and focus seemingly back in her control.

"Not literally, what's the full date?" she said as she strolled back towards Chantel.

"It's Thursday 5th April," she replied.

The woman's gaze intensified.

"What *year*?" she asked.

"2063."

The woman's eyes widened even further than Chantel thought possible for a human being. But then again she had not demonstrated the abilities of a normal human being so far.

"Fuck me."

The woman moved towards the bar where the remaining candles were, and leaned on the structure rubbing her eyes. Chantel wandered over to her, remaining cautious, but equally *curious*.

"Who are you?" she asked directly.

The woman looked at her, and took a deep breath, before exhaling slowly.

"Sorry. My name is Grace. And it sounds like I may have just travelled through time."

26

The gunshots were doing more harm than good. The more Grace fired, the more attractive they became to their hunters. Despite the initial massacre of the zombies surrounding Kathryn and Jack, more had soon followed, and they were still several hundred feet from the base of the tower. Jack was now more able, but was still losing blood, and unlike Kathryn, he couldn't handle a weapon. As Grace blew a .40 calibre through the skull of a six-foot mutated mime artist, she heard a cry from ahead.

"Grace! I'm getting ready to drop the dolly!"

Grace signalled a thumbs up to Chantel, who was on the base platform along with two others, preparing to lower what looked like a moving truck.

"Who are your friends?" Kathryn asked in between shots.

"Oh didn't you know? I'm a scientist now."

Kathryn smirked and continued firing. It felt good to have her niece fighting alongside her again. But something was different. She looked older somehow. And much more confident. But right now they didn't have time to reminisce. Their priority was getting somewhere safe. That, however wasn't going to be easy, as a new form of obstacle now stood in their way.

"What the actual fuck is that?" asked Jack, still unsure if he was dreaming or not.

"Oh shit, not again."

Grace's response suggested to Kathryn that she had not had the best rate of success with their new opponent. In front of them, just fifty yards from the tower gift shop, were five rabid dogs. Their teeth were glistening with drool, their growls were low and thunderous.

"Seriously? Zombie dogs?" Kathryn asked bewildered.

Grace shook her head.

"No, but they have spent the best part of three years snacking on zombie flesh, so they're a bit… demented."

Regardless of the likely outcome, the former human army were closing, which left them no choice but to plough on. Grace ran ahead, spraying her fire in a linear pattern, attempting to hit as many of the dogs as possible. Three went down, but the two on the outside, broke off and attempted to flank Kathryn and Jack. As one leapt over a bench, Kathryn turned and pulled the trigger, blowing its head clean off, the mangled torso collapsing on the road surface with a splattering noise.

The second attempted to lunge at Jack, but it was a previously unseen sixth dog which knocked it out of the air, and they began fighting and tearing chunks out of each other. With their distraction in place, Grace re-joined the others and they helped get Jack to the gift shop.

Chantel and the others lowered the dolly down the elevator shaft and when it hit the ground, Grace helped Kathryn to lower Jack into it. With only enough room for two, they decided to send Jack up first and keep the two angles of fire rather than just the one. The three people on the platform hauled Jack up, and dragged him off the dolly, before lowering it back down. Grace and Kathryn hurried onto it, keeping their guns aimed, and firing as soon as any of the undead got close enough.

The dolly began to rise, although due to the weight, it was much harder work and moved incredibly slowly. Three more rounds of fire later, and Kathryn's gun clicked to indicate her ammo was gone.

"Shit," she said. "I'm out."

213

Grace reached into her pocket, and pulled out a small squashed box of bullets, but as she went to hand them to Kathryn, the dolly jolted, and she dropped them. They bounced off the edge and down into the crowd of hungry flesh eaters below.

Another jolt, and this time, the dolly tilted slightly to one side. Grace looked up towards Chantel and the others and threw her hands up in the air.

"What's going on up there?" she shouted.

"I don't know, something is wrong with the pulley!" shouted the woman beside Chantel.

Without any warning, the rope holding the left hand side of the dolly snapped, and the whole thing dropped on that side. Kathryn dropped her gun as she fell, and Grace slipped, reacting just quick enough to grab hold of the rope on her side. Kathryn was now clinging onto the bottom of the dolly, and upon first glance, Grace could see the second rope was beginning to weaken and fray.

"Hang on!" she shouted at Kathryn, but the rope began to split.

Kathryn's fingers were losing grip, and the roars from the crowd below intensified. If the fall didn't kill her, then the zombies surely would. Another jolt, and one of Kathryn's hands slipped away.

"Hang on Kat! Just hang on!" shouted Jack from above, now alert to the situation.

Grace looked to her side, and she saw the ladder was almost within reach. They were just six missing rungs away from a potential way up. Instinctively, she threw her gun as hard as she could up the shaft. It travelled like a bullet itself, much like she had upon her arrival, and the barrel got just close enough to the platform for Chantel to grab.

214

Grace looked up at her, and nodded towards the pulley. Chantel nodded back, and cocked the weapon, before aiming it. Grace then looked down at Kathryn, fear now consuming her.

"Kat, I need you to trust me okay?" she said very sternly.

Kathryn's fear grew as she suspected she wasn't going to like what was about to happen. But given the fact she was about to plunge to her death, she knew she had no choice but to trust her niece. She nodded, and closed her eyes.

Grace looked back up at Chantel, braced herself, and shouted "NOW!"

Chantel pulled the trigger, and the pulley unjammed, and the rope began unwinding at speed. The dolly along with Grace and Kathryn plunged. As they did so, Grace let go of the rope she was holding, and as she reached Kathryn, grabbed hold of the bottom of it, and pushed Kathryn off. Kathryn's eyes widened as she began to fall, but Grace grabbed her with her other hand, and as the rope extended enough to become taught again, their motion was slammed, and the dolly swung out into the open air.

Kathryn's screams were deafening and in any other situation would have been comical, but as the dolly slowed, and began swinging back the other way, she felt Grace's hand tighten around hers, and noticed her muscles bulging. As the dolly swung back to its highest point, Grace swung Kathryn up, the screams continuing and let go. She flew upwards, and managed to grab hold of the first rung of the ladder that was intact. Clinging on to it for dear life, she desperately tried to pull herself up, but she no longer had the strength in her arms. Chantel and the other young woman had climbed down to help pull her up, but she was reluctant to move.

"Kat, we need you to move, Grace is gonna need that spot!" said the woman.

215

Reluctantly, she let go and the others helped her up to the platform where she embraced Jack, before turning back to see where Grace was. The dolly swung back out again, and Grace was focused on her target. As the dolly made its return journey once more, Grace took a deep breath and let go, just as the rope finally gave way. She clattered into the iron framework of the tower, several feet below the first rung, and held on tight. Below her, she watched the dolly and the rope fall into the crowd where it disappeared.

It took Grace and the others a good twenty minutes to climb back up to the Jules Verne, and when they reached it, Kathryn found there was a lot of activity. There were desks, and a wall full of weaponry, but there was also a converted bar which was now serving as a lab table, surrounded by vials and beakers, and Bunsen burners. On the back wall where the alcohol would have previously been, there were various chemicals, crudely labelled by hand. The sound of sizzling was coming from what she presumed was the kitchen, and she could smell food cooking. Finally, she saw over by the windows, an intravenous drip, gurney, and a monitor.

This appeared to be a fortress in the sky. Kathryn was in awe as Jack was taken over to the gurney and several people began to examine him. She turned back to Grace, who was now strolling towards her, and the two of them shared a hug for the first time in years. The last time she had embraced her niece had been after the funeral of Duncan and Daniella. But again, she felt Grace was now different.

"How did you get here?" was the first thing Kathryn could manage to say.

Grace directed her to a sofa near one of the large windows, and the two sat down and Grace began telling her aunt about how she had fought Monarch, and come through one of the doorways. She detailed how she first thought she had travelled into the future, but then discovered there were significant differences between this reality and theirs. Kathryn then relayed their adventure so far and detailed how they still had no idea how they were going to get home.

It was several hours later that more details about this iteration of France came to light. The young woman, Emma, and the man, Danny, who had assisted Chantel in rescuing them were of particular interest.

"I'm sorry, run that by me once again please?" asked Kathryn.

"When I arrived here two years ago, we captured one of the zombies and administered Chantel's serum into their bloodstream. Within two hours, the effects of the mutation began to recede, and within a week, we had ourselves a Danny. Another capture, another serum delivered, another cure. We had ourselves an Emma. This cure works, and we have been able to bring back almost fifty people. But supply runs are dangerous. In the two years we have been working, we have only managed to get enough materials to make sixty vials of serum. That means we only have ten left."

Kathryn listened to everything that she had just said, but was focussed solely on two words.

Two years.

Grace had been in this alternate Paris for two years. Zombie apocalypse aside, which she was disturbed at not being as surprised about as perhaps she should have been, that made her want to cry.

"Grace… we've only been gone from Wealdstone for six days."

Grace stopped talking, and allowed herself to ponder that for a moment. She presumed her aunts had been searching for her for the past two years, but given up when she had found no way out herself. How was that possible?

"But, it's been two years for me. How has it been six days for you?"

Kathryn rubbed her hands over her face in an effort to clear her mind. Obviously the notion was ridiculous, but it did make Kathryn feel more prepared to explain.

"Each reality or realm we go to, time seems to pass differently, depending on when we arrive. In the Triangle, we arrived at different time. Kristin and Annie were there around two weeks before I showed up, even though we went into the doorway at the same time. In the alternate Wealdstone, Monarch had been there for two years trying to excavate their version of Crossroads. At most you've been gone two weeks."

Jack stumbled over, his head wrapped in bandage, clutching a glass of water.

"Kinda screws with your mind a little, doesn't it?" he asked Grace.

"Just a little bit, yeah. Oh and welcome back from the dead, by the way."

Jack did a pretend curtsey and sat down beside Kathryn. Grace continued.

"So you're telling me there is a way out of here, but we have to find a doorway?"

Kathryn nodded. Jack then placed the caveat.

"The only problem is, the only place so far that we have managed to guarantee there would even be a doorway, is Crossroads. In your reality, Kimberley and Annie's energies helped top off the required level to open dozens of them. In my reality, once excavated, there were a dozen more. Different realities, same location, same result."

Grace looked around the room.

"So what you're saying is, we need to somehow get to the US, and reach this reality's version of Wealdstone to have a shot of getting home? How are we meant to do that in a zombie apocalypse?"

218

Jack opened his mouth to answer before realising he didn't have one. He turned to Kathryn who simply shrugged her shoulders. Grace looked at them both, and when neither could answer her, she shook her head.

"Brilliant. Thanks for your help."

She gestured to Chantel and Danny, and they wandered over to join the group.

"What's up?" asked Chantel.

"Well, we need to get across the Atlantic to the States, and then drive across the country somehow to get to your version of my hometown. Any thoughts?"

Chantel looked at her friend as if she had lost her mind. Danny, however, was formulating a plan. Grace cottoned on to this and enquired.

"Danny?"

"I may have the foundations of an idea."

27

The track through the forest was not the easiest to navigate. Nybor refused to allow any potential for others to know where they were going. There had been too much conflict and stigmatism attributed to the Blue Spirits, and too many painful memories for people involving Monarch. This meant that although they were trying to get to the Green Dragon as quickly as possible, they could not take a known route, and Nybor did not want to risk flying ahead. Annie walked alongside her and Chan in silence for the most part. She had so much information to process, and feelings running through her that she had not yet assimilated. She had not had time to grieve the loss of Kimberley, the fact that her friends were either missing or dead, and to process the information she now had regarding her father. The threat was just too large to ignore and to compartmentalise was now the only concept she could cling to in order to prevent her having a breakdown.

Chan was starting to tire, but like an eager school child, wanted more and more information.

"Nybor, what happens when we reach the Green Dragon? Are they actually dragons like the lore says?"

Nybor, despite her attempts to keep a low profile, burst out laughing which was infectious and caused Annie to giggle too.

"No Chan, they are not real dragons."

Chan appeared disappointed. There were many wonderous creatures and beings in Beyond. He was walking alongside two of them. But the idea of real dragons had captured his imagination.

"But why not? You're a real falcon, Annie is a real Blue Spirit. She glows blue, and her powers come out blue, so why aren't the Green Dragons, real dragons?"

Annie, not finding an answer to that question, looked at Nybor to elaborate.

"I am not a real falcon, Chan. The members of the Order are enchanted, and endowed with special abilities which we use to protect the realm across the five kingdoms. Before we are inducted, we are just as ordinary and mortal as you. Blue Spirits get their name from their powers, not the other way around."

Annie was now as invested as Chan.

"And the Green Dragons?"

Nybor gave her a look to say she should know better than to encourage pointless conversation, but nevertheless gave her answer.

"The Green Dragons are similarly endowed with abilities in order to protect the gateways. But they're abilities include advanced strength and agility. Their armour can be conjured with a single thought and is made of dragon skin."

Chen got over excited again and started jumping up and down directly in her path.

"Ah! Made of dragon skin! So there *are* dragons!"

Nybor stopped walking, looked towards Annie for support, but just received a shrug of the shoulders in reply. She took a deep sigh and explained.

"There *were* real dragons. A long time ago. They died. And when they died, the first Green Dragons were created and given armour made from their skin. That armour is passed down from one Dragon to the next."

221

Chan nodded and moved out of her way and the trio resumed their walk. Annie's mind, however, generated a rather ludicrous idea. Of all the things running around in there, she was a little surprised that this thought shot to the front of her brain. She figured the only way to expel it was to speak it.

"Did you just tell me the plot of *Game of Thrones*?" she asked.

Nybor looked confused.

"I don't know what that means," she replied.

"You said there are five kingdoms, obviously that's two fewer, but then said there were dragons that died out, and there's been treachery and royal murder plots... anyone would think George RR. Martin came from Beyond."

Nybor stopped and shot her a look.

"Don't mention that mischievous troll's name again!"

Nybor then continued her stride, leaving Annie stood there dumbfounded. She looked at Chan.

"Did she just confirm..."

"Come along you two! We have a long journey ahead!" Nybor shouted over her shoulder, and the two ran to catch up, Chan still dreaming of meeting a real dragon.

28

The landing this time was significantly rougher. As his face hit the cobbled street, Monarch felt as if he had been struck by lightning. The amulet now lay several feet away from him, smouldering, the centre of the jewel now destroyed.

"These damn transitions are going to be the death of me."

The rain cascading from the sky was now so heavy, in just a couple of minutes, he was soaked through to the skin. And something strange happened. Something that disturbed him greatly.

He shivered.

Initially, the sensation didn't register with him. The only feeling he tended to experience was pain and that was very rarely. But then it occurred to him that he had felt a pain in some manner or another numerous times during this quest.

He shivered again.

"What the hell is this?" he said aloud.

He picked up the destroyed amulet, and jammed it into his pocket, and felt an uncontrollable need to get under cover and find somewhere warm. Pounding the cobbles with his feet, he wrapped his arms around himself in an effort to retain some form of heat, splashing through puddles, and slipping on the cobbles as he tried to pick up speed. Ahead of him, he saw a pub, and could see the glowing of a fire through the window. He staggered over, now consumed by cold and looked through the glass. But he didn't see the fire or the patrons inside.

He saw *Dorn*.

Looking back at him in the reflection was the mortal vessel he had occupied for so very long, unoccupied by his presence.

And then he *spoke.*

"You will not win, Monarch. I am still here. And I am getting stronger. I will be free again."

Monarch closed his eyes tightly, shook his head, and when he opened them and looked back at the glass, Dorn was gone. He moved to walk through the door and entered the pub, bumping into tables and chairs as he made his way towards the fire. The people within the pub began to stare at him, bemused by his strange clothes, and his apparent difficulty in walking straight.

"Got another strange one here, Alf."

"Think he's had a skinful already, don't you."

Monarch wasn't listening. He sat himself as close to the fire as possible, consumed by the desire to get warm. His mind was beginning to unravel. Had he truly seen Dorn in the reflection? Why was he feeling so many sensations, so much pain, cold. And then it dawned on him as he began to feel the warmth of the fire. The doorways. The number of realms, times and realities he had crossed must be affecting him. It must be weakening him. The more he thought about this, the angrier he started to feel. The laughing in the background from the drunks and the locals only served to feed that anger.

He felt his eyes begin to burn, and his breathing became more intense. He heard Dorn's words in his mind once more.

"I will be free again."

Monarch leapt to his feet, and let out an animalistic and deafening roar. The windows of the pub shattered outwards, glass spreading across the

224

cobbled London streets, the rain now cascading inwards. He span around and roared again, firing a stream of yellow energy directly at the head of the landlord, obliterating it sending blood splattering all over the patrons, fragments of bone shattering the bottles of spirits standing in their optics on the wall. Two of them attempted to flee the building, but Monarch launched forward with lightning speed, and pinned them both against the wall by their neck. He squeezed his fists closed until their eyes filled with blood, and their necks were crushed to dust. The fear and rage now surging through his body had created an implosion within. Streams of golden ribbon lashed their way around the bar, furniture was obliterated, the door was smashed off the hinges and the final patron in the bar remained cowering in the corner. Monarch, now with a mouth as wide as his shoulders, teeth bared stomped over to him.

"No, please, don't!"

He reached down with one hand, and lifted the man as if he was a rag doll. He opened his mouth and roared once more, before clamping his teeth into the man's throat. He ripped the side of his throat out and spat it on the floor, the lump of raw flesh mingling with the blood of the other patrons. The victim's face remained frozen in the expression it had sported when he was attacked. The dark wooden floor was now slick with blood and glass, and broken wood. Monarch discarded the now limp man, throwing his corpse over the bar. From within, he heard Dorn's voice speak to him again.

"That's it, Monarch. Use all of your energy. It will only make you weaker."

"NOOOOOOOOOO!" he roared and his entire body became consumed by his golden energy.

Yellow lightning and clouds of golden fog erupted from every point on his body, and the entire building exploded in an enormous golden fireball, the walls, window frames and ceiling all blown out. As the flames consumed the building, the roof began to collapse. Monarch staggered

225

forward through the burning door frame, untouched by the flame, now completely returned to his normal appearance, and staggered down the street, now feeling weaker than he had since this all began. The smoke began to rise from the rubble as people flew towards the building to try and help.

Monarch turned a corner into an alleyway, and collapsed to his knees. The rain continued to pour and he examined his face in the large puddle in front of him. Again, he saw Dorn looking back at him.

"What's happening to me?" he asked aloud.

Dorn's image vanished, and his mind began to rest. But then he heard conversation behind him which peaked his interest.

"Come away, Miss Annie. It looks dangerous. We need to let the professionals handle it."

"What happened Herman?"

"I'm not sure, but I've never seen flames like that, have you?"

"No. And I've got a feeling it may have something to do with the coven we've been hunting."

As the younger Annie and Herman moved away, Monarch felt his confidence and his smile returning. This time, he would find a way to not only return to *his* version of Crossroads without having to travel across the planet, but he would take the power of the coven and of the young Blue Spirit for himself.

29

"This is NOT what I had in mind!"

"Where's your sense of adventure?"

"Have you not had enough adventures in the last ten years?!"

Kathryn was distinctly unimpressed with Danny's so called idea, and Grace's endorsement of it. She had almost forgotten the way in which Grace had reached them upon their initial arrival into this reality. In truth, she didn't think it would ever come up again. And yet here they were. About to leap from the top of the Eiffel Tower with no safety equipment, and no real clue what they were doing.

"Come on Kat, this is the only way we get far enough from the tower to have a clear run at the airport. You've done worse."

That was certainly true. Kathryn thought of all the people she had lost since she had taken the decision to open her museum all those years ago. Things had certainly seemed simpler then. She thought about Kristin and how it hadn't quite settled in that they were no longer together. There was happiness within her that they had both found peace in someone else, but she was of course unaware of the fact that Daniella had rebuffed Kristin. In re-examining these thoughts and feelings, Kathryn had taken her eye off the ball.

"Three…two…one…GO!"

Grace gave her a shove in the back, and she was involuntarily launched over the railings. All of her inner strength and calm was gone and her legs were kicking and she was screaming at the top of her lungs. Jack was floating beside her, loving every minute of the experience. He shouted across to her to try and calm her down.

"Kat! You need to focus on where you're steering! You're drifting!"

Kat pulled one side of the flag, and she began to turn back towards Jack, all the while still screaming. Further back, Danny, Chantel and Grace had also begun their descent. Danny's idea was not the use of the final five flags to parachute down to the ground, but to reach the airport. He was previously a commercial pilot, and he was hoping that there would be at least one plane with fuel and in a stable enough condition to fly.

Below them, Kathryn's screams were beginning to alert the never decreasing army of undead, and despite their inability to see particularly well, they were moving towards the airport. From behind her, Chantel was yelling.

"Kathryn! Shut the fuck up!"

Grace turned to Danny as they adjusted their flight, and he just shrugged his shoulders.

"I didn't know she knew English swear words?" he replied.

Grace smiled, and Kathryn began to stifle her screams as they began to descend towards the top of the trees lining the avenue ahead. She noticed Jack had angled his flag parachute downwards slightly, and had begun to lower at a faster rate than her. She wanted to ask what he was doing, but they were finally ahead of the horde and didn't want to risk drawing them back towards them. Or anymore of Chantel's colourful metaphors. Instead she watched, as Jack pulled on both sides, making the pocket of air smaller, and as he did so, he descended quicker, and looked like he was aiming for a large clearing in a park off to the left.

She attempted to do the same, and after some inaccurate manoeuvres, managed to turn in the same direction, although she wandered a little too close to Chantel, and received a few more expletives before all five of them came in to land. The impact was hard. Jack hit the ground and bounced, rolling into a park bench, wrapped in the fabric, smashing the

228

wooden frame. Kathryn did much of the same, but landed on a tarmac footpath, skinning her knee and tearing her jeans. Chantel managed to land near a tree, and the top of her flag chute became embroiled in the branches, snapping her back, and left her dangling from the branches. Danny misjudged the landing entirely and ended up dropping from his chute and into the nearby pond. Watching on, Grace lifted her legs up upon landing, and planted her feet firmly, and calmly on the ground, running off the extra speed before turning and surveying the disaster zone before her.

"Guys, two of you have fought demons and entities, one is a scientist and one is a pilot. Can none of you figure out a simple landing?"

Kathryn and Chantel looked at her, but both thought better of starting an argument. Each member of the team was retrieved from their crash landing and they pulled their weapons, moving forward cautiously.

"We are about fourteen miles from Orly Airport. We are gonna need some transport that's quiet or off the land."

Grace and Chantel looked around and the land that surrounded them, and raised their eyebrows at Danny, still dripping from his dunking in the pond.

"Bikes then," Jack suggested.

"Bikes," Kathryn agreed, wiping the blood from her leg with her sleeve.

A few streets later, they discovered a bike rental hut, and with a little inventiveness from Grace, the chains were cut, and they were on their way. They cycled past several groups of zombies, but with the low humming noise from the chains on the bikes, they were not alerted. After they had cleared the worst of them, Jack looked over to Kathryn.

"Just like the Borg," he said.

Kathryn looked over at him, and raised her eyebrows.

"What? We do have *Star Trek* in our reality you know."

Kathryn chuckled.

"I wouldn't wanna live in any reality without *Star Trek*."

It took two hours to reach the gates of Orly Airport. The direct route was not possible due to blockages and smaller groups of undead blocking their path. The new problem would be getting past the group of former passengers that were lumbering their way around the terminal building. With no direct access to the runway without navigating the building, it would prove difficult. But then Danny came up with an idea.

"We could make a bit of noise to save a lot of time."

Grace walked up to him.

"How do you mean?" she asked.

"If there's gas in that shuttle bus, and we can get it started, we can plough through the wire fence on the far side, and drive right up to the planes. By the time they realise what's going on and focus on the source of the noise, we should be on a plane."

Kathryn and Chantel joined them.

"That sounds very risky," Chantel said, sounding concerned. "If that plane won't start, or is out of aviation fuel, they could be on us before we've gotten away."

Kathryn nodded.

"I have to agree with Chantel. In the time it takes to figure that out, we could be dead meat."

230

It was then that Chantel shocked them with a statement about her decision.

"You guys get to the planes, and I'll distract them."

Jack jogged over, having checked the condition of the bus.

"Woah, we're not using you as bait. We'll find some other distraction."

Chantel shook her head.

"I can't leave Paris. My cure works, we have saved people. If I leave, there's nobody to continue the work. I can save all these people."

Grace placed her hand on Chantel's shoulder, and looked her directly in the eyes. They glimmered with a deep green that until now she had not noticed.

"And if you die, there will be nobody to continue the work. If we get home, you can develop the cure on an industrial scale, and we can find a way to get you back afterwards."

Grace almost seemed to be pleading with her friend not to leave. Chantel had admired Grace from the moment they met, and she could feel herself choking up. She placed a hand on Grace's cheek.

"I'll be fine. I can't just leave these guys. Besides, there's no guarantee that when you get back these doorways will still be open."

Grace felt tears welling in her eyes.

"Please. Don't do this."

Chantel leaned forwards and placed a gentle kiss on Grace's lips.

"The way I'm feeling right now, now zombie would dare mess with me."

She removed her hands from Grace's face, and ran towards a discarded motorcycle, lying on the floor behind the bus. She smiled when she saw the keys in the ignition.

"Good day to be a hero."

She cranked the key, and after a few false starts, the bike roared into life. Suddenly, the windows at the front of the terminal building exploded outwards, glass showering down everywhere, and the crowds of undead poured out and began jogging towards her. She looked back towards Grace, gave her a cheeky wink, and gunned the bike.

"Come on, we need to hurry."

Kathryn led Grace and the others towards the bus. Chantel's plan was working, and the crowds were charging after her. She was keeping a pace that wouldn't move her out of range of their attack, but would keep her from harm for the time being. Jack leapt into the driver's seat and found that the bus was a push button start with no key required. He hit the button, but nothing happened. A second try, and just a faint whine from the engine.

"Come on you baguette smoking piece of shit!" he yelled.

"You know," Grace said softly, "if Chantel heard you say that, she'd beat your ass."

He smiled, and jabbed the button again, this time holding it down, and after a few coughs, the engine roared to life, and a huge cloud of black diesel smoke poured from the exhaust at the back. The fuel gauge read close to empty. They wouldn't get much chance to get between planes if the first one failed them. In the distance, they heard the motorcycle rev up even louder, and tyres screeching.

"Come on, we don't have much time."

Jack closed the doors, and everyone sat down, gripping the bar in front of their seat, as he floored it. The bus veered to the left, and began moving off course.

"What the hell are you doing?" shouted Danny.

Jack glanced in the wing mirror, and saw the rear driver's tyres were flat.

"Ah shit. We got two flats back there!"

Kathryn looked down out of the window, and saw the rubber bulging on the rims. The tyres wouldn't last long under this speed. She turned towards the front of the bus.

"Jack just do what you gotta do!"

Jack nodded, and yanked the wheel hard to the right. The bus screeched and leaned hard as the back wheels began to slide. Another yank to the left and he managed to aim it straight just in time to plough through the metal chain fence. The barbed wire atop the fence snapped, and whipped back at the bus, shattering the windscreen, and slicing Jack across the chest. As he yelled in pain, he momentarily let go of the wheel, and the bus went into a spin. The rear tyres finally let go, and rubber flew everywhere, exposing the rim which then dug into the concrete of the runway. After skidding for a few seconds, the metal of the rim dug into a groove in the concrete, and the bus rolled.

Danny was flung from his seat, and landed in the aisle hitting his head on the bar on the edge of the seat. Kathryn and Grace clung to their seats for dear life as the bus bounced as it rolled, the metal crunching, and glass flying everywhere. When the vehicle finally came to rest on the driver's side, they heard Jack groaning from the front. Crawling along on their bellies through the broken glass, they managed to reach him.

233

"Are you okay?" asked Kathryn, desperately worried he was badly hurt.

"Yeah I think so. That wire got me good though."

He looked down, and his shirt was torn, and there was a deep laceration across his shoulder and down to the centre of his chest. Kathryn tore off one of her shirt sleeves, and pressed it down onto the wound. Jack screamed in pain, but grabbed her hand and held it pressed against the cut. After a few moments, he calmed as he acclimatised to the pain.

"Where's Danny?" he asked.

They all turned around and saw Danny towards the back of the bus, lying on the now empty window frames, eyes wide open, head split on the right side.

"Fuck." Grace took a deep breath and looked down at the floor that was now made of windows. "What do we do now? I don't know how to fly a goddamn plane, do you?"

Kathryn shook her head, but Jack didn't answer immediately. Kathryn noticed this and looked him in the face.

"You? You can fly a plane?" she asked.

"Well, kinda. Maybe."

Grace rolled her hand in the air to indicate she needed more elaboration on the subject.

"When I was twenty-two, I was flying chinook copters in the air force."

Kathryn let the cloth drop from his wound. Suddenly she was even more attracted to him than she was before.

"You were in the military? You?"

234

Jack looked hurt by that.

"You don't need to sound surprised! You said your Jack was a cop right?"

Kathryn had to concede that point, but this was somehow more impressive.

"Yeah but, he wasn't like full metal jacket level badass."

Grace let out a deep sigh.

"Guys, we made a hell of a noise there, and I dunno about you, but I haven't heard any motorcycle noises for a little while. They're gonna come for us, and the nearest plane is clear across the runway. We gotta go!"

Jack and Kathryn shared a knowing smirk before they helped slide Jack out of the drivers seat. They clambered up the side of the bus and out over the top facing windows. Grace took one more look at Danny, before she jumped down. The nearest plane was indeed across the runway, and was a commercial airliner.

"Are you sure you can fly that?" Grace asked as they ran.

"How hard can it be?" Jack replied.

"Would a private jet not be better? Smaller? Easier to fly?" asked Kathryn.

Jack shook his head.

"A private jet of the size kept here wouldn't have the fuel capacity for a flight like that, and even if it did, we're assuming it would have a full tank to start with."

Jack had a point. But before they could discuss it in depth, the roar of the motorcycle returned, as Chantel appeared at the opposite end of the runway. But she wasn't being chased by zombies any longer.

"What the fuck is that?" Grace asked, bewildered at what she was now seeing.

Chantel was now running the bike at top speed, but gaining on her was kind of huge mutated beast. It appeared to be at least eight feet tall, composed of rotting flesh, and its roar was almost as loud as the motorcycle engine itself. The speed it was running at was almost impossible. Chantel attempted to weave around the runway, but the creature continued bounding straight down the middle, and she narrowly avoided several swipes from its elongated, and claw tipped arms.

"I have no idea, but we really need to get in this plane."

Kathryn clambered up the aircraft steps, closely followed by Jack, but Grace held back.

"What are you doing?" Kathryn asked.

"You get this thing started, I'll be back."

Without another word, Grace sprinted forward, rounded the plane and into the open hangar. Off to the side near the entrance was a second set of aircraft steps, a plane tug, and a catering truck.

"That'll do."

Grace broke the side window with the butt of her rifle, and swung it onto her back. She climbed through the gap and clambered over to the driver's side. Feeling around for keys, she checked the sun visor. The keys dropped into her lap from above, and she couldn't help but smile.

"Just like the movies."

The roars outside were getting louder, and much closer, and from the sounds of the engine, the motorcycle was beginning to die. Grace turned the key and the truck burst into life. She glanced down at the dials, and the fuel gauge was full to the top.

"Finally, some good luck."

She slammed it into gear and jammed her foot as hard as she could on the accelerator. The truck tore out of the hangar, narrowly missing the steps connected to the jumbo jet. Grace pulled the wheel hard to the left, and the truck went into a power slide, tyre smoke billowing from the tortured rubber. She spotted Chantel, and the creature was now just feet behind her. The speed increased quickly. Fifty miles-per-hour. Sixty. Seventy. The truck tapped out at seventy and Grace aimed the truck for a parallel run. She caught up to the creature, and it dipped a shoulder and barged the truck. Grace grasped at the wheel and the vehicle veered off to the side from the impact.

"What the hell is this thing?!" she shouted as she regained control.

It moved in for another hit, and Grace swerved wide to avoid it, but as it moved back central, and raised its arm to take a final swing at Chantel, she yanked the wheel hard to the left, and crashed into the side of the beast, knocking it off its feet. As it fell, it grabbed the side of the truck and pulled it up off the ground. In full action mode, Grace turned and clambered over the passenger seat, pushed the door open and leapt out of the top as the truck went over. Ahead of her, Chantel screeched the bike to a halt, and turned it around. As Grace landed on the concrete, she felt her shoulder snap, and she careered along the hard surface for thirty or forty feet before coming to a stop.

Chantel pulled the bike up next to her and leapt off, crouching down and checking over her frantically.

"Grace! Grace are you okay?" she shouted.

"I've felt worse. At least this time, I don't have to pull myself back together."

With no idea what she was saying, Chantel embraced her with the tightest hug she had given anyone ever, which made Grace's shoulder crunch a little more, and she yelped in pain.

"Merde, excuse-moi," Chantel said.

"I love how you get even *more* French when you're upset."

Behind them, the engines of the jumbo roared into life, and they saw Kathryn standing at the top of the steps, gesturing for them to hurry up. Something they were even more desperate to do when they heard the giant undead beast begin to stir again.

"Time to go!" shouted Grace.

She leapt up, and with a swift jerk, popped her shoulder back into the socket, causing Chantel to gag a little more than she expected, and the two of them sprinted towards the plane.

"Guess I'm coming with you after all!" said Chantel.

Grace smiled, gripped her hand and led her up the stairs into the plane.

"We all good?" she shouted to Jack.

"We've got three quarters of a fuel tank to do a full fuel tank journey. Yeah we're sound!"

The plane increased in speed as it moved down the runway, toppling the aircraft steps over as it moved away. Behind them, the creature had gotten back to its feet, and smashed the truck away, roaring in anger. But it didn't get the chance to catch up with its aggressors. Jack pulled back on the controls, and the jumbo lifted up into the sky.

The question now was would they make it to the United States, and if they did, would Crossroads finally lead them home.

30

Kristin suddenly felt cold. A shiver went through her entire body. Except she wasn't *in* her body. She could now see, but she wasn't opening her eyes. The cold sensation dissipated, and as she looked down, she saw a glow. Her vision began to clear up, and as it did so, she saw a sight that mesmerised her.

She was no longer in a room, or a landscape. She was in an energy vortex of some kind. There were ribbons of violet light strobing all around her, with occasional sparks of lightning. She looked around, but she had no head to direct, it was simply instinctive. Looking down again, she saw ribbons of energy, but no limbs to speak of.

"What the…?"

She spoke, but no sound was audible. The words were in her mind. In her consciousness.

"I don't understand… what is this?"

All of a sudden, a bright strand of white and purple mass swirled into existence in front of her, and seemed to take a humanoid form. As Kristin watched, a familiar face began forming. Had she had a mouth, she would have covered it in surprise.

"Hello Kristin."

"Ariella?"

"Well you've certainly gotten yourself into a mess this time, haven't you?"

Ariella was not entirely opaque but she was recognisable even at distance. Kristin had thought her dead after the battle with Jasmine. She was killed with the elder blade.

And then it finally clicked into place.

The suffering, the pain, the torture.

Kristin had found herself in the Realm of Screams.

"Ariella, how am I here? How are you here?"

Ariella seemed to hear Kristin despite the lack of a mouth or way to communicate audibly. She smiled and gave her old friend a gentle shake of the head.

"I've been here since my mother dispatched me with the elder blade. I managed to keep the cracks open wide enough for your friend Kimberley to pass back through, but I'm trapped here now. As for you, I saw what's happening in your realm. I've seen what Monarch is doing. I cannot leave this realm, but I am able to see what is occurring to some degree.

Mortals are not meant to enter our realm. Your bodies are not designed to cope with the experiences a pain wraith goes through. We did not know what to do with you. At first we thought you were an intruder, and so the council began putting you through those horrifying scenarios. I am so sorry for that. I cannot imagine how that must have felt for a human.

As soon as I realised it was you, I had your consciousness brought here."

Kristin was still seeing flashback of some of the horrible deaths she had experienced since she got here.

"Where is here exactly?" she asked.

"This is our equivalent of... a window."

241

Ariella waved her projected arm, and a gap appeared in the vortex. Through the gap, Kristin was able to see images of Earth, and the multiple realities. She saw Monarch engaged in a fierce battle with a younger Annie in Victorian London. She could see the older Annie alongside what looked like a giant angel and a short teenager throwing spells at some kind of energy barrier.

And then she saw Kathryn, on a plane with Jack, and a girl she didn't recognise… and Grace.

"Oh my God, they found Grace!"

Ariella nodded.

"She had spent the last two years fighting an army of undead. The girl she is with is called Chantel. She attempted to cure the plague. They're currently about to run out of fuel over the Atlantic and all plunge to their deaths."

Kristin gasped internally.

"What? We need to do something, we… what can I do?"

Ariella again held up her hands, and Kristin fell silent once more.

"Your demonic friend Monarch, here, is about to kill my daughter, five years before you meet her, and take out most of Victorian London with him. He's after her power, and the coven that made the immortality amulet you were all so fond of. When he succeeds, he will destroy all of the realms, and the Yellow Demons will reign over existence."

The anger was now building up inside Kristin, and she could see her own presence beginning to glow a hotter and hotter white.

"Why are you telling me this? Is it all just more pain? Is there nothing we can do to stop all of this?"

Ariella walked over to the gap, and waved it away. The vortex returned, and she glided back over to Kristin.

"There is a way we can return you all to your own reality in your own realm. But there is a price."

Kristin could feel her heart pounding, even though she was nowhere near her body. Whatever it was she was already decided that she was going to be signing up for it.

"I'll do it! Whatever it takes!"

Ariella, again held her hand up in patience.

"Kristin, the price is a life. And it cannot be your own."

She had no words for what Ariella was telling her. She had expected it to be a high price, but she was prepared to pay for that with her own life. But now she had to make a choice.

"I don't understand. Why a life? And why not mine? Why is that the requirement?"

Ariella's image blended away and she became the same swirl of violet and white energy as Kristin. As she spoke, the light pulsed gently. She approached Kristin, and hovered in front of her.

"The council recognised that when you arrived here, a threat was emerging not only to your realm, but to them all. We put plans in place to stop Monarch, but when your friend Kimberley was displaced by him, we realised we would need something far more powerful. Only a few of us are strong enough to leave this realm after the damage the battle of Wealdstone did to us. If we were to allow you to now leave, we would

243

require that energy to be replaced. And in order to put you all back to where you should be, we would require an enormous amount of energy. The kind of energy that can only be generated by the creation and existence of a new pain wraith."

Kristin was growing increasingly frustrated.

"But why can't that be me? I've been here and gone through so much, I know how it works, I've already experienced the pain! Let it be me!"

Ariella drifted closer.

"Don't you understand? We cannot leave. If you don't return to Earth, nobody will know what they have to do to stop Monarch's plans. You have to go back to tell them. And then you need to send someone back to us. Each journey is a one way trip."

"You mean, once I leave, I can't come back?"

Ariella moved in a way that mimicked the nodding of a head.

"How can I possibly choose who that is? I can't kill one of my friends. I can't do it!"

Ariella swayed to the side slightly and her glow intensified, as did the urgency in her voice.

"Kristin, if you don't go back, then existence will fall to the Yellow Demons. And all of our friends will die. You have to do this. You have to choose."

Before Kristin could say another word, she felt herself being dragged backwards, Ariella drifting further away and the lights growing dimmer and dimmer. In the distance she heard Ariella whisper to her.

"Tell my daughter I love her."

Kristin's vision became disorientated once more, and she suddenly felt as if she was falling from a great height. She cried out loud, but only heard her voice echoing in the now dark void she was in. Her mind began to refocus, and she saw what she thought looked like daylight beneath her. She looked down at herself, and she saw a violet glow beginning to form around her. A surge of energy shot through her, and she felt electric. The daylight rushed closer and closer and suddenly she bolted forwards as if shot from a canon, completely enveloped in purple lightning.

Then… nothing.

Severe pain shot through her back and head, and after a moment or two, she realised that her eyes had clamped shut. She gently opened them and she saw an eagle flying by overhead. Clouds moved above her. Beneath her hands, she felt wood. Broken wood. She felt her limbs begin to return to normality. She felt her fingers and toes move. She turned her head to her side and saw that she had landed in an old cart outside the saloon.

"Holy shit, I'm back."

Kristin pushed forwards, her back cracking in a few places, and she winced at the pain as she steadily rose to her feet. She looked around the now empty settlement, and in the bright daylight, she could see just how much damage had been caused in their initial battle with Monarch. There was not much left standing, and there were no visible doorways remaining, at least not in the main part of the camp.

And then the noise she had dreaded. The same sound that she had heard as she returned from the realm of the pain wraiths. Her friends and family were about to return. She moved to straighten her jacket, and felt a heavy object in the inside pocket. Kristin opened the jacket and saw a white bone handle protruding out the top of the pocket.

As Kristin removed the elder blade from her jacket pocket, her mind began to race. In a few moments, everyone would return, including Monarch, and the final battle would ensue.

It was time for Kristin to choose who to kill.

31

As the window exploded from the impact of the shot, Annie leapt behind a parked horse carriage. She did not know enough to take on an enemy of this level. More golden beams of energy impacted the side of the house next to her, sending bricks tumbling down from above, and people running for their lives. Across the street, Herman was still lying unconscious under the rubble of a storefront. She prayed that he would be okay.

"Desmond, how I wish you were here," she said to herself.

But he wasn't there. Desmond had returned to the future in an effort to track down the mysterious yellow amulet. Another barrage of energy flew towards her, and she dived out into the street just before the carriage exploded.

Monarch was *loving* this. The young woman had not yet discovered her true identity, nor her powers. Her magical knowledge was minimal at best. So far he had rebuffed everything she had to offer. He was *toying* with her. And yet with every assault, he felt a slight drop in his strength. He began to move in, his plan to take her life and absorb her power, definitive in his mind. There was no chance of failure here. She was not strong enough to defeat him.

However, as he approached the mangled carriage, he felt a shift in the energy. Several sparks flickered in the air, and the sky began to darken. Monarch looked up and saw the clouds begin to shift. The wind picked up, and began to blow the wreckage around the street. As the younger Annie watched on, Monarch was struck in the left shoulder by a bolt of violet lightning. He dropped to one knee, but shrugged it off and climbed back to his feet.

Another bolt struck him in his right thigh, and again, he dropped to his knee.

"What is this?" he called out into the street.

He began to wonder if he had misjudged the development of this young woman, but as a third and fourth strike hit his body, he could see that she was as surprised as he was.

Monarch shook off the hits which had caused him significant pain and began a fast march towards Annie, preparing to strike. But this time a ribbon of purple energy shot down from the sky, and shackled his left arm to the ground, pulling him backwards and on to his knees for a third time. In quick succession, a second, third and fourth strand tethered all four of his limbs. He struggled against the restraints, and began to resist. He roared with anger as he moved closer to breaking free of these mysterious bonds, but more flew down from above, until his entire body was consumed by these energy tethers.

It was then that behind him, a crack began to appear out of thin air. As he watched on, still fighting his restraints, the crack began to widen and crackled with violet light. It was a portal. A manufactured doorway. He stopped struggling for a moment as he realised what he was seeing.

"Well, I'll be damned."

In the ever widening gap that formed the portal, he could see Crossroads. *His* Crossroads. The *right* one. He glanced up towards the sky.

"It wasn't quite the way I planned it, but I'll take it."

A wide grin returned to his face, and with a huge burst of strength, all of the pain wraith shackles that had anchored him to the spot split away from him, and with an almighty roar, he leapt through the gateway. As the younger Annie watched, the doorway closed, the skies began to clear, and all evidence of Monarch's presence were gone.

Annie ran over to Herman, who was now beginning to stir and come round.

"Annie, oh Miss Annie, are you okay?" asked Herman.

Annie nodded as she helped him to sit up.

"It's okay Herman, I'm fine. But I think we're going to have to step up our defences."

"Agreed. Where did he go?"

Annie explained about the mysterious lightning and the portal that had appeared before vanishing and taking Monarch with it.

"My goodness. Why was he attacking you in the first place?"

"I don't know. I don't even know who he was. But when Desmond comes back, we're going to have to have a chat about some kind of wraith defences. This... creature had powers that I've only read about with wraiths."

Herman gradually got to his feet, nodding as he did so.

"I've heard of a potential hinderance to them, but I'm not sure how accurate it is. It involves holy water, a special incantation, and a silver tipped arrow."

Annie helped Herman down the street towards the doctor's office, glancing over her shoulder at the damage that was now strewn throughout the street. She didn't know who that man... that entity was, but if anything like that ever came to their door again, she would be prepared for it.

32

The instrument panel on the plane was now awash with blinking lights, and unsettling noises, and the vibrations now shuddering through the cockpit and passenger compartment were unsettling Kathryn and the others. They were still over the Atlantic, and the fuel reserves were all but gone.

"Jack what are we gonna do? Is there any way we are gonna make it to land?" asked Grace.

Jack looked down at the dials, and looked back up at her.

"We're an hour from land. We have fuel for ten minutes. There's nothing I can do, except try and get this thing as close to the water as possible to lessen the impact. I'm sorry."

Grace turned and walked out the cockpit and back into first class, where Chantel and Kathryn were sat, staring out of the windows. Kathryn saw her approach and her face fell.

"We aren't going to make it are we?" she asked.

Grace didn't answer, and simply shook her head. She was indicating their imminent demise to Kathryn, but was looking at Chantel the whole time. She thought she had lost her, only to rescue her. Now she faced the prospect of losing her all over again. She sat opposite her and smirked as she spoke.

"I guess now I won't have the chance to ask you out on a date."

Chantel smiled back.

"I just assumed the date was a certainty. I was more worried if we'd have French or Italian."

The two of them shared a brief laugh, Kathryn watching on. She glanced toward the cockpit, where Jack was still trying to figure out a solution. She felt the plane's trajectory alter slightly and she looked out of the window and saw they were now beginning to dip below the clouds. Looking at how Grace and Chantel were invested in the moment, she decided it was now or never for her and Jack too.

She slid past the others and walked along the aisle, reaching the cockpit door as the descent continued.

"Hey," she said, placing a hand on Jack's shoulder.

"I'm sorry Kat, I really thought we'd make it."

Kathryn walked in, and closed the cockpit door behind her, sitting in the co-pilot seat and looking Jack directly in his deep brown eyes.

"Listen, Jack. I know we aren't the version of each other that we fell in love with in our realities. I know we are both different people. But I want you to know. Wherever we are and whatever reality we are in… I do love you."

For the first time, certainly that Kathryn had ever seen, Jack's eyes began to tear up. She couldn't remember ever seeing him emotional. She had certainly seen him react with emotion, but not in this way. He activated the auto-pilot and turned towards her, taking her hands.

"Kat, there are differences between you and the woman I spent the last five years with. But the core things are the same. I was worried I was investing too much into this because I just wanted *my* Kathryn back. But I quickly realised that she was gone, and the feelings I was having were for you. That night in the cabin wasn't a mistake to me. It was confirmation. I love you too."

The whirlwind of emotion encapsulated them both, and they leaned in and shared a passionate kiss, and a long deep hug. However, the emotional turbulence within the plane was now being mimicked outside. A flash or bright light caught Jack's attention, and broke the mood.

"What was that?" he asked.

Kathryn looked around, but all she could see was the sea below and the clouds above.

"What was what? I didn't see anything."

Jack's eyes scanned the sky and the horizon, but saw nothing. Just as he was about to dismiss it as a glint off the ocean from the sun, it flashed across the windscreen causing them both to jump back in their seats.

"Okay, I saw that," said Kathryn.

Another four or five flashes later and Kathryn suspected she knew the source.

"Oh no, please no. We really don't need them to make an appearance right now."

Jack looked across.

"Who?"

Kathryn looked back at him.

"Pain Wraiths."

Looking back out the windscreen, they saw several purple bolts of lightning striking the middle of the sky, not touching down anywhere, and as they watched, they began to become faster, increased in number, and began knitting themselves together. This was not quite the attack Kathryn had been expecting.

"What are they doing?" she asked a bewildered Jack, who had no idea what was going on.

The cabin door opened and Grace and Chantel stood in the doorway.

"Pain Wraiths?" asked Grace.

"I thought so, but the lightning isn't hitting us, it's creating some sort of pattern in front of the plane."

Chantel examined the phenomenon, and with her scientist brain, she began to piece together what was happening, despite the fact she knew nothing about these pain wraiths.

"They're striking the same places. It's a pattern. They're making a concentrated effort to break something."

Everyone turned and looked at her.

"What? Do you not see it? What do you do when you want to rip open a shirt, or a dress? You grab it on both sides, and pull, right?"

Grace raised her eyebrows.

"I heard the French were freaky, but damn."

Chantel tilted her head and gave her a cheeky wink, before returning to the matter at hand.

"That's what they're doing out there. They're trying to rip something open. Look!"

Everybody turned to look back outside once more, and sure enough a tear was appearing in front of them. As the lightning strikes became more concentrated, the gap widened until an image became visible.

"Well fuck me sideways, would you look at that."

Kathryn's demeanour received the biggest boost since this nightmare began. Directly in front of the plane, through some sort of portal, was Wealdstone."

Jack on the other hand was not quite so celebratory. While the others had been staring at the view, he noticed the plane's engines had stalled, and the controls had frozen. The plane began to dip sharply, and the portal was vanishing above them.

"No, NO!" screamed Kathryn.

The plane began to nosedive and everyone grabbed the nearest solid object and clung to it tightly.

"We were so close!" Grace exclaimed.

Almost as if through some form of telecommunication, a loud bang erupted far above them, and an enormous, thick bolt of energy erupted from the clouds above, and hit the portal as if it was a pool cue hitting the ball. The portal spiralled down at speed, and began to gain on the plane.

"I don't know what is going on up there, but thank you!" shouted Kathryn.

The plane was sixty feet from crashing into the ocean, when the portal overtook them, and consumed the plane in its entirety. As the portal vanished, a delayed gust of wind hit the water, and caused several large ripples, before returning to tranquillity once more.

33

Three hours had gone by without either Annie or Nybor managing to break through the energy barrier they had encountered. Even Chan had tried some of the incantations Nybor had taught him during his training, and nothing had penetrated it. Clearly the defences erected by the Green Dragons were formidable.

"I don't know what else we can try," Annie said, collapsing into a sitting position on the grass.

Chan also agreed and sat down next to her.

"I knew their magic was strong, but I didn't realise even a White Falcon and a Blue Spirit wouldn't be able to break it."

Nybor strolled past them, and continued to examine the defences, running her hand along the rippling energy field. It tingled against her fingers, and her reflection sparkled back at her.

"They have great reason to be cautious. Whatever is occurring in the other realms because of Monarch, clearly has them worried about our safety."

Annie hadn't thought about it potentially affecting Beyond. But her instant feeling of being home, despite having never been here, had thrown her off completely. Right now the only thing forcing her to continue to try and return to Wealdstone, was stopping Monarch.

"Is there no way we can communicate with the Green Dragon on the other side?" she asked.

Nybor held her staff up in her direction.

"I don't believe that will be necessary. He's coming to us."

The semi-transparent effect of the barrier suddenly became entirely clear, and while it still remained, they could now see through to the other side. Approaching from the shadows under the nearest line of trees was a broad figure, at least six feet tall, a long grey beard and shoulder length wavy auburn hair, tinged with white streaks.

As the Green Dragon emerged into the light, the sun shone off his armour. Each scale was so detailed, that you could see them all from distance. The sword contained within his holster was also incredibly detailed. The blade was almost white in colour, and the handle was black, also encrusted with the dragon scales. But the thing that threw Annie, was that he did not appear to be moving with the speed that Nybor did, or the alertness she would have expected from a Guardian of the doorways.

He approached the barrier and stood directly in front of Nybor.

"What do you want, falcon?" he asked in a gruff tone.

"I am Nybor, leader of the Order…"

"I know who you are, I'm not fucking stupid. I said what do you want."

Nybor was taken aback by this response. Dragons were meant to treat all members of the Order with the highest respect. Annie however, suspected something. She moved alongside Nybor and looked at the Dragon through the barrier.

"You're *human*."

Chan looked at Nybor, who in return looked at Annie.

"Then this is the man Monarch threw into this land half a millennia ago?" she asked.

The demeanour of the Dragon changed, and his hand instinctively reached for his sword.

"Do not say that name, Falcon. Or it will be you on the end of my blade."

Annie wracked her brains trying to think of the name Grace had given her for her contact inside Crossroads. And then it hit her.

"Tommy?"

His head snapped around to look at her, and she saw tears in his eyes.

"You know me?" he asked.

"My friend, Grace, she knew you. You were at Crossroads together."

Tommy's eyes widened. He had not thought about these memories for a very long time.

"Grace. What did he do to her?"

Annie looked down at the ground, before replying.

"We don't know. She went missing a couple of days after you did. Me and my friends were split up and we're trying to get back."

Tommy said nothing for a moment. He looked at his sword, and from underneath the handle, opened a small compartment, that the others hadn't seen. A small bag fell into his hand. He walked up to the barrier, opened the bag and emptied some kind of green dust into his gloved hand. Replacing the bag in the hidden compartment with his other hand, he stepped back a few paces, and then blew the ground crystals out of his hand. They swirled and began to expand into a cloud. The cloud then moved towards the barrier and settled on its surface.

As it came to rest, the barrier dissolved, until it was gone completely. Tommy then walked up to Annie, and spoke to her directly.

"I chose to guard this doorway when my predecessor died. I knew it was the gateway home, but I chose not to go through it. The horror that Monarch was planning to inflict on every realm had been spoken in hushed tongues across all five kingdoms here for centuries before I even came along. These people were good to me, and I decided to protect the entrance to this world with my life. It is the one doorway that Monarch would never cross. He called it the third doorway."

Nybor was confused.

"Why the third?" she asked.

"Because it was the third route he had taken to escape Beyond. There are other ways to cross realms without using the doorways."

He looked back at Annie.

"You should ask your friend the Phantom Wraith about that."

Annie's stomach dropped. Scarlett had been to Beyond? For what purpose? Was she dead, or simply returned to her own realm? Either way, she had left Beyond alone. Clearly she was looking for something.

"Scarlett was here?" she asked.

Tommy simply nodded. Nybor, however, pushed for more.

"There was a Phantom Wraith in Beyond, and you told nobody?" she asked, anger rising in her voice.

"She was not interested in attacking Beyond. She was looking for something that Monarch had claimed he used to escape. In reality, it was one of his twisted ways of spreading rumours that had no foundation in order to remain… slippery."

Annie tapped him on the arm. His armour was warm to the touch.

"Why would she need something to help her move between realms if she could do that anyway?" she asked.

"That, I don't know. I never saw her again."

Nybor approached Tommy, and she didn't stop until she was inches from his face.

"Dragon, we are trying to return Annie to Wealdstone. She must get through the doorway in order to battle Monarch, and help defeat him once and for all. This is not just about our realm, but all of them. You must allow us to pass."

Tommy turned and began walking back towards the trees.

"Tommy, please?" shouted Annie.

Tommy drew his sword, and thrust it forwards, rotating in the air. It then dipped, and plunged into the ground. As it did so, the barrier began to grow up from the ground at the point the sword had hit. Within seconds, it was fully erected once again. Tommy strolled up to his sword, pulled it out of the ground, and returned it to his waist.

"This doorway has been camouflaged on the other side. It took a lot of my power and a lot of effort to conceal the entrance on the Earth side, without leaving this one. I will not reveal its location to Monarch again. I'm sorry, but you will have to find one of the other ways."

Tommy turned and walked back down into the trees until he was no longer visible. As he left their line of sight, the barrier once again became translucent.

259

"God damn asshole!" shouted Annie.

Nybor however, was sympathetic.

"That one has been through great pain. More than I believe any of us know. There is more to his story."

Chan brought the conversation back to reality.

"If we can't use the doorway, then how do we get Annie back to Wealdstone?"

As if by magic, purple bolts of lightning began falling from the sky. They struck the ground all around them, and Nybor reached for her staff. She began twirling it, and her wings unfolded.

"Everyone get down!" she yelled.

But Annie recognised the lightning, and held her hands up.

"NO! WAIT!"

Nybor lowered her staff, and her wings began to retreat.

"I know this phenomenon. It's Pain Wraiths."

More lightning strikes hit the ground, scorching the grass where they struck. As the three of them watched, the purple strings began to move towards the centre of the circle where they were standing. They all bunched up as tight as they could, Nybor desperate to react. Just as they began to run out of room, the ground beneath them opened up, and two seconds later, they were gone. The portal closed, and silence returned to the forest.

From the edge of the trees, Tommy watched on, before walking away.

34

Kristin stood in the middle of the street, clutching the elder blade in her right hand. A hundred feet away, stood Monarch, clenching his fists, and shaking his head wildly from side to side.

"Get out of my head!" he shouted.

Kristin had no idea what was going on with him, but she was strongly considering launching an attack. Her own mind was still swimming with images of death and pain, and it was taking all of her strength to keep her focus. She still had no idea how to stop Monarch. Ariella had said she was the only one who could deliver the message, and yet had not given her one to deliver. She also still had no idea how Monarch planned to draw all the realms together. But none of that mattered. There were two facts before her.

The first was that he had to be stopped, whatever the cost.

And second, she would have to kill one of her friends to replenish the energy lost by the Pain Wraiths in getting them all home, or their realm would fall, such was the delicate balance from the destruction Jasmine had caused. Her attention was soon recaptured though, as Monarch had now stopped talking to himself and was standing fully upright. He glanced around and then back at Kristin. His eyes caught sight of the knife, and they glowed.

"That relic won't help you. It has no effect on my kind."

Kristin took a few steps forward.

"A knife always cuts. Whether the cut hurts or not depends on the person you use it on. Either way, it does the damage."

Monarch made a mocking pained face.

"Ooh, that felt like it ran a little deeper than a literal meaning. Do I detect all your pain coming to the surface? After all, I did kill all of your friends."

Kristin smiled slightly, and stopped moving forward.

"You really are a showman aren't you? You claimed that you'd killed my niece, but I know that's not true. You claimed you broke free of your realm with violence and power, but you left via a distracted innocent bystander. You say you killed all my friends, but I know they're alive. You spread the rumour you moved through realms with a little trinket, so that more powerful beings would track you looking for it, when it didn't exist. You're just a con artist. A deluded power hungry creature, who really thinks he has a grip on everything."

Monarch was slightly uncomfortable with the fact Kristin seemed to know that he had been somewhat gratuitous with the truth, but despite this, he was still only facing one human woman, with an old knife.

"That's quite a speech from somebody I could obliterate without lifting a finger. Your friends may be alive, but they aren't here. Are they?"

Kristin's smile widened, and Monarch's in response, dwindled a little.

"How do you think you got back here, Monarch? Who do you think opened that portal?"

Monarch's smile completely receded. He had not considered where the portal had come from, he simply took advantage of it. Yet again, he felt concern that he hadn't felt much in the last thousand years. And all at the hands of these mortals and second rate witches. The anger began to bubble up within him. As he went to take a step forward, however, a huge crash echoed through the sky and from above him, a portal appeared.

Briefly mesmerised by the whole thing, he didn't react fast enough, as Annie, Nybor and Chan dropped from the sky, Annie and Chan clinging on to Nybor's back as her wings were at full stretch gliding through the air. She let go of them both, and Annie and Chan fired spells at Monarch, knocking him back a few feet. They then used their magic to cushion their fall as they landed. Nybor leaned back, and lifted her feet. She planted them square in the middle of Monarch's chest with such force, he was slammed across the street, through the front of one of the houses and straight through the back, landing in the dirt on the other side. Nybor then landed in the spot he had just vacated, as Kristin looked on with amazement.

Another loud crack of sound in the sky, and as the four of them looked behind them and up, an enormous jumbo jet emerged from a second portal, just metres from the ground. Kristin sprinted in the opposite direction, as did the others. Looking back over her shoulder, Kristin could see Kathryn and Jack in the cockpit, and smiled to herself.

Monarch pulled himself to his feet, and his eyes began to burn golden fire, his mouth widening in a vicious snarl. It was only then that he became aware of the noise from the plane, and as he turned around, he saw the landing gear hit the ground, and rip away from the plane. The impact of the nose hitting the ground caused the underneath to crumple, and as the left wing caught the edge of one of the buildings, it veered around, the entire plane now sliding on its belly. Monarch fired an energy burst towards the plane, and blew the second wing clean off the aircraft, but he was again, not fast enough. He turned and ran as the plane crushed him beneath it, and continued onwards.

Inside the cockpit, Kathryn, Jack, Chantel and Grace were cowering on the floor, tightly packed, just hanging on for dear life, as the plane crashed through the blacksmith barn, and then through an entire row of houses. The embedded wing wiped out the rest of the church and the Sheriff's office before it too was sheared from the plane and came to rest. The main body of the plane did not come to a halt until almost the entire settlement of Crossroads had been flattened.

As the dust cloud began to settle, one by one, the team began to emerge from the plane, the door simply dropping to the ground. Kristin was focussed on Kathryn. She looked like she had a head wound, but was walking fine. She started sprinting towards the plane, but then Jack emerged, and put her arm around his shoulder, helping her down to the ground, and she stopped running. She clutched the blade until her knuckles glowed white.

Jack.

The painful memories she had been forced to relive, and the physical pain from the wounds she had been victim to in the realm of screams flashed before her eyes like some kind of '*previously on*' reel. He was the cause of all of this. He put the rift between her and Kristin. He had to be involved with an alternate version of Kathryn. And now he had stolen her in this reality too. She had made her decision.

35

Kathryn and the others ran over to Annie and Kristin slowly walked across to join them, her eyes never leaving Jack's movements. She watched as Grace, who she was delighted to see alive and well, made the introductions to Chantel, and Annie introduced Nybor and Chan. She knew she would not have much of a chance. Annie could send her through the air in a nanosecond if she got this wrong.

"A… White Falcon? Blue Spirits? Interdimensional doorways? I don't know if I'm gonna be able to keep up with all this… this weird shit."

Chantel was overwhelmed with everything she had experienced in the last twenty-four hours. And it was far from over. The ground began to rumble, and it stopped everyone in their tracks. As Kristin broke her gaze on Jack, reluctantly, she saw the wreckage of the plane begin to lean to the side, before lowering again. Silence for a second, and then the centre of the fuselage blew apart into the sky, sending shards of metal, glass and rubber into the atmosphere. A now glowing Monarch stomped his way forward, striding with pure anger.

"HOW DARE YOU LESSER BEINGS ATTEMPT TO STOP ME! I WILL BRING YOUR REALM TO IT'S KNEES BEFORE I MERGE THE OTHERS. BUT BEFORE THAT, I'M GOING TO TEAR YOU APART!"

Monarch then leapt into the air, arms spread out wide, yellow beams shooting from his fingertips. Nybor spread her wings and launched into the sky, and swooped directly towards him, Annie running along the ground below sending balls of concentrated blue flames up to divert some of his impacts. Kathryn checked her gun.

"Shit, only six bullets left. I sure miss being a Blue Spirit."

Jack laughed, and checked his own weapon. Five bullets left. He gestured towards Grace who still had her rifle over her shoulder.

"Twelve."

Chantel rolled her eyes.

"Well, I guess we aren't going to win this fight with bullets and firearms then."

The lack of hesitation in Nybor was impressive. Kristin watched as she twirled in the air like a fighter jet. She launched streams of white fire from her staff as she dodged, and looped around Monarch's attacks, and as she got close enough, actually struck him across the face with the staff, knocking him down to the ground.

Nybor landed alongside Annie, and Chan ran to join them.

"What's the matter, Monarch? Not used to dealing with such strong opponents?"

Monarch gradually got to his feet, and wiped a drop of blood from his lip. He nodded in recognition of the strength of her strikes.

"I must admit, it has been a very long time since I fought a White Falcon. I suppose if I'm going to kill one, it makes sense to be the daughter of this vessel."

For the first time since Annie had met her, Nybor appeared rattled. The bullets came flying from the left, and Monarch was sent careering through the window of the only remaining building in the immediate vicinity. The spray of firepower lasted less than ten seconds.

"Well, that's all of those gone," Jack said sarcastically.

The front of the building was blown apart as Monarch smashed his way through and bounded in huge leaps until he reached Jack, Kathryn and Chantel. He launched a yellow strand of energy towards Chantel, wrapping around her like a whip, and he pulled her towards him at speed, before flicking the energy rope upwards and sending her high over his shoulder. The crack of bone as she hit the ground on the other side was clearly audible to Grace, who had dived out of the way of the initial attack. Monarch swiped his left arm directly into Jack's jaw and he was sent rolling a hundred feet away. A kick from a boot, and Kathryn was sent careering backwards.

More blasts from behind him, and blue and white firepower hit his shoulder and span him backwards. All the while, Kristin remained on the side-lines. Jack was now too far away to get to successfully. Then she saw Kathryn, lying on the ground, holding her side. And then it dawned on her. The last thing Kristin wanted to do was hurt Kathryn. If she was in love with Jack, then sacrificing him would do irreparable damage to her. As much anger as she had towards Jack, she now knew that she couldn't kill him.

Kristin took a couple of steps towards Kathryn with the intention of going to help her, but then more images of the pain she had suffered flashed in front of her. Her body being torn apart, her heart being ripped from her body, and then the message Ariella had given her.

Tell my daughter I love her.

And suddenly everything became clear. She had been given the message on how to stop Monarch. She turned her head towards the fight, and saw Nybor blasted through an abandoned jeep, the entire vehicle somersaulting along the ground. Moments later, Annie was the one barrel rolling along the ground after taking a heavy hit. Monarch was now in his stride.

"You think you can beat me? I'm going to kill you first, Blue Spirit, and take your power. Then I'm going to kill your new falcon friend for extra

267

juice. And with the damage I had the Phantom Wraith do to the barriers between realms, I will be able to draw all the doorways together. All of this is just a mere formality. Soon, it will all be mine!"

Annie looked up, blood pouring from her mouth. Her chest was consumed with stabbing pains, and clearly several ribs were broken. But now she knew. That was how Monarch was planning to do it. He'd led Scarlett on a wild goose chase through the realms, damaging the barriers between them on the way. He'd planned to increase his energy levels by killing all of the cult members he had amassed. That had to be it. He didn't know there would be other entities to draw from, surely? Either way, the plan was laid bare, and now she had to launch a more strategic attack.

It took every ounce of strength for her to clamber back up to her feet. She took a deep breath and took one step forward. She didn't feel the blade penetrate her back at first. The initial heat of the blade slicing through her back had stopped her in her tracks. It was only when she looked down and saw the tip of the elder blade protruding from her chest, blood dripping from it, her shirt darkening, that she realised. She felt a hand on her shoulder, and a whisper in her ear as her breathing began to fade.

"Your mother says she loves you."

Kristin's voice caused Annie to attempt to turn around, but when she pulled the blade back out, Annie dropped to the floor. The dirt began to darken quickly with her blood. As she gasped her last few breaths, she looked up at a tearful Kristin, holding the blade. Her lips moved to mouth the word 'why'. Kristen knelt down beside her friend, the tears now falling to mingle with Annie's blood.

"You will see your mother soon. I'm sorry Annie."

The breath finally left Annie's body, and her head came to rest on the ground, eyes rolling back into her head. The tears were now flowing down Kristin's face, as she placed the elder blade in the hand of her now

268

dead friend. She moved back and just looked at Annie lying there. Before her very eyes, Annie's body began to transform. Her figure began to blur, and within seconds, her body had turned into a bright blue mist. It lifted from the ground as if being carried by an imaginary being. The elder blade moved to the centre of the mist, and a crack of thunder echoed overhead. There was a single flash and a bolt of violet lightning shot down from the sky, and struck the cobalt mist of Annie's energy.

And then she was gone.

All that remained of Annie was the huge puddle of blood from the knife wound. Behind Kristin, the battle was still raging. She had to focus and help her remaining friends. She sniffled, took a deep breath and turned around. Directly in front of her was Nybor, one wing slightly torn at the edge, blood trickling from her eyebrow. She was wide eyed and looking down at the blood on the floor. She snapped her eyes back to Kristin, who was now backing off slowly.

"What did you do?" she asked, in a hauntingly devastated voice.

"You… you don't understand."

"WHAT DID YOU DO?!" Nybor bellowed, attracting the attention of Kathryn, who was trying to regain her footing after yet another blow.

Kristin staggered as she tried to move backwards, and she tripped, landing in the pool of blood and trying desperately to scramble out of it. Nybor's rage continued to grow, and her eyes began to glow so bright, it was like looking into two identical planets of water.

Jack was thrown into the wreckage of the jeep Nybor had been tossed into, which left Chan and Grace trying to subdue Monarch. Chan only knew basic incantations, and Grace was doing her best to protect him, but she only had physical strength and agility. She was no match for Monarch. A point that was proven moments later when he fired a blast of pure energy from his chest, and she was struck in the shoulder, flying

269

backwards and taking Chan with her, the two of them bouncing along the dirt and coming to rest feet from Nybor, who was now beginning to twirl her staff.

"Kris, what's going on? Where's Annie? And where did all that blood come from?"

Kristin couldn't look at her wife. The image of her killing Annie now joined the jumble of things in her mind, and searing pain was now shooting through her brain.

"She killed her!" bellowed Nybor. "She stabbed her in the back, murdered her in cold blood!"

Kathryn felt sick. She looked at Nybor, then at the blood, and then down at Kristin.

"Kris, tell me she's wrong. TELL ME SHE'S WRONG!"

Kristin closed her eyes, blinking away more tears, and then turned her head up at her wife.

"I can't."

Kathryn placed a hand across her mouth, and tears began to form in her own eyes. Nybor let out a tremendous roar, and span her staff with such speed it turned into a blur, and then directed a blast of pure white energy directly at Kristin, and she flew instantly through the air, through three smashed up cars, a partially collapsed house and right into the side of the wrecked plane.

Monarch had paused his attack, and realised what was going on. He looked over at the crumpled unconscious form of Kristin, and back towards Nybor. The smile returned to his face.

"Oh dear. Fighting in the ranks. I thought you were going to make it hard for me, but I guess I'll just sit on the stoop over there and wait for you to kill each other. Taking out your best weapon? How stupid are you mortals?"

Kathryn snapped her head towards Monarch, gritted her teeth and marched towards him. She screamed in rage, and ignored all of her broken bones and cuts and grazes. Monarch just sighed, and rather than waste his energy, waited until she reached him and then smacked her down to the ground with one swipe. He raised his foot and brought it down sharply towards Kathryn's head, but a blast from Nybor's staff knocked him backwards before he could make the final blow.

She leapt into the air, twirling her staff, but her anger had affected her logic and she shot straight for him, giving him plenty of time to blast her out of the sky. Chan was terrified, but seeing his friend crash to the ground, where she was no longer moving brought out some reaction in him that he hadn't felt before. The bottom of his legs began to vibrate and an orange glow began forming by his toes. Monarch watched on, bemused.

"Well this is new," he muttered to himself.

Chan's eyes clamped shut, and the glow moved up his legs, and when it reached his waist, a shockwave of energy flew out from his body, strong enough to cause Monarch to take a step or two back. The light continued to consume Chan until it reached his head. His eyes opened and they burned like fire. In fact Chan's entire body appeared to be burning, and consumed by flames. Nybor lifted her head to see what was happening. Even she didn't understand what was happening. Never before had she seen a creature of fire.

Grace stepped back from Chan, as the heat became so intense she had to shield herself. He let out a growl similar to a lion, and like a bullet from a gun, fired forwards. Monarch didn't move. He wasn't entirely sure what he was now facing. Chan collided with Monarch with such force, a

271

second shockwave erupted, and anyone still standing was knocked to the ground. The two of them twirled through the air like wayward missiles exchanging punches and blasts of fire and golden light. On the ground, Kathryn and Nybor were helping each other to get back to Grace. Jack was only just recovering from being implanted in the side of the jeep. One of his eyes was now swollen shut.

"I don't understand. Why would Kris do this? There has to be a reason!"

They were not expecting an answer. But they got one.

"There is."

Everyone turned towards the aforementioned jeep wreckage where they saw a glowing figure standing. Kathryn raised her hand to her mouth once again, and Grace inhaled sharply. Standing before them, large as life, was Ariella.

36

The lights were blinding. Streams of violet and white light everywhere. Every shade of purple, every possible design of lightning fork. Annie attempted to shield her eyes, but found she had no hands to shield them with. As she gazed down, all she saw was a blue glow, and a rough outline of her body. So many images were running through her mind, but the last thing she remembered was the one that troubled her.

"What... what's going on here? I don't..."

Then came a reassuring voice resonating all around her.

"It's okay Annie. I'm here."

To her disbelief, Annie watched as her mother appeared in full human form in front of her. Was she dreaming? Was this a life after death experience? She couldn't compose her thoughts, she couldn't focus. Everything was creating a sensory overload. Her feelings and sensations were heightened like she had never experienced.

"Mum? Is that you?"

Ariella nodded and walked forwards. She reached out her left hand and as her fingers touched the glow of blue light, Annie's body began to reform. She saw her legs appear, slowly followed by the rest of her. When she was her again, she took a deep breath, and as she breathed out, an aqua coloured mist emerged, and dissipated.

"I was hoping Kristin understood the message."

A moment of uncertainty began to fester in Annie's mind.

"Am I dead?" she asked.

Ariella nodded.

"In a manner of speaking, but I'll explain that in a moment."

Annie did not appreciate the lack of urgency, but could not help but be consumed by her surroundings.

"Where are we?"

Ariella raised her arm, and gestured all around them.

"This is the Realm of Screams as your mortal friends like to call it. I never did like that name. You're in the realm of the Pain Wraiths. This is where we exist. And we nearly ceased to be thanks to what is going on with the humans."

Annie looked away from the splendorous sight before her, and looked back at her mother.

"You mean Monarch?" she asked.

Ariella nodded.

"After the damage Jasmine, my mother, did to this realm, we were too weak to intervene and help stop Monarch's plans. We were able to observe but no more. But then after the Phantom Wraith split you all up, Kristin ended up here. She went through a lot before I found her. The equivalent of a thousand lifetimes of pain. I was able to help convince the council to send her back, and bring all of you back together too. The problem was, using all of our residual energy meant our realm would destabilise. It required rebalancing. A new form of power."

Annie's eyes were flicking back and forth so quickly, they were almost a blur. She was trying to piece this all together.

"So you told Kristin to kill me with the elder blade, so I would come back here, and stop you all from dying?"

Ariella nodded.

"More or less. Annie, you are not a pain wraith. You are also not human. You're a Blue Spirit. You are one of the most powerful beings in existence. Once you learn the true strength of your abilities, you'll become almost immortal."

Annie held up her hands to get Ariella to stop.

"Wait, I haven't reached the peak of my abilities yet?"

Ariella began to laugh. She shook her head, and gestured towards a gap in the violet light show. She could see Crossroads, and the battle below.

"Wait, is that… is that Chan?" asked a very bemused Annie.

"Yes. Seeing his best friend hurt by Monarch, triggered a response in his core DNA. Your friend is a very ancient type of being. He is a Fire Demon. The creatures of Beyond thought them extinct, but they are beginning to re-emerge. Your friend Chan is the first to be born in six thousand years. Even that is not the full potential of a Blue Spirit."

Annie was finding all this very difficult to assimilate. Her mother asked her another question.

"What is the last thing you remember?"

Annie scoffed, and suggested she had already answered that question. When Ariella still didn't continue, she repeated what they had discussed.

"Kristin plunging a knife through my back, and choking on my own blood. How's that? Will that do you?"

She tried to turn away, but the room or vortex she appeared to be in, seemed to shift around her.

"And do you know why you were killed with the elder blade?"

Another sigh from Annie as she repeated herself.

"So it would bring me here, but I don't…"

Annie trailed off as she began to piece it together in her mind.

"A new form of power. I'm the new form of power. You needed me specifically!"

Ariella nodded.

"Your Blue Spirit energy stabilised this realm, but not only that, it has supplied us with enough residual energy, that we can leave our realm once more. And this time, we will help you and your friends save existence."

Annie's heart started pounding with excitement.

"You mean…?"

Ariella nodded.

"We're going on a field trip."

37

The reaction was everything Ariella had secretly hoped for. But when Annie stepped out from behind her, Kathryn couldn't help herself. She sprinted, or at least limped, as fast as she could. Annie met her halfway and they shared a tight hug.

"Ow, ouch, okay maybe a little softer."

They pulled away from each other, and a very beaten up Kathryn looked Annie over. There was a perpetual blue glow around her. Something was different.

"How? I thought…"

"Kristin killed me? Yeah she did. But she had a reason. It was the only way enough energy could be returned to the realm of Pain Wraiths to stabilise their realm. It was them who sent us all back here, so we could defeat Monarch."

Ariella stepped forwards, and Kathryn and Grace both gave her a tight hug. For a moment, they all forgot the firefight going on over head with Chan and Monarch, but they were soon reminded of it when Chan's limp body was deposited at their feet, and the thump of Monarch landing created a dust cloud. He tilted his head in curiosity as he examined Ariella, and again when he saw Annie.

"I'm pretty sure you are dead, Spirit?"

Ariella stepped forward.

"What's the matter Monarch? Afraid the numbers might be getting too much for you? Oh and how's that little voice inside your head? I bet Dorn is scratching at you from the inside as we speak, isn't he?"

Monarch began to feel uneasy. He was so close to victory, and this was an obstacle he hadn't anticipated during the course of his grand scheme. He generated some bravado in an effort to catch Ariella off guard.

"Look around you. I've wiped your little friends out multiple times. I think the fire boy is dead, and I'm pretty sure our winged friend here killed the murderess who stabbed that one."

He pointed at Annie, who scowled back at him.

"So tell me why I'm supposed to feel uneasy?"

Ariella moved forwards, stopping just in front of Chan's body. She turned her wrist around, watching her fingers as little sparks began to shoot from their tips. She pointed her hand down at Chan, and gave a slight flick of her wrist. A bolt of lightning struck him in the chest, and he opened his eyes and sat bolt upright as if awoken from a bad nightmare. *That* caught Monarch off guard.

"Annie, I think your friends could do with fixing up a little."

Annie looked around for a minute, unsure as to what she was expected to do. Then she remembered what Ariella had told her. She had not yet reached her full potential. She looked at Kathryn, and closed her eyes. She tried to focus on Kathryn in her mind, and where her wounds were. Her body began to glow intensely, and the others moved back. Monarch was too surprised to even react. Annie stepped forward, and reached out her hand. Placing her palm on Kathryn's left shoulder, she opened her eyes, and the glow from her body moved across to Kathryn's and expanded until they were both consumed by it.

As the others watched on, Kathryn's cuts began to heal. There was audible cracking as her ribs began to move back into place, and all of her bruises disappeared. After no more than thirty seconds, Annie moved away. Kathryn was completely healed.

278

"Holy shit."

Kathryn looked herself over and felt her entire body. She was not only healed, she felt as if her muscle definition had improved, her core felt stronger, and her mind was free of all pain. In truth, she had never felt better. Annie leaned in and whispered to her.

"I gave you a little something extra."

She winked at Kathryn, and as she looked down, her fingertips began to glow with blue flames. Kathryn snapped her fingers and her entire body began to glow blue to match Annie's.

"Now THAT'S what I'm talking about!" she exclaimed excitedly.

Monarch was now nervous. His power was gradually weakening and his hold over Dorn's body had taken such a hammering from travelling through the weakened doorways that it was possible that he would not have enough energy to merge the realms as well as take down these pesky individuals. Again, he played the showman.

"So what? Now you have two blue spirits, and a broken Falcon. It won't save you."

Ariella fired a blast of purple lightning directly at Monarch, and he flew back through the air, and smashed clean through the plane's already decimated body. She turned back towards Annie.

"Fix up the rest of your friends, honey. I'm bringing friends of my own."

Annie nodded, and made her way to Jack. Grace ran over to Chantel, who she had moved to the side-lines out of harm's way, picked her up and carried her back to Annie. Ariella strode forwards, and reached out an arm. A violet ribbon wrapped around Kristin's limp body, and pulled it swiftly through the air, and placed it at her feet. She thrust her hand forwards into Kristin's chest, and she took a sharp intake of air. Eyes bulging, heart racing, she looked up at Ariella.

"Holy shit, was I…?"

"Dead? Yeah I think so. I mean you got thrown through like four buildings and a plane, so yeah. Pretty dead."

"But it worked?" she asked, wincing as her broken bones began to click back into place.

"Oh yeah. It worked."

Kristin grinned, and Ariella helped her to her feet.

"Oh, and I figured I'd bring some friends to the party."

The air above them crackled and fizzled with energy, and six lightning bolts hit the ground at various points around Ariella. As the light dissipated, the bolts had been replaced by people. Four more. Four more people. The team now fully healed, and slightly enhanced by Annie's energy, albeit temporarily, watched on with excitement as more Pain Wraiths descended from the heavens. When the lightning stopped, Jack counted thirty-two wraiths including Ariella. The number did not go unnoticed by Kathryn.

"Ariella?" she shouted. "Thirty-two? You trying to be funny?"

Ariella looked over her shoulder.

"Hey, I thought you liked in-jokes?" she shouted back, smiling.

With a burst of energy, everyone sprinted forwards to join the Pain Wraiths. They stood their ground and waited. But Monarch did not return. Then the ground started rumbling. The smiles vanished from Ariella's face.

"What is it?" asked Annie.

"He's started. He knows he doesn't have the energy to take us all on, so he's trying to merge the realms. He pulling all the doorways in."

38

The image was quite something. As the vast group of wraiths gathered behind the destroyed plane, and the team joined them, they all looked on as Monarch was floating above the river. His arms were fully outstretched at either side, his head tilted back, and strands of his golden energy beams were latching on to various parts of the air. As each one struck a seemingly invisible object, the frame of the doorway began to shimmer into view.

"What's he doing?" asked Chantel.

He's using all of his remaining energy to pull the doorways together," replied Grace.

"How does he know where they are?" Jack asked.

Kathryn had also wanted to ask that question, considering how until he struck them, they appeared to be invisible.

"He can sense them," Ariella replied. "They give off immense amounts of energy. It's what drew him here to Crossroads in the first place. It was the one place in your realm where there was enough energy to bring so many here."

"Woah," interrupted Kathryn. "So they weren't always here?"

Ariella shook her head.

"The energy at this site in particular for some reason is able to draw the doorways in like magnets. Before she was phased, your friend Kimberley surmised that it was her energy that was activating them. And she was right in a way. But the energy has been building here for some time."

Kathryn walked up to Ariella.

"Just how much spying on us have you been doing?" she asked with a smirk.

Ariella looked back at her.

"Well, we can't get HBO. Earth is the next best thing."

The two shared a brief laugh, before they turned back towards their nemesis.

"So this is it, then?" asked Kathryn.

"This is it."

The area surrounding the group illuminated in combinations of purple, blue, white and orange as every single one of them leapt into the sky. One by one they landed in a huge circle surrounding Monarch's position. Sensing their presence, he opened his eyes, but his magic continued to search for the doorways.

"You're too late. It has begun."

Kathryn and Annie both stepped forward. They were joined on either side by Grace and Chantel, and Jack and Kristin. The six of them created a front line of attack. It was Kathryn who addressed Monarch.

"We will stop you. You will not destroy these realms."

Monarch laughed, but in his current state, it sounded truly demonic. A much deeper and more echoed tone from deep within his chest.

"I told you, it has already begun."

The ground shook violently, and the green glow of the exposed doorways flickered violently. A crack appeared in the ground near to Ariella, and she followed its path all the way to one of the doorways, where the crack took a fork, and reached a second one. As she watched, the two doorways slowly began moving towards each other.

"We have to stop him, NOW!" Ariella shouted.

In a scene reminiscent of a Hollywood superhero movie, the pain wraiths began a bombardment of violet and white energy blasts, all concentrated on Monarch's position. Each one however, diverted from its path as it approached him, and flew through one of the doorways. None of them could strike him, and as each one went through a doorway, that doorway moved closer to its neighbour at an accelerated rate.

"STOP!" Annie cried out. "The blasts are speeding it up! It's increasing his energy. We have to find another way."

Ariella instructed her fellow wraiths to stand down. The ground began to quake, and a section of the river began to rise up, creating a chasm beneath it, the water now running into it. More cracks and shifts in the hills behind Monarch sent rocks tumbling down into the now raging torrent being created from the seismic activity. Jack was eager to utilise his new abilities before they expired, but something triggered in the back of his mind. He shouted across to Annie.

"The incantation! On the back of the bus!"

Annie's eyes flicked back and forth for a moment, and then the light bulb illuminated.

"YES!"

Kathryn, Kristin and the others looked at them both as if they had gone mad, but were distracted again as a huge chasm opened up beneath Chantel's feet, and she narrowly avoided plummeting down into the Earth.

"What are you two up to?" asked Kathryn.

Jack and Annie knelt on the ground, and began scratching symbols and designs into the dirt, mumbling to each other.

"Have you got this?" Annie asked Jack.

He nodded.

"Yeah. Whatever shit you juiced me up with is enhancing my memory too, but I can feel it slipping, so let's hurry."

Kathryn cleared her throat again.

"Hello? Apocalyptic event going on here? Realms at risk?"

Annie tried to explain whilst still drawing in the sand.

"In the spell book that Scarlett booby trapped, there was an incantation for removing a demon from its host. It's how they separated Monarch from Dorn's body in Beyond. Me and Jack were trying to learn it on the bus."

Kathryn turned to look at Ariella.

"And you missed that part? What was that, a commercial break?"

Ariella shrugged her shoulders, and staggered as another crack split the river. This one was big. The river was now diverting towards them with great speed.

"Uh, guys?" Grace pointed out.

"Merde."

285

Chantel was discovering that perhaps this was not the best time to have joined this group of adventurers.

Without hesitation, the Pain Wraiths leapt in front of the wall of water, and began generating an invisible wall. The water hit their energy, and Ariella motioned the wall into a curve, sending the water back towards the other side of the river. But this was only a minor problem. As she watched on, the first two doorways touched.

As they did so, the ground shook with such violence that everybody was thrown to the left. There was a very loud, almost mechanical grinding noise as the doorways turned from green to a dark red. Monarch appeared to get a boost from this, and as the two doorways completed their merging, screams were audible from the other side. There was no way to tell which realms had been lost, but the screams numbered in the millions.

"My God."

Ariella did not expect to lose any realms. To lose two so quickly was devastating. She only hoped that it was not hers. There would be no way to know until the fight was over. Jack and Annie had now erected a protective bubble around them so that they were unaffected by the seismic activity. The Pain Wraiths were continuing to divert the water, and Kathryn, Kristin, Grace and Chantel were attempting to repair some of the cracks and chasms in the ground. Their power, however was not strong enough, and they found they were only able to hold the ground from spreading further.

Nybor and Chan were circling the skies, attempting to launch a direct attack on Monarch, but each time they got close enough, they found themselves being drawn towards one of the gateways, and having to alter course before they were sucked in. Nybor landed on the ground beside the protected Jack and Annie, and Chan soon joined her.

"This is no good," she said to Chan. "We need to find the doorway to Beyond, and bring reinforcements."

Chan agreed but didn't see a way to find it. And there was another problem.

"What if we do manage to find it, and Tommy won't let us through?"

Nybor shook her head.

"We'll cross that bridge when we come to it. We need to find it first, before he does. If he latches onto it, we've lost it."

She leapt into the skies again, and Chan followed her. Back on the ground, Jack and Annie had finished drawing their incantation, and were now reciting words in a language that Kathryn could not understand. She just hoped they knew what they were doing.

Two more doorways were getting very close to merging, and Ariella began to feel helpless. She began to think that she had finally been reunited with her daughter, and saved their realm, only to lose it all now. To her left, stood Chantel and Grace. Chantel was way out of her depth. Just hours before she had been a simple scientist, developing a cure to a mutation. It may have been zombies, but compared to what she was witnessing and experiencing here, that had been child's play.

Another crack shot from the river, through the rubble of the town, and a chasm opened so wide, that the remains of the plane fell into it. Had there been any fuel left in there, it would surely have exploded. Kathryn shouted across to Ariella.

"We can't keep this up much longer!"

As she spoke the words, their temporary powers began to dissipate, and the ground began to move apart again. Chantel gasped as she lost her powers and the second two doorways merged. This time the screams numbered in the trillions. Ariella could hear every single one. That was the curse of a Pain Wraith. Across the other side of the clearing, Kristin was also hearing the screams. Her experiences in Ariella's realm had broken her mind in a way that mortals were never meant to experience. She too heard every scream. As the third pair of doors began to move together, there was a whooshing sound as the protective bubble disappeared, and Jack and Annie were now stood on their feet.

Kathryn gasped, as she saw the scripture that had previously been on the ground was now etched into their skin. The words, images and texts were etched in blood. They slowly walked forward towards the edge of the river, until they were directly in line with Monarch. His eyes began to lose their intensity as he saw the two of them approaching. He knew that scripture only too well.

"No. NO! Not when I am so close!"

He momentarily allowed two of the doors to be released, and they began to drift apart. He fired several blasts of energy towards Jack and Annie, but high above them, Nybor had returned to the fray and shot her own blasts, striking Monarch's down before they reached the pair.

Jack and Annie raised their arms, and Kathryn saw their eyes glow bright blue. As if they were charging like a power station, white electricity began to build up around them. Crackling sounds accompanied the visual scenes. Monarch became increasingly fearful, and increased his bombardment, releasing two more doorways, but Nybor was too fast and in his weakened state, too powerful, and she continued the rebuttal of his attacks from the air.

The electricity around Jack and Annie reached its peak, and as a high pitched noise built up around them, a pure white beam of light launched from their hands and struck Monarch directly in the centre of the chest. He flung his head back in pain, and began screaming in agony. Kristin could not take the noise and dropped to her knees, covering her ears as best as she could. Grace, Chantel and the others watched on in astonishment and the doorways began to move apart and away from the area. Monarch's screams had now reached a deafening volume, and alternated between a scream and a roar. As the group watched on, a yellow fog began to emerge from the top of Monarch's head. Kathryn was in disbelief, as the words etched onto her friends bodies moved up their bodies, and when she squinted, she could see them flying down the beam of energy towards Monarch. The yellow glow vanished from his eyes, and his mouth closed. The body went limp, and the yellow fog rose above Monarch's body into the air.

As the white light ceased, Jack and Annie dropped to the floor exhausted. Monarch's body dropped to the floor in a heap, and all remaining doorways vanished. The yellow fog swirled around darting in one direction, and then another. It seemed to recognise that the host body was still below, and attempted to move towards it again.

Nybor landed on the ground at the edge of the river, and began twirling her staff until it once again became a blur.

"I don't think so."

With an intense blast of energy from her staff, she struck the fog in its centre, and what sounded like a secondary scream filled the air. In its weakened state, the Yellow Demon could not resist the attack. As Nybor ceased her motions, the group watched on as the fog appeared to turn a dark brown, and begin to blow apart in the breeze like burnt paper. Silence fell on everyone as the realisation that the battle was finally over, began to settle in.

On the ground on the other side of the river, which had now returned to a normal flow, Dorn began to move. He rolled onto his back, and Nybor moved towards him slowly. As he dragged himself up to his knees, he opened his eyes and attempting to take in his surroundings. The others then began to notice what was happening, and watched on as he climbed to his feet.

Nybor stopped at the edge of the river, and tilted her head as she examined her father. He looked at her.

"Nybor?" he asked, unsure of his words.

"Father," she returned in her typically curt manner.

"Oh my goodness, thank the kingdoms its you…" he trailed off, and began to burst into laughter.

Nybor stepped back, and Dorn looked down at the ground. As he looked back up, there was a golden glint in his eyes.

"Did you really think you could destroy me that easily!"

A remnant of Monarch had remained in Dorn, much as it had all those years ago with Arthur.

"And now, I shall finish what I…"

A whistling sound rang through the air, and as Dorn looked up, his eyes bulged wide. Tommy landed, sword in hand and plunged the end of the blade straight through Dorn's heart, gritting his teeth tightly as he did so.

"You will never enslave anyone again, demon."

There was a brief moment of recognition in Dorn's eyes, before the glow vanished once more, and the body of Dorn, gave in to death. Tommy stood up, and removed his sword from the ground, turning to face the awestruck crowd. Chan gently landed by his side, and his visage appeared to return to normal. Nybor walked up to Tommy, and reached out her hand for him to shake. He obliged.

"Thank you for coming to help after all."

Tommy nodded.

"You were right. I may not be from Beyond, but it is my home. I had to bring this full circle."

With their work done, the Pain Wraiths began to return to their realm, bolts of the violet lightning carrying them away. Only Ariella remained. The entire group met up together at the edge of the river, except Kristin. As the others moved together, she took the opportunity to wander away. She took one last glance at Kathryn, and headed down the road towards Wealdstone.

39

"I have never been so glad to have a drink in my entire life."

Jack held up his glass and the others clinked them together. It had been a long time since he had been in a bar. The same went for Chantel, who was absorbing the atmosphere in Sisko's like a sponge.

"I have never been in an American bar. This is very... grungy," Chantel explained.

"Excuse me?" Grace asked. "Grungy? I'll have you know, my bar is not grungy!"

Chantel held up her hands in apology, and the crowd laughed. Kathryn looked around the table. They had faced their worst challenge to date, and while it had nearly killed them, they had survived again. They had new friends, and allies, and the team was stronger than ever. Almost. It had not escaped her notice that in the two days since the final confrontation with Monarch, they had not seen Kristin. When Kathryn had returned home, she found that all of her wife's belongings were gone, and there was a signed copy of divorce papers on the kitchen table. No note, just the papers.

She contemplated how much Kristin had changed. She had been unaware of just what an experience she had gone through until Ariella had explained to her the graphic nature of it. It was that experience that not only led to her reaching a willingness to kill a close friend, but to also leave the group that had loved her so dearly. And then she glanced at Jack. This was a new beginning for them. Life had given them another shot at happiness, and maybe this time they'd be able to take it.

"Can I just also propose a toast to the people of Beyond?" asked Annie, who had discovered that alcohol no longer had an effect on her.

"Please do carry on," said Chantel, as she downed her fifth shot of the evening.

"To my new friends Nybor, Chan and Tommy. May their return to Beyond with the tale of Monarch's defeat bring joy throughout the land."

"CHEERS!"

More glasses clinking, and more drinks drank. Jack excused himself from the group, and went outside into the cold night air to take a breather. Kathryn got up from her seat and joined him. It was much quieter out there and she appreciated the silence. She grabbed Jack's arm, and rested her head on his shoulder.

"Where do you think they are Jack?" she asked.

"Who?"

"Kimberley, Daniella, Kristin. I mean, they have to be out there somewhere. There are so many realms and realities."

Jack nodded.

"The universe just got a whole lot bigger didn't it?"

She chuckled as she nodded.

"It's going to get even bigger too, I know it."

Jack leaned down and placed a gentle kiss on her lips.

"Come on, let's get back to the gang. Don't wanna give Ariella anything else to watch in reruns, " Jack joked, pointing to the sky.

Kathryn laughed, and they went back into the bar, thankful they had found each other, and thankful they were here to live another day.

293

EPILOGUE

The heat on the back of her neck was so intense, she could feel her skin burning. Her head was pounding, and she tasted grit in her mouth. As Daniella sat up, she cried out in pain. Her hand moved up her chest, and she felt at least two broken ribs. She was dazed, and couldn't focus her vision properly. She held her hand up above her head to provide some shade. Once her eyes adjusted to the bright light, she looked around. Desert. Sand. No sign of civilisation, just the distant rumblings of what sounded like wheels on gravel.

She gradually pulled herself up against the rock she was propped up against, the surface burning her hands. The sound of wheels was getting closer. She turned, again shielding her eyes from the sun. Approaching her appeared to be a horse and cart, btu she couldn't be sure. She appeared to be standing on some kind of dirt road.

"Where the hell am I?" she asked aloud.

Her throat was bone dry, to the point of pain. She squinted again, and sure enough, it was an old fashioned horse and cart approaching her.

"This must be one hell of a backwards town. When in Rome."

She waved her arm, and flagged down the coach. The driver was unsure as to whether or not they should stop, but decided Daniella looked like she needed help. She drew the coach to a stop, and the horse let out a mild complaint.

"Uh excuse me," began Daniella. "This is gonna sound really weird, but do you know where I am?"

The woman driver jumped down from the coach. She looked Daniella up and down. Her clothes were very strange, and certainly not of this time.

She was disorientated, and confused. This could be the sort of person she had been looking for.

"You're about fifty miles north of Eureka. It's a hell of a trek on foot. Where did you come from anyway?"

Daniella chuckled.

"It's a long story, but I need to get back to a place called Wealdstone."

The driver's face appeared confused.

"Wealdstone? Never heard of it."

Now it was Daniella's turn to look confused.

"Never heard of it? The town that's been cut off for years, went missing? Was probably all over national TV?"

"National what?"

Daniella's stomach sank. Never heard of Wealdstone. Questioning TV? She had a terrible sinking feeling that it was not so much a case of *where* she was, but *when*.

"Excuse me, I'm gonna be making no sense again here, but what year is this?"

The driver, surprisingly, was not phased by the question.

"The year? It's 1886."

Daniella collapsed to the floor, and rubbed her hands over her face two or three times, trying to expel some imaginary ailment. She struggled back to her feet once more. This time it was the driver who asked the question.

295

"Where is this Wealdstone place, you're trying to get to?"

Daniella gave a brief chuckle.

"That is the question. My Wealdstone was south of Trinity Bay. But I suppose you've never heard of that either?"

The driver shook her head.

"Sorry."

Daniella held up her hand.

"It's okay. Listen, I need to get to San Francisco. How far would you be willing to take me?"

The driver stared into Daniella's eyes with a burning intensity.

"You ain't from this time are you?"

That question surprised Daniella, but she answered it nonetheless.

"What makes you say that?"

"Darling, I'm several centuries old. I know an outsider when I see one."

The driver removed her hat, and placed it on Daniella's head.

"I've got another one in the back. You'll need that."

Still unsure as to what to say, Daniella simply said thanks.

"I'll take you to San Francisco. Didn't have a particular destination in mind anyway. What's your name, stranger?"

"Daniella."

"Nice to meet you Daniella."

She reached out her hand and the two women shook.

"My name is Deanna."

AFTERWORD

So many twists and turns, I hope you got your head around them all!

Before I start talking about the book and what is to come, I'd like to take a moment to say something. Since I began writing this story, I sadly learned of the passing of Jason David Frank, the original Green and White Power Rangers.

Now a lot of you won't know what I'm talking about, but when I was a child, *Mighty Morphin' Power Rangers* was one of my favourite shows. I would play it out with my sister at home and my friends at school and watch it every day on TV. When Jason David Frank joined the show as Tommy Oliver, I found my childhood hero.
I wanted to *be* the Green Ranger. Tommy was so cool; he was a leader, and he saved the day. I would go to school, and when I would get bullied, I'd come home, put on *Power Rangers,* and watch Tommy kick ass and I'd feel better again. He inspired me to be a better person. And when he became the White Ranger... well that was even cooler!

I wanted to be the White Ranger. I wanted to be a leader like Tommy. And of course, I wanted to date Kimberley.

As I grew up, Jason continued to be an inspiration. He set up schools around the US, developed his own martial art style, and continued to inspire people with his speeches and videos about

298

mental health. When he died in November 2022 at the age of just 49, I was devastated. It put me into a spiral for 24 hours of just sadness and misery. I rewatched the *Power Rangers Movie* and lived my childhood all over again.

But the real sadness was that someone so dedicated to inspiring others, felt he had nowhere to turn. He couldn't take anymore, and so he chose to leave this world.

We suffered a great loss that day, and so when writing Wealdstone : Crossroads, I decided to introduce a new character and name him after Jason's character. What resulted was the Green Dragon. I can't do much to celebrate this man or what he meant to me as a child, but I can honour him in a small way.

May the power protect you always, Jason. Rest in Peace.

I only introduced the character based on JDF at the start of the book, and in cameo at the end, but we will see more of him in future instalments of the Dark Corner Universe very soon, but for now let's reflect on what just happened and where we are now.

So the notion for this book was not only to continue what had come before, but to plant the seed for what is to come. It's no secret if you follow me on social media that I intend to expand this universe beyond the confines of Wealdstone, and to do that I designed Crossroads as not only the main location anchor of the story, but I chose the name Crossroads because that's what this book is. It's the divergent point for the Dark Corner Literary Universe.

We have in this story, the origins of at least five spin-offs that I have ideas in development for. I told you previously that the name of Trinity Bay would be important, and hopefully at the start of the book, you'll understand why. We will be revisiting Trinity Bay very soon.

I also wanted to drive home the fact that Resurrection was part of this universe, and so included the Deltarian in the Bermuda Triangle part of the story. That realm in particular was something I was keen to expand on, but I just didn't have enough material for a whole story. Maybe we will revisit it at some point in the future.

As usual, I dropped in many, many easter eggs for my regular readers. Everything from Star Trek references, to references from earlier in the universe. I take great joy in inserting those, and seeing how many people pick up on.

And now for some of the characters.

You will have seen that a lot of effort went into creating and emphasising the drama between Kathryn and Kristin. I decided before I started writing the book that given the strained relationship in the previous book, that it should continue into this one, bearing in mind it is set 2-3 years later. When I decided I would be visiting not only other realms but also other realities, I knew there were two characters I wanted to bring back. One was Daniella, because I had a lot of people on Twitter tell me that I'd done her dirty by wiping her out like that, and others telling me I had done the same to Jack.

The reintroduction of Jack was designed to break Kathryn and Kristin up from the word go. The introduction of Daniella being gay, however, was something that I had thought about only briefly. I didn't want to just bring every character back from the dead. That would give their deaths in the last book no real meaning. It also gave the relationship a bit of a push. If Kristin started feeling more towards Daniella, and Kathryn felt more towards Jack, then the relationship may just come to a natural conclusion.

The arc that I have in mind for Kristin, though, meant that it was vital she became the outcast. And while she has left Wealdstone, it is by far and away not the last we will see of her. As I have stated before, Kristin is my favourite character that I have created so far.

Which finally, brings me to my new characters. I've already mentioned the character of Tommy, but let's discuss the other three. At the start of 2023, I became obsessed with a live stream on TikTok called TTFood. I bought some snacks and some Prime from them (yes I wanted to try it, no I'm not obsessed with it!), and noticed they were getting a lot of hate towards the host. He was funny, and really cool, and had such a good personality, and the moderators couldn't keep up. So I decided to engage maximum sarcasm and help them out.

I was such a hit, that the moderator in the chat, Chantel, asked the host Josh to make me a moderator too. He said yes, and now we dish out punishments to trolls and haters worldwide! I decided to create a character for each of them in their honour, but you won't see Josh until the next book. More details coming soon!

Josh's fiance, Robyn, co-founded a peer support group called Flare. They help young people and adults suffering with mental health issues when they don't feel they have anywhere else to turn to. They help them find the support and help they need, and they were having a giveaway. I signed and donated some of my books to their fundraiser, and we struck up a friendship between the three of us. I support them whenever I can, and they do the same for me. And that is where the character of Nybor came from. Robyn often calls herself Nybor on social media, and if you can't figure out why…

then read Nybor backwards. And finally, Chan is on the live streams hosting with Josh. He's always in the background helping with orders, creating bundles and basically ensuring the thing keeps running. So it gave me a little boost of joy to include them in my books so they know that I appreciate their friendship and banter, and it's the least I could do. Here's to many more adventures in this universe for all of them.

Now before I sign off and reveal the name of the next book, I wanted to say that I created some artwork for these characters in an AI generated app, and I've decided to include them here so you can get a feel for what Nybor, Chan, Chantel and Tommy actually look like in your minds. Josh, sorry buddy but your artwork will be in the next one!

As always, thank you all for your continued support, I wouldn't be doing this without it, and here's to the future.

Stay safe, and be kind.

Dave.

Chan

Nybor

Chantel

305

Tommy

COMING SOON...

Printed in Great Britain
by Amazon

22901377R00175